Heart of Steel

JENNIFER PROBST

All rights reserved. 2nd Edition First printed 2012
Manufactured and printed in the United States of America

ISBN-13, eBook: 978-1-938568-00-8
ISBN-13, pdf: 978-1-938568-02-2
ISBN, Mass Market: 978-1-938568-27-5

PUBLISHER'S CATALOGING-IN-PUBLICATION DATA
(Prepared by The Donohue Group, Inc.)

Probst, Jennifer.
    Heart of steel / Jennifer Probst. — 2nd ed.
        p.; cm.
    Issued also as ebooks.
    ISBN: 978-1-938568-27-5 (Mass Market)
    1. Businesswomen–United States–Fiction. 2. Financial
executives–United States–Fiction. 3. Man-woman relationships –
Fiction. 4. Conspiracy–Fiction. 5. Love stories, American.
I. Title.

PS3616.R62 H42 2012
813/.6

Amanda Poulson, Editor, 2nd Edition
Brian Ferrin, e Book Formatting
Cover & Interior Design: Chris Dec

Published by Blue Star Books

Blue Star Books
903 Pacific Avenue, Suite 207-A
Santa Cruz, CA 95060
(831)466-0145
www.book-hub.com

Books are available for special promotions and premiums.
For details, email news@book-hub.com

This book is dedicated to
all the good friends
who have helped me on my journey:

Jodi Prada, Marlaine Scotto, Lisa Hamel-Soldano, Kimberly Cornman, Colleen La Pierre, Nancy Chaudhry, Angelique Devlin, Theresa Depierro and Kelly Cronk.

Without their friendship and support,
this would never be possible

•

Special thanks to the members in
my writers group,
The Hudson Valley RWA, who never failed
to inspire me and tell the truth.

And finally, to my two boys,
Jake and Joshua,
and nieces,
Taylor, Kaitlyn and Amanda.
You all make the world a
more beautiful place.

Acknowledgements

Many writers don't get the opportunity to publish their first book, let alone the chance to publish it twice. *Heart of Steel* was the very first novel I ever penned. It went through many editors, who believed my alpha hero was "problematic" before hitting the desk of *LionHearted.* My first editor, MaryAnn, believed in this story enough to publish it. We eventually lost her in this world, and the company decided to close. When I received my rights back to the story, I knew I wanted to revise and freshen it up a bit. I now have the opportunity to re–issue the book in e–format with Book Hub. Chandler and Logan will now have another chance to reach my readership.

Writers grow and change with experience, but I didn't want to alter my original, much younger voice. The revisions made are more surface – a bit more technology is now incorporated for my powerful CEO. A few tweaks. The rest remains the same.

I believe *Heart of Steel* is still a keeper; a true love story about change, redemption and the power of love.

I hope you all enjoy my very first novel – ready for the digital age.

— Jen

Chapter

1

Chandler Santell studied the man behind the sprawling mahogany desk and wondered if she'd lost her mind. She took a deep breath and tried not to fidget, but her expensive celadon wool business suit was beginning to itch.

How could she make a business deal with one of the most powerful men in the finance industry? Every firm she had contacted in New York City had rejected her proposal. Desperate, and almost out of time to save her Yoga and Arts Center, she decided to take a shot on one last name.

Logan Grant.

She knew why they called him the "man of steel."

Chandler ran down his list of attributes: owner of L&G Brokerage—one of the most successful companies in the city; dubbed the "man of steel" by the business community due to his ruthless reputation in closing a deal; a man whose word was law—and whose name commanded respect. His hard, steely presence in a room made people step out of his way. One word from the man's lips caused companies to double their profits or go bankrupt from loss of investors.

Now Logan Grant held another fate in his very

capable, very large hands. He held her entire future.

He read her business proposal without looking up. She studied the strands of dark sable hair cut slightly longer than fashionable. A hint of silver at his temples helped Chandler place him in his mid-thirties. His features were too bold to be called typically handsome, but he had an interesting face. A tanned, almost olive complexion set off hard cheekbones and a strong jaw. Dark eyebrows lowered into a frown as he flipped through the pages of her proposal. His mouth tightened into a thin line, but his lower lip hinted at a devastating smile that could change his whole demeanor. Unfortunately, Chandler bet the man didn't smile too often.

He wore a dark charcoal gray suit, and though conservatively cut, the quality of the fabric and elegant lines told her his clothes were custom made. When he stood to welcome her, he towered easily over six feet and radiated a tightly contained raw energy. Even as he studied the figures in front of him, his presence pressed down upon her in a purely masculine intimidating manner. Another advantage the man held when closing a business deal.

Chandler pulled discreetly at the itchy neckline of her suit and wished she was back in her studio, conducting a class in her own comfortable clothes. Four years ago, she'd walked away from the corporate world and vowed to never return. The irony of the situation hit her full force. The Fates certainly possessed a sense of humor. She was now about to use all the skills she'd acquired from her past to convince Logan Grant to help save the Yoga and Arts Center, the school she'd built from scratch.

She hoped the Fates were also kind.

Logan dropped the proposal back on the polished wood and looked up. His gray gaze, as clear as ice but with a smoky intenseness, made her stare helplessly back, as if she had no choice. A shiver rose up her spine. She knew immediately he was not a kind man. Chandler fought against the sudden urge to walk out of his office and hide in a safe place.

An inner voice mocked her thought. If Logan Grant wanted to find her, there would be no safe place. She took another deep breath and braced herself for his decision.

"You are one gutsy lady."

She blinked. "Excuse me?"

He leaned back in his chair and surveyed her. The leather creaked gently beneath his weight. "I've seen many projects looking for funding, but never one with so many—how should I put it? Good intentions. I've heard of financing a health club, but a class that helps my employees manage stress? The results are impossible to measure. How do I make a profit?"

Chandler leaned forward and resisted the urge to pull down the hem of her tight skirt. Her legs itched from the scratchy material, but she wasn't about to draw his attention there. "Your investment will come back to you time and time again, Mr. Grant. As you've just read in my research, employees today aren't working to their full potential. L&G Brokerage, like many firms, suffers from high turnover. An employee hired by your firm shows productive results for an average of two years. Then the employee exhibits signs of burnout, and your firm hires a batch of fresh blood. Teach an employee to deal with stress, and he or she will keep productivity steady over the years. This saves you from hiring and retraining a new work force."

He studied her in silence. Chandler felt his piercing gaze try to strip away the cool, professional image she presented. She hoped he never saw her desperation, or she would fail. A man in his position respected strength, and she guessed he'd expected a mild mannered yoga teacher with no developed business plan. She'd spent weeks begging his secretary to schedule this meeting. Chandler knew she'd have one shot to sell her proposal.

She reached up unconsciously to push back her long hair, and then realized the strands were confined in a tight bun. "Mr. Grant, if you'd let me—"

"Logan," he interrupted smoothly.

"Logan, if you'd let me give you a brief rundown of my plan, I'm sure you'll see the benefits."

A soft knock on the door made her pause. A tall man with light brown hair entered the room and stopped beside her chair.

"Chandler, this is Richard Thorne, one of my attorneys. I asked him to sit in on this meeting if you don't mind."

She forced a smile and stood. Offering up a quick

prayer that her palms weren't damp, she reached out and shook the attorney's hand. Somehow, the idea of a lawyer listening to her proposal drove home the fact she was dealing with major league players. She fought back a nervous giggle when she remembered she'd never even scored in the minor leagues. "Nice to meet you," she said.

The attorney's hand held hers for a moment longer, and he smiled as if he knew her thoughts. Chestnut-colored eyes showed a teasing glint. "Don't let my being an attorney intimidate you," he said, with a wink. "I'm really harmless."

She laughed. His lean, angular face seemed kinder than Logan's and his smile came quick and easy. He took a chair near the window and settled a legal pad on his lap.

Chandler managed to give one leg a quick scratch and her skirt a discreet tug as she sat back down. She re-focused her attention back to Logan.

"You've made some good points but still didn't answer my question." Logan handed the proposal to his attorney, then tapped his gold pen against the arm of his leather chair. "Why funnel money into a program that can't guarantee a profit?"

Chandler dug bronze fingernails into the seat cushion, and reigned in her frustration. Businessmen only liked the bottom line—money. People didn't interest Logan Grant. Profit did.

She concealed her rising irritation and gave Logan

her most convincing business smile. "When employees suffer from stress, job performance also suffers. My workshop will teach them to be calm under pressure, and attack problems with a clear mind. Employees will show a more positive attitude toward their jobs. Maybe my workshop won't make you a million dollars, but investing in people always brings profit in the long run."

She almost bit her tongue when she caught the hard steel gleam in his eyes. Damn, she wasn't softening him up. In fact, he looked a little angry. She tried to casually re-cross her legs. Perfect. Both mens' eyes went immediately to her hemline. The meeting was becoming a disaster, and she was definitely allergic to wool.

"Interesting point," Logan said, his gaze rising to her face. "But you don't sound as if you approve of million dollar profits."

"Oh, but I do, as long as people aren't sacrificed."

He nodded. "Spoken like a true yoga teacher." His gray gaze drilled into her. "I'm curious how you became involved in this field of work. Your proposal is impressive. If I didn't know better, I'd swear you graduated with a business degree."

"I hold a bachelor's degree in psychology with a minor in business." She tried to keep a straight face when she saw his surprise. "I confess I'm a vegetarian—or at least I try to be—but I hate green sprouts and tofu. I still have trouble standing on my head. But I do take a multi-vitamin, daily."

A smile tugged at his lips. "Am I that bad?"

Chandler nodded her head and laughed. "Most people equate the term yoga with an image of a guru in a turban. I was equally doubtful the first time I took a class. I completed a paper in college on the effect of meditation on society. I researched yoga and was hooked. Learning to focus so clearly gave me the feeling I could accomplish anything. It also gave me the freedom to be comfortable doing nothing at all."

She shook her head at the memory. "Everyone is so caught up in the rat race. Complete a degree, make loads of money, and support a family." She leaned forward. "We start to forget the feel of sunshine on our face, the salty smell of the ocean, the taste of chocolate. We sleep through the sunrise and ignore the sunset. We don't know how to stand still and enjoy the moment."

She watched as a slight frown creased his brow.

Logan studied her for a moment, saying nothing. When he'd first heard he was scheduled to speak with a yoga teacher, he'd been ready to wring his secretary's neck. The last thing he wanted was to waste time discussing a proposal with a flower child of the new millennium, so he'd decided to cut the meeting short.

He changed his mind the moment she entered the room. Maybe it was the fiery glint in her emerald eyes, or all that dark honey hair begging to be set free from her severe spinster bun. He wondered how far it would tumble down her back.

She moved with a natural grace and had greeted

him in a low, husky voice that soothed his ears. As they exchanged pleasantries, he'd decided to humor her for awhile and look over the proposal. After all, the time was blocked on his calendar, and he'd have the opportunity to satisfy his curiosity.

He hadn't expected her business plan to be so good.

But what was even worse, Logan decided as he watched her fidget beneath his stare, was his reaction to the woman herself. Her passion for her plan caused an odd hunger to stir deep in his gut. When was the last time he'd gotten impassioned over a sunset, or even thought about something other than his next business deal? Maybe Chandler Santell lived moment to moment, with no intentions of settling down with a husband and family. Logan ignored the faint prickle of unease that shot through him at the image of her making love to anyone but him.

"You sound like you decided to give up the kind of life most people strive for," he said.

A shadow passed over her face as she fought back the memories. Then she forced a smile. "There's a certain amount of reality in that world. I follow a different path. I'd like to see people made more aware of simple daily pleasures, and then they can make their own choice."

"Sometimes there are no choices, Chandler. Sometimes people do the best they can."

She blinked in surprise at her body's sudden, feminine reaction to his words. Her mouth became dry. Her stomach clenched into a tight, silken fist. Funny, how the sound of her name from this man's lips evoked a sensation she'd never experienced before. Her body seemed to vibrate, humming to a tune she couldn't quite catch. Maybe it was just the way his voice caressed her, deepening to a low, dark pitch as he spoke. Maybe it was the sudden glint of regret she caught in his eyes that made her wonder what events had shaped this powerful man's life. Or maybe she was just finally losing her mind.

This time she caught her hand in mid-air before she pushed away honey brown strands that weren't there. She tried to re-direct the conversation back to business. "This program will keep you on the cutting edge."

"How would you implement the workshops?" he asked. "To be perfectly blunt, I can't see my executives seeking out a stress reduction class."

She nodded. This was the delicate part of the negotiation. She tried to keep her mind clear and calm her nerves. "I've given the matter some thought. When a seminar is offered in a company the employees take note of which groups attend and how important their function is. For example, if top management signs up for a seminar, the lower level managers usually follow, until it works its way down the hierarchy."

She clasped her hands together and knew she had his full attention. "So, if we institute a stress reduction workshop, there's only one way every employee will attend." Chandler paused. "You have to be the first person to enroll."

A short silence fell as her words hung in the air. Then he smiled. Chandler pulled in her breath at the sight of his dangerous, masculine smile which displayed a row of straight, white teeth. Logan Grant looked as if he'd found interesting prey and wanted to toy with his catch. She shivered at the thought.

"You want me to go to these classes personally?"

Chandler gathered her courage and took the plunge. "Yes, I do, Mr. Grant. It's the only way this program will work and—"

"Logan," he interrupted softly.

"I think this class will be the best thing for you."

"How so?" he drawled, leaning back in his chair.

She crossed her arms in front of her and vowed not to be intimidated by his tone. The words bubbled out of her mouth before she stopped to think.

"I'd guess by the dregs left in the coffee pot and the tired look in your eyes that you've been up half the night, going on caffeine and raw adrenaline. I'd also guess your temper hit full steam first thing this morning by the way your secretary looks at you with fear. Papers are stacked on your desk, it took me over a month to get an appointment, and I bet the door behind you leads directly to a bathroom and sofa. You probably work day and night here. All in all, I think a class teaching you to deal with stress couldn't hurt."

She inwardly cringed and waited for the explosion.

No wonder she hadn't done well in the business world. Her father always warned her blunt honesty never closed a deal. But how could she stay quiet and watch someone go blithely through life, without really living? Collecting the next degree or earning the next million didn't ensure peace or happiness. She once lived her life by a similar philosophy, always searching for something to help her forget the emptiness. Alexander Santell taught her about money and power, confident his only daughter would follow in his footsteps and inherit control of his company. She'd watched her father ignore his own family to pursue the path of success, and he lost everyone who'd ever cared for him or loved him. She didn't want to someday see the man across from her in the hospital because of a heart attack, where all the money in the world wouldn't help. If she implemented her stress seminar, he'd finally understand. If he gave her the chance, she would teach him to understand.

Logan studied the woman across his desk with amusement. Obviously, she regretted her impulsive words but decided to brazen it out. She held her chin high in defiance. Admiration flashed through him. Of course, he'd be insane to accept her offer. There was no sure way to measure the results. There was no guaranteed profit.

There was no way he'd agree to her proposal.

He tapped his pen against the desk in a steady rhythm, and tried to analyze his deep pang of regret at the thought of Chandler Santell walking out the door and out of his life. He heard honest concern and anger in her voice when she lectured him on his work habits. In his long climb up the ladder of success, many people gave advice regarding his next business move, and many shared in his rewards. But no one expressed interest in his personal health, or suggested a way to help him.

His eyes raked over her figure for about the twentieth time. He took in her professional appearance, from her tawny polished fingertips matching her honey-hued hair pulled back into a strangled bun, to the high neckline and short wool skirt of her "show-me-the-money" green business suit, to her too sensible low-heeled black pumps. She projected the image of a serious businesswoman who desired to be accepted into a man's world, but not be particularly noticed by anyone, especially a man.

The problem, Logan decided, was that Chandler Santell was destined to fail at her goal of men not noticing her.

He knew by the way she unconsciously lifted her hand to check her bun that her hair would spill around her shoulders in riotous waves. Anger made her green eyes flash, which would challenge a man to turn temper into passion. Her lips may be drawn tightly together, but Logan glimpsed the gentle fullness to her mouth, hinting at a certain softness and vulnerability. Her business suit couldn't hide her ripe curves and long, slender legs. Even her scent bewitched him; a subtle fragrance of vanilla that teased his senses and kept him from concentrating on their conversation.

As she spoke, he realized beneath her constrained appearance lurked a passionate spirit yearning for freedom. He became intrigued at the thought of tapping into a hidden part of Chandler Santell. He wondered if such a spirit could be tamed to live with one man, or if she'd ever even met a man with enough guts to try.

Chandler expected ice, but his gunmetal gaze drilled into her core as if searching, testing. His eyes were the color of smoke, trapping her with their heat.

"You know a lot about me and my company. But there are certain things in life that even I allow time for." His voice lowered to a deep, caressing pitch breaking the silence. He held the gold pen horizontal between both hands and his fingers met in the middle as he stroked it with slow, fluid motions. "Certain pleasures take away even my driving need to work…"

The pen gleamed against his bronzed skin as strong masculine fingers wrapped around the object and continued the pushing, pulling movements. His touch was light and fleeting. His gaze told her he was thinking of stroking other things. The thought caused liquid fire to race and singe every nerve ending, then pool between her thighs. Her tongue involuntarily dampened her lower lip. She saw him catch the movement, then lay the pen back on his desk. "…for a while," he added softly.

Chandler knew he made a deliberate choice to refrain

from questions, even though many were reflected in his eyes before he looked back down at her proposal. The rustle of papers cut through the pulsing silence.

She struggled for composure as she glanced over at Richard Thorne. The attorney's eyes narrowed thoughtfully as he watched her, seemingly interested in her reaction to Logan's words. She cleared her throat. "I apologize for my outburst. I never meant to imply something was wrong with your life, I know you made a choice to work hard for your success." She smiled. "I worry about people too much. I once worked in this type of corporate climate so I've seen the kind of drive and dedication needed to climb to the top. I've also seen the damage. I'd like to help your employees handle their stress so they don't wake up one morning and wonder what their lives are about. I think they deserve more."

Logan Grant was probably one of the most controlled, self-contained men she'd ever met. She bet he carefully analyzed every emotion before he decided to express them, or bury them deep. A pang of regret confirmed her belief about corporate executives. They never let their emotions overrule business decisions. They pushed away messiness and made logic their god. A shiver ran down her spine when she thought of the way his fingers had glided over the pen. Something deep inside told her Logan Grant held many secrets behind a steel barrier, but it would take Superwoman to unveil the ray of vulnerability she glimpsed within his eyes.

She was not Superwoman, and she mustn't forget

that he reached the top by being cold-hearted. She needed to have her guard up.

Logan nodded. "Apology accepted. I know you have good intentions. But good intentions don't necessarily mean good profits." Chandler braced herself for his next comment. "Your outline is excellent. Your idea is creative. These figures show how well your clientele is expanding, but I also see your profits aren't what you need to keep the business going. Even with your research, there's still no proof these employees are doing more productive work. So, Chandler, the bottom line is that you want to use my company as a guinea pig because without my money, the Yoga and Arts Center is going under. Richard, do you agree?"

Richard Thorne looked regretful, but gave a nod. "Sorry, Chandler. Personally, I think you have a great plan, but Logan is right. We can't take the chance."

She almost closed her eyes in defeat. She'd been hoping, no betting, that with the proper appearance and some impressive paperwork, he may see the truth. Of course, she should have known her ruse was a mistake the moment she met him. Logan made CEOs of billion dollar corporations fidget beneath his stare. A novice never had a shot.

"Yes, Mr. Grant. Your bottom line is correct." Surprise flickered over his face, before the mask slammed back down. "So, I'll guarantee a profit."

"How?"

This was the riskiest part of the deal. "Test the

program out for a six month trial period. If you don't see a difference, our relationship will be terminated and I'll reimburse you in full."

It was a while before he spoke. When he did, it was in a bedroom voice, the mere sound of it conjuring up a number of disturbing images: heavy velvet pulled over naked skin; steel sheathed in satin; smooth silk dragged over gravel. It was a mass of contradictions she wanted nothing to do with. Chandler pushed away the thoughts and concentrated on his words.

"Do you realize your position if I decide to terminate this arrangement?" he asked. "You'd lose everything. If you invest all your capital and efforts into this program and it fails, your client base will be reduced along with your cash flow. Your whole business could go under."

Chandler nodded. "I'm willing to take the risk. If you don't want this offer I have a new list of names to approach. I'm sure one executive will give me a trial run."

Logan glanced at Richard. The attorney shrugged his shoulders. "If she's willing to back up her offer, we have nothing to lose."

Minutes ticked by. Chandler sensed angry waves of energy radiating around Logan, and wondered why he seemed disturbed since she was the one risking everything. She waited patiently for his decision. She knew she'd done everything possible to save the Yoga and Arts Center.

"One gutsy lady," he muttered under his breath.

Her lips curved in a smile. "Do we have a deal?"

"Yes. We have a deal."

He rose from the chair and walked around the desk, reaching out to shake her hand. His fingers wrapped around hers.

Fire.

Possession.

Safety.

She fought for breath as the strange emotions whirled and crashed within her. The touch of his skin against hers made a million butterflies take flight in her stomach. She tried to reassure herself that he held her entire future in his grasp, but her body responded only to her fear of his control.

A smile played about his lips, as if only he knew the outcome of the game they decided to play. She tugged her hand out of his and caught the amusement in his face.

"Richard will draw up the contract," he said.

"If you don't mind, I'd like to use my own attorney. Harry needs the practice."

One black brow shot up. "Harry?"

"Yes, he's a friend of mine who recently passed the bar exam." Her tone reflected a warm affection. "I promised I'd give him all of my business once he passed the test."

A dark scowl passed over Logan's features. She rushed to alter his anger. "Oh, don't worry, he's perfectly capable of drawing up the contract. He's really a hard worker, besides having a big heart."

"I see." Actually, he didn't. Logan didn't like the raw jealousy that shot through his system when he thought of Chandler belonging to another man. He frowned. This Harry couldn't be right for her. She revealed too much passion beneath her proper business suit, and obviously her current lover couldn't handle her.

Knowing he wasn't acting in the rational way he normally handled matters, Logan took a step forward and closed the distance between them. Satisfaction surged through him when he spotted the flicker of awareness in her green eyes. Hmmm, maybe he need-ed to explore these strange feelings more in depth. To satisfy his curiosity, Logan decided to move quickly.

It looked like she intended to ignore the current of sexual energy crackling through the air, and chose flight. He decided not to let her. "Why don't we get together for dinner tomorrow night?" he asked. "We can discuss the program. We'll be working closely together for awhile."

Chandler tilted her head back in order to meet his gaze. The clean scent of soap, lemon, and musk teased her senses. Waves of heat radiated from his skin, pulling her towards him. Chandler took anoth-er casual step backward and prayed he wouldn't notice her panic. "Oh, I guess I thought you'd dele-gate another executive to work with me. I know you're very busy."

He gave her a lazy smile. "When I invest heavily in a project, I like to oversee all aspects of the operation."

He paused. "Personally."

She nodded in agreement and inched further away. "Fine."

Richard moved across the room and stood between them. "Chandler, it was nice to meet you. I'm looking forward to taking your class."

She noticed Logan's surprise at his comment.

Richard laughed and touched her arm briefly. "I discovered yoga and stress reduction a couple of months ago myself." He shifted his feet and grinned sheepishly. "I even meditate."

Her eyes lit up. "Richard, that's wonderful. I can't tell you how rare it is to meet someone in this industry who actually knows about yoga. Do you take classes?"

"I've taken a couple at the local YMCA."

"Hmmm, interesting. I thought you belonged to that fancy country club and preferred racquetball. And I doubt there's a local Y in your neighborhood." Logan's words were laced with ice as he stared down his associate. "We've got a meeting in a few minutes."

Richard's face tightened, but he nodded and said goodbye. Chandler took a step back, and suddenly over six feet of coiled muscle towered over her. She stood frozen in her spot.

"I'll pick you up at seven tomorrow night." Steel gray eyes burned into hers. "We can toast to our new relationship."

With a shudder, Chandler walked out of the office and tried to ignore the flicker of unease, warning her there was hidden meaning in Logan Grant's last statement.

Logan watched Richard Thorne neatly file his papers in his briefcase and set up for the next meeting. His gold embossed cufflinks gleamed in the sunlight as perfectly manicured fingers flipped through the pile of contracts. He was younger than Logan, by a good five years, and possessed an uncanny ability to put people at ease. His eyes reflected pleasant humor clients immediately warmed up to, but Logan had hired him for a different reason. His laughing smile covered up a brilliant mind that could find a loophole in a clause and maneuver a client to sign on the dotted line. His easy-going nature hid an inward ruthlessness Logan spotted from the first moment they met. Richard liked the good life, and had more ambition than most people gave him credit for.

"I didn't know you took yoga," Logan said. He walked to the window and leaned against the wall.

Richard shrugged. "I like to experiment with different things. I didn't announce it because yoga isn't a popular activity for men."

"Hmmm, I suppose you're right."

"An interesting woman, Chandler Santell." The rustle of papers echoed through the air. "I assume you know who her father is."

An uneasy feeling flickered through Logan, but his voice remained bland when he spoke. "I never meet with a person I haven't researched."

"Thought so." Richard looked up from his briefcase. The attorney's eyes held a gleam of determination. Logan suddenly realized this man had the potential to be dangerous, and made a mental note to watch him more carefully. Though he trusted his attorney with business, he knew Richard hungered for success. Logan didn't intend on becoming one of his attorney's victims on the man's climb for power. "I hear her old man still keeps a close eye on her, even though she wants nothing to do with him. I wonder why she cut him out of her life."

"Yes. I wonder."

Richard snapped the leather case closed and smiled. "Well, the stress class should be interesting. I'm looking forward to it."

"I thought your case load was too heavy for extra activities."

"Like yourself, I always allow myself time for certain pleasures."

The air sparked with primitive energy. A slight smile played about Logan's lips as he recognized the challenge. He didn't know Richard's game yet, but he intended to find out. In the meantime, he needed to keep a close eye on Chandler Santell.

"Point taken." Logan pushed himself away from the wall and headed toward the conference room. "I hope you're ready to take on Tony Piscetti. I want Global Electronics on board."

Richard's tone held satisfaction. "Somehow, I feel lucky today, boss."

Logan shut his office door behind them.

Chapter
2

Sunlight poured through the oversize bay windows of the Yoga and Arts Center and enveloped Chandler in a warm, hazy glow. She breathed deep as the soothing strains of a flute drifted in the air. Her name echoed from the distance but she ignored the sound. She floated in a calm, peaceful state of mind, and knew the moment she opened her eyes reality would intrude. As she slowly brought herself back from her meditation, she became aware of the cool, smooth wood beneath the soles of her bare feet. Her unbound hair fanned out on the mat around her and absorbed the heat of the sun. When the voice became more insistent, she opened her eyes and eased herself up.

Harrison Edward Weston III rushed through the door and stopped short. "Oh! Sorry, Chandler, I didn't know you were meditating."

"Don't worry, I was just finishing up." She rose to her feet and walked to the end of her studio to flip off the CD player. "I need to go over the contract with you, anyway. I want to be prepared for my dinner with Logan Grant."

Harry trailed behind her. His tone held a worried note. "I shouldn't have let you handle the meeting alone. I'm your lawyer; it's my responsibility to protect your interests."

Chandler hid a smile. Ever since she'd met Harry in the sixth grade, she'd looked out for him. Being a year older, she treated him as the younger brother she never had, and throughout the years a close friendship evolved, bordering on family affection.

Harry's father still worked for the law firm which handled Alexander Santell's legal matters. They'd often laugh as they reminisced about their common backgrounds, since both of them had been raised in their fathers' offices. After he failed the bar exam, Harry left his father's firm to work as a legal assistant, vowing to achieve success on his own. Her heart broke each time he failed, but she admired the determination her friend showed, swearing he wouldn't quit until he passed the bar.

The mirror on the far wall of her studio reflected an image of a man to be trusted. His curly, dark hair and warm brown eyes drew women toward him, and his friendly smile helped build him a solid base of clients. His five foot six frame bubbled over with energy, and she always had trouble trying to get him to relax and focus on the task at hand. She enjoyed Harry's company, and relaxed in his presence. With Harry she never worried about any hidden intentions.

Chandler led him toward her back office and watched him sink into the worn cushions of the tattered mauve sofa. "Maybe I should go to dinner with you and Grant." Harry opened his briefcase with a frown. "What if he tries to put one over on you?"

She leaned against the edge of the desk and sighed. "No, I'll be okay. This dinner meeting is a way for him to learn my weaknesses. It's a familiar tactic I learned in the corporate world."

Harry chuckled. "I almost feel sorry for him if he thinks he can intimidate you. Beneath your gentle image lies a mighty core. Four years ago, you were prepared to enter your father's corporation and marry his right-hand man. Your whole future was planned. And at the last minute you left everything behind to take the time to find yourself. You've got guts."

She smiled. Harry understood what it took for her to walk away from everything she thought she wanted. Her disciplines of yoga and meditation helped, strengthening both her body and mind. Yet late at night, she still heard her father's taunting words from the day she walked into his office and found her entire life had changed.

She shook off her disturbing thoughts and poured a cup of herbal tea. The hot liquid slid down her throat with ease. "Logan will help me keep my business. I guarantee him his investment, and then we both get what we want."

"The escape clause was a mistake. You never discussed that option with me."

"You know I'm desperate. Logan behaved oddly, too. After I offered him a full reimbursement, he acted angry. Almost as if he cared about what happened to my studio."

Harry gave a snort. "Grant doesn't care about people. He cares about money."

"Yeah, you're right. His lawyer seemed nice, though. His name is Richard Thorne, and he actually studies yoga."

Harry lifted one brow. "An attorney of Grant's doing yoga? That's a new one." He studied her face thoughtfully. "What did you think of him?"

"He's nice. Not like Logan at all. He seemed more, well, light-hearted. Non-threatening."

"Hmmm. Just your type."

She crossed her arms in front of her chest. "Are you trying to tell me something?"

"Yeah, you need a date."

"Harry, you're so subtle."

"It's been too long since you had a man in your life. A lawyer who's interested in yoga is a rarity these days. Go for it."

"Thanks for the advice, but I'm not jumping into anything. I'm content with my life, and men make things complicated. Besides, he works for Logan. He wanted to draw up the contracts but I told them I'd use my own lawyer."

"Good move. I'll add a clause so you can break the arrangement within six months if you think the program won't work. I want you both on equal footing." He grimaced as he took a sip of the herbal tea she handed him. "Damn, don't you have any coffee in this place?"

"Too much caffeine isn't good for you. Besides, this tea contains antioxidants."

"I'd rather die happy. This stuff tastes terrible." He

put the mug back down. "How will you manage the extra workload?"

"Linda will handle the bulk, but I'll have to cut back on some classes temporarily. If this deal works out, I can hire new instructors and expand without a deficit. This contract is the start of a whole new future. Can you imagine how many new students I could teach? I can renovate the building, and get that soft lighting we talked about, and new mats and—"

"What if the deal falls through?"

She raised her chin. "The deal will go through. I'll prove to Logan this is the best program he ever invested in."

Harry shook his head. "No offense, but I can't believe he agreed. Can you picture the 'man of steel' trying to relax and clear his mind?"

"I know. I bet half of his work force suffers from ulcers."

Harry chuckled. "Those finance boys won't know what hit them. I bet after a month of your classes they'll watch what they eat and breathe deeply in stressful situations."

Chandler laughed. "I hope you're right. But the first executive I need to impress is the man picking me up in a couple of hours." She glanced at her watch. "I have to get home and change. I'm sure at exactly seven he'll show up at the door in his usual suit and tie."

Harry went over a few details he added to the contract. "Are you wearing the itchy suit?" he asked.

Chandler made a face at his teasing remark. "No, I'm donating that to charity. I have a different outfit in mind for Mr. Grant. Maybe the white chiffon."

He whistled. "The one with the headdress? Your father almost dropped on the floor when you showed up at that business dinner and caused his client to spill champagne in his lap."

Her laughter floated through the room as she shut the door behind her.

• • •

The situation was not what she'd expected.

Chandler watched the man from across the table as she bit into a slice of crusty French bread slathered in butter. From the moment he'd picked her up in his low slung Italian sports car he'd thrown her curve balls. Instead of the usual suit and tie, he lounged before her in a casual sport jacket and black sweater, which molded to his body and defined his broad shoulders and chest. Black slacks clung to his muscular thighs and a pair of Nikes completed the outfit. Logan Grant actually wore sneakers. She couldn't seem to accept it.

What was probably worse, she thought as she stabbed her fork into her Caesar salad, was his reaction when he'd seen her outfit. She'd prepared for a shocking response, but the pure masculine satisfaction showing in his eyes made her nervous.

Chandler had passed on wearing her white chiffon dress and instead wore a black lace bodysuit that peaked out from under a sheer black blouse in the finest of silk. Her black silk skirt flowed down to her ankles, but when she moved the material parted to reveal a dozen slits cut to her thigh. A wide silver belt completed the outfit. The fabric flowed with her every movement and lightly skimmed her body.

She gave up on hair clips and pins and let her hair fall loose, allowing her dark honey and sun-bleached tawny strands to curl wildly about her shoulders and down her back. She wore no jewelry, having always preferred bare skin to the overdone-in-gold look. Many arguments ensued with her father based on her tendency to dislike clothes suitable in the business world, but Logan didn't seem to mind. In fact, she almost blushed under his direct gaze.

She sipped her Pinot Grigio and watched him carry on a lively conversation with the waiter about the Giants and their chance to win the Super Bowl. The man actually knew how to talk football. This hardly seemed fair given the amount of time he spent in the office.

"Food seems to be another one of life's pleasures. Don't you agree?" he asked in an amused tone, interrupting her thoughts. She paused in the act of reaching for the shrimp cocktail as the waiter left.

"I try to be vegetarian and eat tofu and yogurt, but my heart just isn't in it." She smiled. "I feel guilty when I lecture my students on nutrition. I've already made note of the dessert menu."

He laughed. "A woman whose heart is controlled by her stomach. I respect that." He watched her bite into the shrimp and close her eyes in delight. "I hope your profession can support your appetite."

"If I wanted a fortune, I would have worked as a business executive."

"So you said before. What else do you hate besides money, Chandler?"

Her green eyes glittered with a hint of moisture. "Power. People who control. Lies hidden behind smiles. The usual things most people hate."

"It's not so simple," he said softly. "Most grab at an opportunity with both hands. People raised in poverty see money as their only way out of hell."

She shook her head. "It's a trap. They're really giving up the self, and what they get in return is a lie. Money and power are illusions and only soothe for a temporary period. Then they wake up one morning needing more, and sacrificing more to get it. In the end they lose everything important and find themselves alone. Money can't help loneliness."

"That sounds like a conclusion drawn by one who followed the path and got burned. You talk from experience. What made you change?"

She looked up from her plate, startled. She never meant to get involved in this type of conversation. She didn't like to tread in such dangerous territory, in fact she refused. Chandler forced a bright smile. "Why, my therapist, of course. Doesn't everyone in New York have one?"

She held her breath and waited to see if he'd follow her lead. She relaxed when he smiled back. If he'd wanted answers, she had a sinking feeling she'd have no choice in the matter. She made a mental note to be more careful about the information she leaked.

He focused his attention back to his dinner. "I'll have Richard look over the contract and you can start the workshops on Monday." His voice was cool and brisk. "I know your lawyer is inexperienced, but an escape clause shouldn't have been offered. It puts you at risk."

"Harry didn't know until it was too late," she said. "I came up with the idea myself. He gave me hell when I told him."

One black brow shot up. "Do you usually do impulsive things without telling anyone?"

She shrugged. "I only have myself to answer to, so I take responsibility for my actions."

"Your Harry doesn't take offense?"

Chandler frowned. "He has no say in my decisions."

Logan watched her for a moment, then shook his head. "You haven't met the man who'll set a couple of rules for you." He cut into his prime rib. "You're too impulsive, so you need to be watched. I bet most men in your life don't know how to handle you. You need someone with enough strength to tell you no once in a while."

Her mouth dropped open. She felt her temper flare. "I do not need, nor will I ever need, a man telling me what to do with my life," she said firmly. "I am a capable, rational woman who knows exactly what will make me happy. No wonder I swore off business executives. Too many of your kind think they know what's good for a woman and refuse to converse in a normal manner. They dictate, threaten, and bully their wives into doing what they want, forgetting the bedroom is not the boardroom. I refuse to be put through that experience again."

"Again?"

She ignored his question and forged on. "Furthermore, I'm looking for a man who listens to what I have to say and supports my goals. A man willing to compromise when he disagrees with me."

"You'd be bored out of your mind. You need someone who will yell back in the living room, and make up in the bedroom."

She gasped. "That is the most ridiculous, chauvinistic remark I've ever heard! I want a partner, not a caveman. I'm quite satisfied with my life and refuse to change for any man. Besides, you don't know the men I date. They certainly don't bore me."

Logan clamped down hard on the wave of irritation that flowed through him at the idea of her dating a wide variety of men. His free spirited yoga teacher intended to show him she refused to cater to a man's whims. Unfortunately, he became more determined to put an end to her experiments. Hell, this was crazy, he thought to himself in disgust. He'd never been a possessive man where women were concerned. Possessiveness indicated a messy emotion, which he normally stayed away from. Maybe this woman called to his sense of challenge. Obviously, she'd been burned by a corporate executive, and chose to stay far away from a man who wore a three piece suit.

His lips tightened. Time she learned a lesson. Chandler probably dated men she safely controlled, but she was about to discover he wouldn't stay meekly on the sidelines once he decided he wanted her.

Logan studied her face. She stuck her chin high in the air, practically daring him to challenge her. A dab of red cocktail sauce clung to her lower lip. Almost as if she knew, her tongue snaked out and licked off the drop, unconscious of how damn sexy she looked. He waited a beat before he made his decision.

He wanted Chandler Santell.

"You haven't met the right man yet," he repeated.

Her hand trembled around the stem of her wine glass. The certainty in his voice and the heat in his eyes made her stomach slide downward, as if she had just plunged off the peak of a roller coaster. She fought the sudden urge to fidget, but reminded herself the deal was closed, and she didn't have to plead her case. Of course, she still needed to placate him throughout the six month trial period, but refused to allow him to pry into her personal life. A strangled laugh rose to her lips. "You're impossible." She reached up and pushed back her hair. "Is this how you wear down your enemies?"

"Words won't convince you. Action will."

A chill ran down her spine. She ignored his remark and chalked it up to one of his control moves.

He devoted the rest of the conversation to neutral topics. She enjoyed matching her wits against his sharp mind and was surprised at his dry sense of humor. No doubt, Chandler thought, he had his fair share of offers given the way women in the restaurant snuck glances at their table. She wondered if his good looks or his money held their rapt attention. The combination was a deadly mixture.

As he escorted her into his sports car, she admitted Logan made a nice dinner companion. As long as she kept the subject firmly averted from her personal life, he'd be the perfect advisor to help her business expand.

He pulled up to her apartment building. "Why don't we finish celebrating our deal over brandy?" he asked.

Chandler hesitated before she decided she'd be rude not to agree. "Sure, come on up." They walked up the flight of stairs and Chandler slid the key in the lock. She flipped on the lights and waved toward the sofa. "Make yourself comfortable, I'll only be a moment." She walked into the kitchen and kicked off her shoes.

Logan smiled at her sigh of relief before turning his attention to the room around him. He wandered around, pausing now and then to finger an object or study a painting. The cream walls, pale yellow carpet and off-white furniture helped set off a whirling array of colors and sights that attacked the senses. Cheerful, bright watercolors hung on the walls in a blinding intensity; they practically jumped out of their frames at him. They were so full of life.

Lush, green plants dangled above him as he checked the view out the window. A large ficus tree dominated one corner and half a dozen smaller plants he didn't immediately recognize surrounded it. Some sort of Christmas-looking pine tree and bunches of flowers claimed the other corner and an entire wall. Chandler obviously had a green thumb—he was curious to see how green she would make his bottom line.

Sitting among the foliage were three large marble sculptures struggling for attention. Each figure stretched in a different yoga position. He made a safe assumption they were not high art, but more of an emotional attachment. Books and magazines were tossed over the floor and furniture, and Logan caught the faint smell of incense which still hung in the air. He studied the sculptures with curiosity.

"One of my teachers gave me those." She placed two snifters on the coffee table and sat down on the sofa. Logan sat next to her. "They were supposed to represent the new commitment I made to my life."

"What commitment?"

Chandler smiled. "Truth in speech, simplicity in manner, firmness of mind—three things to constantly strive for."

"Have you succeeded?"

She took a sip of brandy. The heated liquid trickled down her throat and warmed her body. "I don't think many people end up succeeding," she said. "Peace is a constant journey. I know I'm happier and more satisfied than I've been in the past. Giving up the drive for wealth and power wasn't as hard as I thought. I've gotten back so much."

"Why does it have to be all or nothing? A person can still have money and reach spiritual height without giving up his dream."

She shook her head. "I think the path sounds easier than it really is. Most people think they can have both, which may work for a while. But someone who is truly reaching for spiritual height will eventually have to choose between truth and lies. Truth must be chosen. When money's involved, the decision becomes harder."

Logan reached for his brandy and studied the amber liquid. "I disagree. If a person knows himself, he knows what path must be chosen. Money doesn't corrupt, Chandler. People do."

"Perhaps." She settled back on the couch. "I think we talk too much about me. I want to know how the 'man of steel' received his nickname."

He groaned. "If I ever get my hands on the journalist who wrote that article, he will sorely regret it. I feel like I should wear a cape," he said putting his fists on his hips and comically staring off into the distance.

Chandler laughed. "Oh, your reputation can't be that bad," she teased. "Your last coup with Larson Securities was very successful. Investors knock down your door to get a hint of your next target." She swished the brandy around in her glass. "Now, I know you started off as a stockbroker and cultivated some high number of accounts, but you've expanded since then. You're buying corporations outright now."

He nodded. "I look for companies that are solid but in trouble. I buy them out, fix them up, and make more money. If I decide it's not profitable, I just take the business apart and sell it off."

"Like Richard Gere in *Pretty Woman*."

Amusement gleamed in his eyes. "Yes, just like the movie."

"In such a competitive market, you've made quite a name for yourself."

"I've managed."

"You've more than managed. But you didn't tell me how you got your nickname."

A shadow passed over his face. His voice chilled when he finally spoke. "Does it matter?"

She blinked in surprise. "No. I just thought we'd get to know one another. Since we'll be working together, of course."

"Of course." A muscle worked in his jaw, but he seemed to want to answer her question. "When I first started L&G Brokerage, I needed to score some particular deals in order to keep afloat. Steele Investments was an up and coming company earning a lot of press. I decided if I was able to acquire them, I could easily double my company's profits."

The name skittered on the edge of her memory.

"Wasn't that a family owned company?"

"Yes. I researched all the members in the family. I learned their strengths and weaknesses, in their professional and private lives. It took me months, but I finally found the weak link."

"What?"

"The younger brother was a gambler. Oh, they kept him tightly under wraps, but he started gambling with some of their investors' money. His family couldn't do too much since he owned a large chunk of stock, and of course, jail was out of the question. So, I hired a friend of mine to pose as an investor and meet with him personally."

A cold chill raced down her spine. "You tempted him with money, didn't you?"

He spoke with no emotion. "I gave him a million dollars to invest."

She gasped. "You had that much capital available?"

A slight smile touched his lips as he took a sip of brandy. "That was everything I had. I took a risk, and it paid off."

"He took the money?"

Logan nodded. "Yes. His family found out too late. I offered them a deal. If they sold me the company, he'd stay out of jail. They signed the papers that week."

She gripped the stem of her glass tighter. "Did the press ever find out?"

Logan shook his head. "They didn't find out about the gambling. But after I signed the deal, the brother talked to a reporter and told him I practically threatened them to sign over the company. Said I was a cold-blooded monster who wouldn't rest until I got what I wanted. The article stated no company was safe from me."

"The 'man of steel,'" she whispered.

He looked up. "With a heart to match." His mouth set in a firm line. "I don't look back and I don't have regrets, Chandler. But I always try to protect the people close to me, even at the expense of myself."

His gaze met and held hers. She knew Logan Grant held secrets buried deep inside; secrets revealed only in brief flashes in his gun-metal eyes. The man lied, he held many regrets—but he wasn't about to explain, and he wasn't going to look back.

Her breath caught in her throat as an unexpected wave of protectiveness flooded her. Why did she have this sudden need to put her arms around him and offer comfort? Why wasn't she horrified at his story, shocked at the way he manipulated another human being?

She didn't know. She'd met many hungry executives before, and counted her own father among them, but there was a unique difference in the man beside her. She believed Logan when he said he'd be fiercely devoted to the people he loved.

"I believe you," she said softly. "I don't hold every businessman in a negative light, and I try not to make judgments on what I hear or read. People deserve a chance."

"Does everyone deserve a chance? Or just the people you can keep at a safe distance?"

She pushed back her heavy mane of hair. "I don't keep myself at a distance. I always try to give something of myself to people."

"Even men?"

She bristled at his comment. "Everyone. Men and women. I don't draw distinctions between the two. If you're talking about a romantic relationship, I'm bound to disappoint you. I never get involved with my students or my business partners."

He raised an eyebrow at her warning. "Doesn't leave a lot of territory open now, does it?"

She rose from the sofa and wondered how this man made her so defensive on the subject of her love life. Or lack of it. She glared at him. "Quantity is not my concern, Logan. Quality is what makes a relationship work, and I can guarantee I won't find that with a man making a six figure salary, but is too busy to come home at night. I need more."

He studied her in silence. Intensity radiated around him. She struggled to take a deep breath, suddenly afraid of him, of the powerful emotions that crackled in the room like a burst of summer lightning. She backed away a bit. He was no longer her charming dinner companion, but a dangerous man who seemed to feel something she couldn't understand.

And she was alone with him.

Slowly, Logan stood up and placed the snifter on the table. He crossed the room in two strides and stopped before her. "Your apartment suits you." His voice vibrated through her body. "It reminds me of how you're a woman filled with life—who uses every moment to feel pleasure."

His hot steel gaze burned her. She stared, transfixed by his words and his voice and the heat that emanated from his body. "But at the same time there's a part of you that remains in control, selfishly contained in a small, dark space. That part is cold and clinical, and vows never to melt into the other."

He took the glass from her hand, set it beside his, then moved closer. The back of his hand caressed her face. "You hold yourself back, Chandler, waiting for someone who will never come; a fantasy figure who seems safer than a man of flesh and blood, a man who will probably make mistakes and possibly hurt you. But the man you deny yourself could also make your spirit soar. You're too afraid to reach out and take him."

He pulled her towards him with slow, deliberate movements. His warm breath penetrated her hair as his arms pressed her body into his. "Don't run from me." His voice commanding, whispered in her ear. Then his mouth came down on hers.

Caught in the fog enveloping her mind, Chandler held herself perfectly still in his embrace. Her senses were overwhelmed by his unique scent as it mingled with his cologne. The heat of his kiss and the coiled power of his hard body ignited a raw sensual energy that threatened to engulf her.

Frantically, she realized the position she'd put herself in. Chandler knew he intended to prove her wrong regarding her attraction to corporate executives. By her denial, she'd waved a bright red flag in front of him and challenged his ego. She needed to remain calm and let him kiss her. He'd realize his mistake, apologize, and they'd continue their business arrangement and avoid future pitfalls.

Logan immediately felt her refusal to respond to him. Obviously, his yoga teacher held on to her rational thoughts and treated him as an experiment. He clamped down hard on the fierce need that raced through his body to make her surrender to her emotions, as he'd been forced to. He deliberately relaxed his hold and eased the pressure of the kiss, moving his lips teasingly over hers, inviting her to kiss him back. Slowly, he sipped at her mouth as if she were a precious drink of water in the hot desert sun, learning her taste and texture. Nibbling at her lower lip, his tongue teased its pouty outline as he continued a maddening game of arousal and retreat attempting to both sooth and ignite her.

Chandler unconsciously pressed her body closer to his, seeking something more to quench the fire in her belly that suddenly flamed to life.

The strong hands that had first dragged her to his embrace now glided over her shoulders and down her arms in a gentle caress. His fingers smoothed her flesh through the sheer black silk and made her wonder what his touch would feel like on her bare skin. Her mind clamored for her to push him away when his grip loosened, but her body longed to feel the promise behind his teasing kiss. The blood pumped through her veins with each deliberate movement of his hands and mouth.

Logan's mouth brushed hers, then withdrew. He pulled his hands through her thick hair, rubbing each strand between his fingers in slow, easy movements. He lightly touched the tips of her breasts which immediately hardened under her stretch lace bodysuit. A moan escaped her lips.

"Open your mouth for me, Chandler," he whispered. And then he was inside. His tongue pushed through the seam of her lips, glided over the smoothness of her teeth, and plunged into the slick recess of her mouth to engage in a passionate battle. He drank in her taste with a hunger she could no longer fight. Her arms slid up and around his shoulders and pulled him closer.

He crushed her soft, full breasts against his chest and insinuated one thigh between her legs, pushing her slightly off balance. Deftly, he undid the buttons of her silk blouse down to her waist and slipped it off her shoulders. The material fell away and cool air kissed her flesh, making her shiver. He dragged his mouth away and took in her swollen lips. "Do you realize how much I want you?" She trembled as his fingers stroked her breast. Her nipple rose into his palm as his thumb made teasing circles. "I knew it would be like this between us."

Logan eased the stretchy black bodysuit over her shoulders and exposed her naked breasts to his gaze. He plucked her tight nipples, murmuring in satisfaction as she arched upward and silently begged for more. His fingers sunk into the hair at her nape and tugged her head back to drop over his arm. "God, you're beautiful."

Chandler felt like a pagan goddess about to be sacrificed. Her hair hung down her bare back, her breasts tilted upward, naked to his gaze and waiting for his mouth. Her body greedily demanded the pleasure this powerful man could give her, needing to be rid of the constraints her mind imposed over her many years of discipline. When was the last time she let a man pleasure her? For the first time, Chandler realized by letting her body take over, she felt gloriously free.

His warm breath teased her nipple as he lowered himself over her and opened his mouth fully over her breast. Throaty moans escaped her lips as he bestowed pleasure, bringing her to a fevered pitch of longing, knowing there was more. She became sensitized to the scrape of his teeth, the stroking of his tongue, the touch of his lips. A throbbing ache settled between her thighs. Overwhelmed by the sensation of being totally possessed, she sank into a place where only pleasure ruled. All her seething emotions and erotic desires, long hidden, suddenly burst free.

When Logan swept her up into his arms and carried her to the sofa, there was no thought in her mind to protest. He pressed her deep into the cushions, fully removed her blouse, and further pushed her bodysuit down to her waist. His leg lay heavily over hers, causing the slits in her skirt to fall open to mid-thigh.

"Touch me."

His softly spoken demand made her tremble as she tugged the sweater out of his waistband and pushed the material upward, sliding her fingers beneath. She lingered over his hard stomach, tracing the swirling pattern of dark hair that covered his torso. He groaned when her nail brushed his flat nipple, causing her to pull back, unsure. When he remained perfectly still, her fingers retraced their path with wonder. His chest rose as he dragged in air. The crisp hairs tickled her palms as her gaze followed the dark line past his stomach to pause at the edge of his belt buckle.

His evident arousal made her ache to reveal more of him, so she let her hands coast downward to explore.

Logan muttered a curse, captured her wrists and pinned them above her head in one swift motion. His other hand slid up her calf, and stroked the sensitive skin behind her knee before he ventured higher and encountered the edge of her stocking. He let his fingers slide on the bare expanse of skin at the top of her thigh. Slowly he unsnapped her bodysuit between her legs and played with the line of her panties, letting one finger slip under the elastic, then moving away.

His mouth took hers in a hungry kiss, and Chandler fought for breath. When he finally raised his head, his gaze locked on hers. With deliberate motions, he settled his palm over the apex of her thighs. A rush of damp heat burned through the fragile black lace.

Slowly, he pressed.

Chandler arched upward and cried his name. Instantly his mouth was back on hers, kissing her without restraint as he continued the rotating, stroking motions of his palm. He drank in the tiny gasps that broke from her lips.

"Tonight I'm going to teach you how good we are together, Chandler. Give yourself to me and I swear you won't regret it. I'll take care of everything."

His husky words had the effect of dumping a bucket of icy water over her. She froze, her mind frantically going over the implication of his last statement.

He would take care of everything.

With dawning horror, she realized how close she'd come to making another terrible mistake. Logan Grant wanted to take her to bed to prove a point. He'd deliberately planned to seduce her, using his coldblooded logic to justify his actions. Her seduction gained him more control, which would be an advantage in their business dealings. His ego also benefitted by conquering her objections to corporate executives. Once he accomplished his goal, he'd tire of her, and then terminate their contract.

One night of passion could cost her her career. Nothing was worth that.

Not even the pleasure she found in his arms.

It took a few moments for Logan to realize the woman beneath him wasn't struggling to get closer, but to free herself from his embrace. Those emerald eyes once sparked with passion now filled with growing panic. Her body stiffened, and the arms that had clung to his shoulders now pushed him away. Logan took some deep breaths to try and clear the fog from his mind, annoyed she now seemed to fear him on some level.

"You don't have to be afraid of me." He tried not to focus his attention on her lush mouth, swollen from his kisses. "I'd never do anything you didn't want. I think you're afraid to admit you want me. I don't fit the image of your perfect lover." His gaze took in her abandoned figure, naked to the waist, ruby nipples wet from his mouth. His voice dropped. "But your body betrays you."

"Please let me up." She crossed her arms in front of her. His gaze clashed with hers in a battle of wills before he slowly rose from the sofa. She pulled her bodysuit up with clumsy hands and turned to face him. "I apologize."

One dark brow shot up in question. "Excuse me?"

Chandler began talking. Fast. "I think this is just a communication problem. I mistakenly made remarks leading you to believe I'd never be attracted to an executive. You subconsciously tried to prove me wrong, and you did. I admit defeat."

He watched her with interest. Her shoulders sagged with relief; she had his attention. Surely, once she presented the complications of getting involved with her, his normal, logical thoughts would take over. He'd agree to put the entire episode behind him. She needed to show him some concrete reasons to avoid an affair.

"Now, I think our best solution is to admit we had a brief attraction which originated from your desire to prove a point, and my surprise at your sudden actions. We both got a little carried away but we stopped our mistake in time. I think we can put this behind us and continue with our working relationship. Keeping distractions to a minimum is crucial for this project to work. Don't you agree?"

She took his silence as agreement; he seemed to listen intently. "We'd have some difficulty keeping our personal lives separate from business, which could affect the result of the program. Second, the reaction of your employees could be detrimental. They could decide you weren't serious about the workshop and only implemented it to satisfy your current lover." Her tongue stumbled over her last word before forging on.

"So, I think it's in our best interests to stick to our original agreement." She laughed nervously when he remained silent. "We would have been a disaster, anyway. We're much too different, and I'd never be able to handle a casual affair. Not that you have casual affairs all the time, but you're probably much better at them than I am," she stammered, trying hard not to blush at his pointed stare. "Well, I think we settled the problem. I'm glad we talked, and again I apologize if I led you on in any way."

Chandler began to walk him politely to the door when she suddenly realized Logan Grant was furious.

Over six feet of muscle towered over her. Dark brows drew together in a fierce frown, and icy gray eyes held her spellbound. Waves of raw, primitive energy radiated from his body in a swirling mixture of anger, frustration, and desire. Her breath caught in her chest. Her body swayed. Her nipples rose to meet him. Liquid heat pooled and throbbed between her thighs. She wished she felt fear. She wanted to be afraid. But her body dared him to take her.

Horrified by her own response, she took a step backward.

He closed the distance between them. She gazed up and knew he glimpsed every naked emotion she attempted to hide—confusion, defiance, desire.

He reached out and roughly caught her chin with his hand. His thumb caressed her swollen lips and gently parted the tender flesh as he watched her struggle to contain her body's reaction. His eyes gleamed with satisfaction, as if he knew what she was feeling and thinking; as if he knew the game would be played by his rules and she was helpless to stop him.

"Good night, Chandler." He abruptly released his hold and walked out the door.

Chapter
3

Chandler stood and stared at the closed door. She struggled against a burst of panic threatening to overwhelm her. Logan Grant would not give up until she was in his bed. She'd made a mistake the moment she responded to his first kiss. He'd sensed a weakness and was going in for the kill.

Just like any ruthless businessman. Except this time she wouldn't let him win.

She gave her bodysuit a firm tug, scooped up the two snifters, and made her way to the kitchen. How long had it been since she let her guard down with a man?

Chandler cursed her stupidity. She believed in total freedom, and had been careful not to tie herself down to anyone who threatened her lifestyle. She took each moment life offered and enjoyed it to the fullest. But she always shied away from sexual encounters. She enjoyed dating, but when she considered taking the relationship a step further, something within her balked. She never lost sleep over her decision. What she really wanted was a man who set her blood on fire. She wanted a man who wanted a family and whose soul burned for honesty and openness, a man who would make her the most important part of his life.

A man who was definitely not Logan Grant.

Chandler undressed as she walked into her bedroom, leaving a trail of clothes on her plush, pale daffodil carpet. She stepped into the shower and let the stinging jets of water soothe her muscles. Her body still tingled from his caresses, and an empty ache throbbed between her thighs. How could she face him Monday and continue as if nothing had happened? She groaned in despair. It would take all of her will power not to blush when she met those charcoal eyes and smug smile. How dare he put her in this position? How could she have let herself respond so wantonly to a man who was practically a stranger?

She scrubbed her skin until it glowed, hoping to wash away the feeling of his hands on her. She'd never reacted to another man that way. Even when she thought she was madly in love with Michael, she never wanted him with the same feverish longing.

The faint memory tugged at the fringes of her mind. Chandler cringed at the innocence of the girl she'd been, of her foolish dreams of love and romance, and the cruelty of her awakening.

The floodgates burst open, and a swirling array of images flowed before her: being introduced to Michael Worthington at one of her father's business dinners, overwhelmed by deep blue eyes, golden hair and his charming, witty demeanor, by her father's booming acknowledgment that he was a rising star in the company. He'd escorted her home with Alexander Santell's blessing. With a brief kiss, he asked her if she'd see him again. She agreed.

As their courtship continued, she was wined and dined by a handsome man who flashed dazzling smiles and whispered words of love. Suddenly, the pieces of her life fell into place. She'd graduate from college and take her position in her father's company. She'd marry Michael and have a family.

And through every step her father would be there, with his silver hair and sharp green eyes, watching and guiding her on the right path as he had done since she was a little girl.

On the night Michael proposed he presented her with a diamond ring on bended knee. She felt like a princess from a fairy tale, so when his kisses became more insistent she gave herself up to the moment. He led her into the bedroom, and she ignored the tiny seed of warning that flashed to life, chalking it up to nervousness.

Afterward, he held her in his arms while she cried, telling her it would get better because her virginity made it difficult. When he left he promised they would tell her father the news of their engagement in the morning.

Chandler stepped out of the shower and wrapped herself in a towel. As she sat on the edge of the lacy Victorian comforter, the years faded away as the memory of her ultimate betrayal played in slow motion before her closed eyes.

She saw herself arriving at her father's office, filled with excitement, breezing past his secretary's empty desk to the partially closed door. Stopping short as she heard Michael's voice say her name, she listened in horror to the conversation unfolding, trapped in a nightmare of her own making.

"It's all taken care of," Michael said. He threw a bunch of documents on the desk. "Chandler was ecstatic. I did my part old man, now it's time you sign the papers."

Alexander Santell chuckled. "Not so fast, dear boy. The agreement was the delivery of the contracts after the wedding ceremony. I didn't hear a set date."

"I'll convince her to speed up the normal process. She's eager to marry me, and I see no need to wait more than a couple of weeks."

"I knew you'd be perfect for her the moment I laid eyes on you, and my daughter's reaction proved me right." A booming laugh rang out. The sound echoed and bounced off the paneled walls of his office. "Three months ago I thought the Walterson contract would be impossible to close. The most prestigious investor in the city almost ran for the door when he heard my daughter wasn't settled down. Can you believe such outdated crap? He actually told me he only felt secure investing in a firm that showed values and stability, which he translated as family."

Chandler huddled at the door. Her stomach lurched as Alexander Santell's words drifted up to her ears. "That's the first man I've dealt with who didn't care about my profits. He was concerned that if I dropped dead Chandler would inherit control and not have a husband." Alexander snorted. "As if my daughter needed one."

"Then why me?" Michael asked smugly. "If you'd been certain she didn't need a husband you would've convinced Walterson she could handle the company. Instead you offered me a full partnership the moment I put a ring on her finger."

"Walterson was impossible to convince. That's when I decided to introduce you to my daughter." Alexander lit a cigar and puffed furiously. "Chandler's a good girl but she's started to stray. It's all those crazy psychology courses and projects. Books can't help you in a business deal when you have to go in for the kill." Silver brows lowered into a frown. "Ever since her momma died when she was young, I promised myself I'd give her something that would last forever. And I've succeeded. My daughter was born to run this company and keep the family name alive, even though she may be a bit soft-hearted. I haven't broken my back all these years just so she could get some notion in her head about finding herself."

"I assume Walterson approved of Chandler's decision?"

"The man lit up like a Christmas tree when I let him know she was safely engaged. He agreed to sign the contracts after the wedding."

Michael sighed. "Chandler's a bit of a romantic. She wouldn't have agreed to this marriage if she didn't think I was in love with her."

"You'll fall in love with her eventually, son. She's a

jewel. But for now a business marriage based on shared values and commitments is nothing to bark at. It's as good as any nowadays."

Michael muttered something under his breath which was overshadowed by her father's chuckle. Chandler slowly backed away from the door and turned, stumbling down the hall in a daze. She couldn't remember how she found her way home. She only remembered the feeling of her safe little world ripped to shreds, and the fear of knowing she'd never be the same person again.

Chandler slid beneath the cool sheets and shivered. When Michael knocked on the door that evening she knew what needed to be done. She remembered his cruelty when she'd given him back the ring; his reminder that her father controlled her life and could force her to marry him.

The stark truth of his words took her breath away. Michael was right. Her father's money financed everything. Her job and future was his corporation. She had no other family, no friends, and no one she could depend on. If he ordered her to marry Michael, what could she do?

Chandler remembered her fear and hatred four years ago. The anger and loneliness at being trapped, forced to play out a role because her father controlled her destiny. Then she'd made the hardest decision of her life.

She left.

Chandler flicked off the light and forced back the memories. She'd made a decision to start a new life for herself, one which would never tie her down to another human being like her father. She refused to think of regrets this late in the game. The present seemed enough of a challenge.

She focused on her breath and consciously let go of any thoughts. Soon, each part of her body relaxed and sank deeper into the pillowed mattress. As she drifted toward sleep, she was grateful the last image flickering before her eyes was not Michael.

But she dreamed of a dark-haired man whose touch set her blood on fire.

• • •

Logan sat in front of the fireplace and stared into the crackling flames as he thought about Chandler Santell. The haunting strains of Beethoven filled the air and soothed his nerves. His gaze took in the sparsely decorated room. He wondered why it felt so empty now that he had seen her apartment. He'd always liked his home, feeling it was suitable to his busy lifestyle. The wraparound sofa was a soft, buttery leather, which matched two easy chairs across from it. The contemporary teak furniture complemented the bare wood floors nicely without adding unnecessary clutter. There was a huge entertainment wall, a desk, and a teak and marble coffee table. The hand rubbed Tuscan beige walls were bare of paintings and pictures, offering no distractions to the elegant lines of the furniture.

Maybe the room needed some distractions. Some paintings. More plants. Chandler.

He sipped his cognac and tried to ignore the odd hunger clawing at his gut. When he stepped into Chandler's apartment, he'd been struck by a sense of joyous clutter, almost like the woman herself. He pictured her floating through the rooms, tossing things over the furniture and floor, flipping through random books and magazines without ever worrying about replacing them in their proper location. He'd wondered if she'd bring the same wild abandon to the bedroom.

Now he knew.

Logan groaned and tried to force the erotic image from his mind. She'd gone up in flames in his arms and surrendered completely. He'd met many women who experienced passion, but he always felt as if they played a game, and he was the prize—his money, his name, his reputation. Never had he felt the sheer honest response of a woman melting beneath him, needing him as much as he needed her.

Until tonight.

A flicker of unease shot through him. He'd been prepared for her to turn in disgust once she heard the circumstances surrounding his famous nickname. Instead, there'd been a light of understanding in those green eyes; a gentleness in her demeanor that touched him. Chandler Santell was a woman who walked in the sunlight, yet she willingly reached out for someone in the darkness and invited him into her world.

He wondered how it would feel to live in such a place.

Logan swirled the amber liquid around in his glass and let the lilting strains of music wash over him. Their encounter presented him with more questions than answers. It had taken every shred of his willpower not to pull her back in his arms during her tidy speech, and force her to acknowledge her feelings. He only stopped because of the sheer panic in those green eyes, and his determination to find out what was the cause. Or who.

A flare of jealousy gripped him, but Logan stamped down hard on the strange emotion. His yoga teacher may not have realized it, but she'd started the game the moment she melted so sweetly in his arms.

He intended to finish it.

His instincts told him he needed to move carefully. He suspected Richard Thorne could prove a problem. The man knew something about Chandler, and in order to play the game properly, Logan needed to find out the rules. First thing in the morning, he'd contact his friend to start some research.

Logan tapped his finger absently against the crystal rim and frowned at the strange restlessness flooding through him. Hell, he'd never bothered to question his life before, it was crazy to start now. He pursued a strict path to achieve money and power, and never looked back. No regrets. After all, there had never been a choice.

Growing up in the slums, he watched his mother

struggle to support them after his father left. He vowed one day he'd be successful. She regaled him with tales of a world that was limitless, urging him to make the most of himself and break away from the vicious cycle of poverty. As his mother grew weaker, he'd been driven by a hunger that constantly ate at his gut, and spent each day working furiously. He was determined to make a home for them someplace safe, where guns and drugs and crime didn't dominate the streets. He'd longed to see his mother happy again, instead of offering a tired smile when she came home from the restaurant where she worked; spending the evening counting every penny from the tips she received.

He delivered newspapers and ran odd errands. He worked as a cashier and waited tables. The neighborhood knew him as the boy who'd do any job as long as the pay was good. And, slowly, he began to build a reputation.

His big break came in college, when he was recommended for a summer internship by one of his teachers. He took the train into the city every day and worked late into the night at a well-known financial firm. By practically living at the office, he soaked up every bit of information. He learned he had a head for figures and a talent for getting what he wanted. Emotions had no place in the world of high finance, and Logan found himself easily slipping into a role that demanded nothing but the accomplishment of profit. At home, he was overcome by feelings of guilt and helplessness. When he stepped into the office, he felt nothing, and as time passed, he realized he had started earning a name for himself. Negotiating the acquisition of companies demanded a businesslike approach and certain ruthlessness, especially in hostile takeovers. Logan realized early on in the game it was easy to tap into those parts of himself. He remained cold when faced with pleas and objections from family companies not wanting to merge. He made a man sign on the dotted line with whatever ammunition he could get, and he learned how to play dirty.

One day his mentor failed to show up for a meeting. Familiar with the deal, he closed the contract personally with a higher margin of profit.

The company fired the executive and hired him immediately. Logan never looked back.

Until now.

He set the snifter on the coaster and got up from the easy chair. No need to start questioning himself. He'd achieved his goals and finally proved his worth. Just like his mother always wanted.

He grabbed the poker and stirred the fire. Hissing logs popped in the silence. He must be tired. He certainly wasn't lonely. His life was too busy to waste precious time exploring the strange emotions bubbling up inside of him. By morning, he'd be back in control and start on his plan to get Chandler into his bed.

• • •

"May I have your attention, please?"

Chandler gazed at a dozen pairs of eyes, all filled with doubt and curiosity. Shorts and t-shirts replaced their business suits. The excess office furniture had been moved into storage and in its place exercise mats were spread out on the floor.

The late afternoon sun cast relaxing patterns about the spacious room. Chandler immediately surmised that her students, which mostly consisted of males, were not too keen on the idea of dealing with stress. Brows lowered in confused frowns. Low murmurs rose and fell through the air. She guessed their distress was caused by the noticeable absence of their esteemed leader, who had yet to show. She fought back a surge of anger and decided to start the class. If the other night caused a change of heart in Logan Grant, so be it. She'd make her workshop a success without him.

"My name is Chandler Santell and I'll be the instructor working with you over the next few months." Her gaze swept the room. "I regret we have to start without Mr. Grant, but I'm sure he'll join us later. As we all know in the business world, sometimes we get caught up in pressing schedules which demand most of our time."

"Ah, but as someone once told me, we must always allow time for certain pleasures."

Chandler turned at the masculine voice behind her. Her gaze collided with amused gray eyes. She felt her cheeks burn as she remembered their prior conversation. She kept her voice neutral. "Please join us, Mr. Grant. I'm glad you could make it."

His eyes swept over her figure as he closed the distance between them. He smiled lazily. "Please call me Logan. I prefer to be on a first name basis with people I work closely with."

She fought the next blush threatening to overcome her, and nodded her agreement, not trusting herself to speak. Logan lowered himself to the mat and stretched his long, powerful legs in front of him. He propped his hands up behind his back and exchanged easy banter with his employees. Grudgingly, she admitted he looked as much at ease in his gray sweatshirt and jogging shorts as he did in his expensive tailored suits. His forearms and legs were sprinkled with dark hair: his lightly tanned skin gave him a healthy glow. His pose made his sweatshirt stretch and cling to his broad chest, reminding her of how his muscles had jumped under her touch. Chandler cleared her throat and forced her thoughts away from the man who haunted her dreams last night. She refused to let him bully her with his deep, rich voice or his sexual innuendoes. She pulled herself back to reality and turned to face her class.

"Most of you don't know what to expect from this workshop so I'd like to give you an overview. First, I want to assure you I won't make everyone sit in Lotus position while we chant to relieve ourselves of stress, at least not the first week." Everyone laughed.

"We all want to learn how to be more productive in

our jobs by taking care of ourselves and our needs. This encompasses not only dealing with stress, but also being aware of our diet, personal habits, and bodies. We'll talk about nutrition, exercise, stress, and awareness. I'll show you some easy breathing techniques and stretches to loosen some of the tension."

She lowered herself to one of the mats and sat in a comfortable, cross-legged position. "I've been involved in the corporate culture," she continued easily, "so I know first hand the pressures involved on a day to day basis. It seems easier to continue to skip meals, drink more coffee, and close one more deal. But if we continue that behavior, all of us are going to burn out. Then we'll be nowhere, except maybe a hospital. What does this have to do with your current job? Let's say you're in an important meeting and the client is ready to close the deal. You've been up all night poring over the contracts and you're tired. There's been no time for breakfast so you gulp down some coffee to get started. You've done all the research, wined and dined the client over lunch or dinner, and it's time for them to sign on the dotted line." She paused. "Let's say the client balks, asks for more time or wants a better deal."

A combined groan rose from the group.

"What are you going to do? If you've been up all night on a diet of caffeine, stressed to the limit, couldn't your temper snap? Or what if you're not thinking clearly, so you offer him what he wants, no matter what the price?" A burst of laughter rang out as Logan frowned and shook his head.

Chandler smiled. "At that moment, anything can happen because you've lost control of your mind and body. In a stressful situation, our adrenaline takes over and we act on instinct. In a business meeting you only want to rely on your wits. So, if you've been taking care of yourself and the client balks, you can clearly see options. You can catalogue his weaknesses and strengths; decide whether to bluff or walk away from the deal; make a judgment whether he needs more finessing or if his mind is made up. That's what we want to learn. This class may not make miracles happen, but it will teach you to become aware, and with awareness comes control. Mr. Grant hopes this seminar will give you a fuller, healthier lifestyle which will be reflected in your work and keep you here for years to come."

Chandler knew she had their interest. The women nodded as if in agreement, and the men looked less skeptical about the entire program. Even Logan seemed to watch her with approval. She ignored the warm rush of pleasure and decided not to probe her feelings too deeply. "I'm going to teach you some breathing techniques and then we'll discuss various causes of stress. I'd like everyone to get comfortable with me at this point."

The rest of the time flew by. From the corner of her eye, she noticed one of the women inch her way toward Logan. She'd never seen a breathing pattern that made a woman's breasts lift so high, nor strain against the material of a t-shirt so tightly—all in perfect view of Logan's eyes.

When the class ended Chandler noticed them

laughing together quite intimately. The woman touched his shoulder in a familiar gesture. Chandler determinedly ignored them as she went about folding mats and chatting with the employees on their way out. It was no business of hers that the boss was on such friendly terms with his workers.

"Do you need some help?"

She turned to face Richard Thorne. "Thank you. Let's put them over there in the corner." They finished clearing the mats and stacked them on top of one another. "It's good to see you in class. What did you think?"

He smiled. "I loved it. My days are so stressful, I find if I don't do something to come down at night, I'm wired. Yoga is a great way to relax."

"I agree. When I first started my practices, I realized how I'd been mistreating my body. Now, I know exactly when I've been pushing too hard."

"Same here. I can't even eat a jumbo burger anymore."

"Are you a vegetarian?"

He shrugged. "Yeah. But I don't like to publicize it too much."

Chandler studied the man before her with growing admiration. Not too many males had self awareness about their lifestyles, but Richard Thorne seemed to have reached a nice balance. He was a successful businessman, but knew how to have a healthy life.

Dressed in a white t-shirt and navy blue sweats, he radiated an open, friendly energy she was immediately drawn to. Light brown hair fell in neat waves over his forehead. Chestnut eyes gazed into hers with a steadiness that soothed her. Nothing like that of the silver heat from the man last night. She couldn't picture Richard dragging her into his arms and seducing her on the couch, swearing he would "take care of everything."

Not like Logan Grant.

"Chandler?"

She shook off her thoughts. "Yes?"

"Would you like to have dinner with me tomorrow night?" he asked. "There's a great new Thai restaurant I wanted to check out."

She hesitated. Then watched Logan say his good-byes to the rest of the employees and stride across the room. He moved with a powerful, masculine energy that made her weak all the way down to her toes. Especially when she remembered last night: his lips over hers, his hands on her body. All his intense concentration focused on giving her pleasure.

Oh, God.

She'd sworn off all businessmen, but Richard Thorne seemed different. Safe. He was the type of man she might be able to explore a relationship with. She tore her gaze away from Logan.

"Yes, I think I'd like that."

A pleased grin curved Richard's lips. "Great. I'll get your address tomorrow, and we'll set up a time."

"Fine. Have a good night, Richard."

"You too. Hey boss, see ya tomorrow." He gave her a friendly wink as he passed Logan, obviously ignoring his boss's thunderous expression. Chandler swallowed hard and tilted her chin up.

"Set up a time for what?" Logan demanded.

She shook her head in exasperation. "For dinner. We're going out tomorrow night."

A range of emotions flickered across his carved features, and then quickly disappeared. "That's not a good idea."

She arched one eyebrow. "Excuse me?"

"You're doing this to prove a point, aren't you?"

Her mouth dropped open. "Why do you think everything has to do with you? I'm going out with Richard because he's a nice guy, and I think we'll have a good time."

"You think he's safe, and you're scared to death of the way I make you feel."

She sputtered with indignation. "That's ridiculous. You have no right to make assumptions about the way I feel."

He didn't respond. His charcoal gaze raked over her face, as if searching for some expression she refused to show. His voice dropped. "Chandler, I want you to stay away from him. He's not who you think he is, and until I find out what's going on, it's best if you don't see him on a personal level."

Anger shot through her. "Businessmen are all alike." She clenched her fists at her sides. "You want to control all aspects of a relationship. A few kisses and you're ready to claim me as your own personal property, and God forbid any other man challenge you."

"Chandler—"

"There's nothing more to Richard than what he shows. He's a hardworking man who's trying to balance his life. I didn't see any hidden motives, or evil plans to take over the world. And I'm going to dinner with him tomorrow night."

"Chandler—"

"I mean it, Logan. We have a business relationship and I will not let you dictate to me who I can go out with."

She took a deep breath, ready to do battle. She waited for an explosion of testosterone-fueled temper and steeled herself for a defense. Logan was being outrageous. Okay, so she'd let things go a bit far last night, but he had no right to bully her.

His lower lip kicked up in a grin. She gazed in astonishment when he shook his head in typical male exasperation. "I thought yoga teachers never lost their temper," he said. "Now I find there's a hellcat waiting to get out. You just cover it up with all that deep breathing and chanting."

She opened her mouth to speak but no words emerged.

He reached out and ran a thumb over the curve of her lips; an indulgent light gleamed from his gunmetal grey eyes. "I figured you wouldn't listen to me. Go ahead and make your dinner plans. Convince yourself you're crazy about Thorne. Pretend our kisses meant nothing."

With that last statement, he turned on the heel of his leather Nikes and strode out the door.

Chapter
4

"Hmmm, that's funny. I didn't know the boss liked Thai food."

Chandler looked up from her spicy vegetable stir fry and watched Logan pull out a chair for his companion. The woman tossed her perfect mane of red curls and laughed at something he said. Her short black dress rode up her thighs as she took a seat, and Chandler noticed Logan seemed pleased with the view. A surge of emotions shot through her and took her off guard. She turned and deliberately focused on Richard. "I guess he decided to take time for certain pleasures, after all."

Richard gave her a strange look but let the remark pass. "A redhead this time. Logan's a killer when it comes to the ladies," he said. "Hair color is a big deal to him."

She narrowed her eyes. "What do you mean?"

Richard grinned. "You know, blondes one week, brunettes the next. I guess redheads are getting their turn."

Her fingers tightened around her chopsticks. "How archaic."

"Yeah, but at least he's fair. Every woman gets a shot."

She raised one brow in warning. "And you think that's okay? I hope you're teasing me, Richard."

He winked. "Now, Chandler, you know I'm not

like that. I firmly believe in getting to know a woman first. Sexual attraction is great, but not lasting." He took a healthy swallow of saki. "I used to be like Logan, but then I decided I needed more."

She smiled in understanding. "Someone to share your life with, right? A woman who really sees who you are, and wants you anyway."

He gazed into her eyes. "Exactly." He reached over and touched her hand. "A woman who believes in the same things I do."

"Richard. Chandler. What a wonderful surprise!"

They both looked up as a deep, gravelly voice cut through the air. Logan stood over them with a sense of masculine satisfaction. She held back a sigh. Somehow, she wasn't surprised at his tactics. The man was impossible to deal with.

"Such an odd coincidence," she said. "We both picked the same restaurant in Manhattan. And on the same night! Imagine that."

The man never missed a beat. "I know, I thought the same thing when I spotted you. Please join us."

Richard gave her an uneasy look. "No, we don't want to interrupt you on a date. Maybe another time."

"I won't take no for an answer. There's nothing I like more than spending time with my employees outside the office."

Richard rubbed his temple. "Uh, Logan—"

"We haven't ordered yet, so we'll join you. I'll have the waiter set two more place settings."

He stalked away and motioned for one of the waiters. Richard groaned. "I can't believe this."

She smothered a giggle. "This is starting to remind me of an old *Seinfeld* episode."

The waiter discreetly adjusted their table setting, and suddenly the redhead stood before them. Her lower lip jutted out in a slight sulk. "Logan, we really shouldn't intrude. They probably want to be alone."

Chandler decided the woman was not happy about the new seating arrangements. Logan waved one hand in the air. "Lisa, let me introduce Chandler and Richard. We work together. I probably just saved Richard from a lecture on nutrition. Chandler's our yoga expert at the company, so she tries to convert everyone to good health. Richard's normal obsession is jumbo beef burgers."

Chandler choked on her water and tried to keep a straight face. She caught a flash of anger pass over Richard's features before he carefully concealed his emotions with a bland smile. Uneasiness flickered deep inside when she realized how quickly he could change his expressions. But he had every right to be annoyed with Logan. She firmly pushed away her doubts as everyone got settled.

Lisa ordered a salad and made a production out of moving around the lettuce leaves on her plate. Actually, Chandler was surprised at the adept way she kept dropping things off the table so Logan could get a healthy glimpse of cleavage. Not that it mattered.

Chandler didn't care about Logan's long list of bimbos ranked by hair color. Not one bit. She was grateful her own escort wanted sparkling conversation rather than a perfect body. Chandler clung to the thought.

"Darling, how do you manage? After working long days, you actually show up for a class that does nothing but twist up your body. What a sacrifice you make for your employees," Lisa cooed.

"I do my best," Logan said.

Chandler rolled her eyes.

"I met a yoga teacher once." Lisa's eyes ran over her with a dismissing gesture. "She believed in saving the environment, especially water. I guess that's why she didn't believe in bathing."

Chandler smiled sweetly. "Yes, I have the same philosophy. Birthdays and holidays I treat myself to a bath."

Her gaze met and locked with amused charcoal eyes. He raised his glass to her in silent salute, and Chandler mentally chided herself for making such a smart remark. Her actions indicated jealousy. But of course, she wasn't.

Moments later, she realized the lovely Lisa actually believed her comment. The woman seemed a bit nervous and adjusted her chair.

The waiter appeared by their table. "May I get anyone an after dinner drink, coffee or dessert?"

Richard shook his head. "Sugar and caffeine. I'll pass."

Lisa agreed. "I'm so stuffed I feel like I'll explode. I'll pass, too."

Chandler winced and glanced down at her clean plate. She'd managed to devour her appetizer, salad, dinner, and all her rice. She held back a sigh and opened her mouth to decline.

"We'll have the brownie bomber sundae," Logan said. One lid dropped in a naughty wink. "With two forks."

At that moment, she knew she liked Logan Grant a bit too much.

• • •

"Let me walk you to the door."

"Thanks." She led Richard up the staircase and paused in front of her apartment. Her high heels sunk into the cream colored carpet as she turned to face him and offered a bright smile. The corridor was quiet, and the lights had been adjusted to the late hour. Their figures cast dim shadows against the wall.

"I had a good time tonight." He gave her a lopsided grin. "At least until the boss showed up."

She laughed. "So did I."

"I'd like to take you out again." The grin faded and was replaced by a serious expression. He reached out and enfolded her hands with his. "I think we have a lot in common, Chandler. It took me a long time to realize what's important in life. For years, I thought power and money were my only options. Now I know I want a woman with the same values, who wants to grow with me on the same path. Does that make sense to you?"

Her gut twisted. She wondered if she was scared because she finally found a man who believed in the same things, or if he just told her everything she wanted to hear.

Everything she wanted to hear...

She nodded. "It makes perfect sense."

His lips touched hers. Tentative, polite, it was a kiss from a man who respected a woman and wanted to take his time. Definitely not like—

She broke off the thought and kissed him back. When he finally raised his head, she caught a gleam of satisfaction in chestnut eyes, before being quickly masked. "Friday night?"

She smiled. "Sure. Friday night."

He squeezed her hands and walked down the hallway. She heard the echo of footsteps on the stairway, and leaned against the door. Richard Thorne was a man who held the same principles. His embrace comforted her and made her feel safe. Surely, those feelings were everything she searched for. Surely, she wasn't shallow enough to think a quick sexual attraction meant more than building a solid friendship with a man.

"At least you didn't invite him in."

She gasped and spun on her heel. Logan Grant stood at the end of the corridor. Still dressed in his evening clothes, every powerful muscle cloaked in elegant fabric, he cut an intimidating figure. His tie had been ripped off, and the first buttons of his shirt undone. Curly dark hair peeked from beneath the pristine white cloth. A muscle worked in his jaw as his silvery gaze drilled into her. His voice was a low growl of a sound. Rough. Sexy. Her stomach slid and dipped to her toes. She made sure her face showed nothing.

"Why am I not surprised? Logan, don't you think this could be considered stalking? We don't live in the Stone Age. You can't drag me to your cave just on a whim."

The corner of his mouth kicked up in a grin. "I never stalked a woman in my life."

"First time for everything." Her eyes narrowed. "What do you want? Have you trained your women so well that your date is sitting in the car?"

He moved toward her like a predator and stopped a few inches away. The scent of aftershave teased her senses. "I took her home. Did you enjoy kissing him, Chandler?"

Her temper surged. "Did you enjoy kissing your redhead, Logan?" Immediately, she realized her mistake and almost bit her tongue with frustration. He'd watched her all through dinner with a possessive gleam in his eyes which annoyed her. The casual intimacy he treated his date with made her angry, too. Those emotions she could deal with. However, it was the way her body jumped at the mere sound of his voice, melted at his touch or look, which made her really crazy.

The amusement was back. "Lisa? I gave her a polite kiss on the cheek and dropped her at the door. Why? Does it matter?"

She shrugged, then glanced around the empty corridor. "No. Look, it's late. I've got an early class in the morning." She turned to dismiss him, but his hand shot out to grasp her wrist. Her heart slammed in her chest. "Is there something else you wanted?"

"If I was sleeping with Lisa would you be jealous?"

Chandler gasped. "Of course not. It's none of my business who you sleep with and I have no desire to know. I wouldn't tell you who I was involved with."

"Are you?"

"Am I what?"

"Are you sleeping with somebody?" he demanded.

"How dare you ask me a question like that? You have no right to ask me anything about my personal life."

Deliberately, Logan leaned in. "It became my right the moment your mouth opened under mine," he shot back. "When you cried my name and your nails dug into my skin with passion, I reserved the right to be your only lover. I'm a greedy, selfish man, and I don't share with anyone, especially Richard Thorne." Logan took in the high color of her cheeks and her trembling mouth. His voice gentled. "The other night we almost became lovers and today you want to pretend it never happened."

She pulled her wrist away and crossed her arms in front of her chest. "I don't see any need to bring that night up. It was a mistake."

"It was the first honest response you've allowed yourself in a long time." He stepped back and plowed his fingers through his hair. "Right or wrong, good for you or not, you wanted me in your bed and now you're too damn scared to admit it. I didn't see you kiss Thorne like that. I didn't hear you invite him in. Why? Because something was missing?"

She shook her head stubbornly. "The night you kissed me I was taken by surprise. You wanted to prove a point. Why can't we let the episode go?"

Logan gazed at her for a long moment. Her chin tilted upward in the air, as if to stand her ground before Goliath. He acknowledged this very well may be the most stubborn, headstrong woman he'd ever met. He noticed the rapid beat of her pulse at the base of her neck and controlled a satisfied smile. No matter how much she denied the attraction, her body betrayed her. If he coaxed her body to step out from her cage, maybe her mind would follow. He needed to try.

Chandler watched the male predator before her and waited for his temper to explode. Instead, she heard him speak in an easy tone. "In your little speech the other night, you insisted you were taken by surprise by my, er, forward actions."

"Yes."

"So, if I had calmly announced my intentions to kiss you, I wouldn't have gotten the same response?"

"No."

"You would have pulled away?"

She nodded. "Yes."

Chandler watched in fascination as he closed the

distance between them. Warm breath struck her lips as his mouth stopped inches from her own. The slow descent held her spellbound. Heat and intense sensual energy radiated from his body. "If I told you I intend to kiss you, you'd refuse to respond, right?"

Her stomach lurched in fear at his obvious intent. She licked her lips nervously and stiffened her body to prepare for battle. "Yes." The word came out slightly strangled.

His eyes focused on her trembling mouth. "Great. Then as two logical people ready to settle an argument, we'll conduct an experiment to prove who's telling the truth." He paused. "Just in case you don't know what's about to happen, I intend on kissing you, Chandler. I'm also giving you plenty of notice so you can't call foul play after I prove your body was made to belong to me."

Then his lips closed over hers.

Chandler prepared for a sensual, teasing game like the night before. What she hadn't expected was the powerful, drugging need that set fire to her body when his tongue penetrated the seam of her lips to thrust into her mouth, hungrily plundering the dark, silken depths over and over again. Like a flower opening to the sun, she allowed him free access. A deep need burned through her; the need to respond to his masculine invasion; the need to feel her body crushed under his; the need to let her soul soar. She could have fought her response if he'd used cold expertise, or a calculated game of thrust and parry. What she couldn't fight was this honest, driven kiss. It had been too long since she'd felt a man need her response so badly, and he seemed to want her with a passion beyond the clinical, ruthless mind of a businessman going in for the kill.

Chandler kissed him back. She learned the texture of his lips, the line of smooth white teeth, the heat of his mouth. She reveled in the hard body pressed against hers. She breathed in the scent of him. As the kiss went on, stoking the fires of desire, she wanted more and more and more...

He slowly dragged his mouth from hers. She took deep, ragged breaths. Her skin tingled from the slight roughness of his five o'clock shadow. She let her tongue glide along her bottom lip and caught his taste. Logan groaned. The pad of his thumb pressed over her mouth and traced its outline, following up to the line of her jaw. He smoothed back the stray tendrils of hair escaping from her twist.

Chandler almost closed her eyes in defeat. No more lies. Clearly, he knew the extent of her physical attraction, and would use the knowledge to his advantage. He announced his intentions and she'd been unable to prove she had no feelings. In fact, the opposite was true.

She definitely had feelings for Logan Grant—and that was dangerous.

Desire within her demanded she throw caution to the winds and get involved with this powerful, attractive enigma. Yet, fear regarding businessmen and their priorities still lingered. If their relationship didn't work out, the contract ended along with their affair.

And what about Richard? Would she be giving up an opportunity to have a real relationship to settle for a short affair?

Her mind took control, disciplined throughout the years to take charge of her lesser emotions. Chandler took a step back and tilted her head to gaze at him more fully.

"I can't cry foul play." She smiled tentatively. He smiled back. "But this doesn't change anything. I can't get involved with you."

"What are you fighting so hard to protect?" he asked. "Who hurt you so badly?"

Her face closed off. Her eyes grew distant. "My past has nothing to do with my decision. I admit we have an attraction, but we don't have to act on it. Can't you see this is wrong?" she pleaded. "We're too different. We belong in two different worlds. I can't go back to yours, and you'd never be comfortable in mine. We would hurt one another and I can't sacrifice the Yoga and Arts Center to find out."

Logan gazed at his worthy opponent and admiration cut through him. Even after her body surrendered, her mind refused to wave the white flag. His lips curved in a smile as he grasped her wrist and pulled her hand to his mouth. He pressed a heated kiss into her palm, and felt her pounding pulse against his fingertips; heard her quick indrawn breath. And he knew he'd never wanted another woman like he wanted Chandler Santell.

"Did you ever stop to think I need you in my

world?" he asked. "Have you ever saved a man from himself? I live in darkness, where deception and lies are at every turn. I learned to protect myself by being cold and hard, the only way I know to survive." Her body visibly shook as her gaze locked on his. "You're like the sunlight. You radiate heat and truth and all the good things in the world." He paused. "Save me, Chandler."

Her lower lip trembled. "I can't," she whispered.

"Try."

Her voice broke. "I think I'm too late."

He saw the fear and knew she wasn't ready. He clamped down hard on the swirl of emotions rising inside him and took a deep breath. When he finally re-focused, there remained only a ruthless determination to claim her. Something told him she could save him. Something told him she may be the one.

"I want you. I'll drag out every damn secret you have. I'll stalk every hiding place, haunt your dreams at night, and make your body burn for mine. When you finally surrender, I'll make you feel more pleasure than you've ever known." He released her hand from his. "Be warned, sweetheart. Cards are on the table. Ante up."

The clock ticked. Slowly, she regained her compo-sure, and watched him from under heavily lidded eyes. She realized she'd unwillingly issued a challenge, and he'd do whatever necessary to make her surrender. The sudden flash of vulnerability in his eyes couldn't be real. And she already knew she wasn't enough of a woman to save Logan Grant.

She stared at him. He wanted to play business games, but he didn't understand she played for higher stakes. Running would only make him pursue. She'd have to fight back with all the skill she learned from her father. Keep your opponent off balance at all times. Never underestimate your challenger. Always be one step ahead.

Logan was about to find out she'd be no easy conquest. She had too much to lose.

She took a step forward and reached for his hand. Slowly, she lifted his fingers to her lips, nibbling on the pad of his thumb, letting her tongue glide along the base. His muscles clenched. She heard the breath hiss through his teeth. With satisfaction, she dropped his hand from her mouth and stepped back once again. The surprise in his eyes made her lips curve in a smile. "Be warned, sweetheart. I was taught to play games by the best. I was also taught to win." Chandler paused. "Ante up."

Then she twisted the knob and stepped inside, firmly shutting the door behind her.

• • •

Logan Grant leaned back in his leather chair and signaled for his secretary to leave. Tapping his pen absently against the edge of the desk, he studied the papers in front of him and searched for a rational solution to his problem.

It had been one week since their confrontation—

five full days and four long nights. And he wasn't any closer to scaling her walls.

He let out a frustrated breath. Besides tying him up in knots, she caused more trouble than any other woman he'd ever known. The logical side to his nature entreated him to walk away, and therefore, solve his problem. But he couldn't.

It already seemed too late to walk away from Chandler Santell.

Logan flipped through the pages of the dossier, feeling like a Peeping Tom as he skimmed through the events of her life. Ever since Alexander Santell approached him with a deal to make his company skyrocket to the top, he'd been suspicious. Ordering Chandler's life story seemed the reasonable thing to do given the circumstances. He needed to be cautious. The rapid growth of his company made it vulnerable to predators looking for a piece of the action. She could be a corporate spy hand delivered by her father. Logan didn't believe in coincidence, and his instincts told him something wasn't right when the deal of a lifetime presented itself a few weeks after hiring Chandler.

He was a businessman who needed to look out for his company. He refused to apologize for doing his job.

So why did he feel like he was making one of the biggest mistakes of his life?

Disgusted with his rioting emotions, he swiveled around to gaze out from his office window. The sun began to sink, turning the river skyline to a dark silhouette against fiery red, orange, and yellow. Towering buildings thrust toward the sky, competing for attention with nature's radiance. The man-made structures fought for dominance, and once again, failed compared to the river and sunset. It was a scene of New York meant for a painting.

God, he was tired. A slight throbbing behind his eyes told him a migraine was on the way. Normally, the view from his office made a rush of pride and energy course through him, refreshing his drive for power and his desire to have the city of New York recognize his name. But today, he only felt more alone. He questioned what he really wanted for himself. More money? More power? After that, would he crave more, always driven to fill an empty space inside?

Whenever Chandler walked into his office something stirred deep inside him. She made him feel things he thought long buried. Normally, when he got involved in a deal it consumed him, leaving no time or thought for anything else. Since he'd met her, business didn't seem as important. Suddenly, it wasn't urgent to be the first one in the office or the last to leave at night. He always wondered what she was doing, or who she was with, until the need to see her overpowered everything else.

You're getting soft.

The inner voice taunted him. Letting a woman break his concentration was dangerous, especially when the future of his company could hinge on this contract.

Logan rubbed his forehead. Why did Chandler run from him, if Alexander Santell hired her as a spy? Wouldn't she drop into his bed in order to learn his secrets? Why had she left her father's company years ago? There was no record of a disagreement between them, unless the ex-fiancé caused her to walk away from such a powerful position. Had he done something to betray her trust? Had she loved him so much she had to run from him?

Tension coiled tightly in his stomach at the thought. He picked up the dossier and stared at the leather binder. Within the pages lay all the answers to his questions. All he had to do was open the cover.

With one decisive motion, Logan swiveled back around in his chair and tossed the report in his waste-basket. To hell with it. His instincts told him to believe in her honesty and integrity. For the first time, he'd go on trust, and assume she knew nothing about her father's offer.

The full impact of his action hit him like a freight train. Trust: a word that meant danger in the business world, pain in personal relationships, and, of course, betrayal. One thought flashed before his eyes, almost like a neon sign, and stopped him from retrieving her dossier again.

She was the woman who could save his soul.

"Hey, boss, got a minute?"

He looked up. Richard stood in the doorway with a pile of papers in his hand. Logan admitted the man exuded an air of confidence as he waited for a response. He wondered if the lawyer practiced his motions in the mirror each morning. Dressed the part in a navy blue suit, silk tie, and custom-made cuff links, Logan wondered what image he presented to Chandler when they were alone. Thoughtfully, he tapped his pen on the edge of the polished wood and motioned him in.

"Sure. Are we ready for our meeting with Tommy?"

Richard nodded and took a seat. His brown eyes took in the room with one sweep, as if memorizing something for future use. Logan casually kicked the wastebasket out of the man's view. "Contracts are ready to go, and I think we'll go ahead with the final negotiations. It's a killer deal, boss."

Logan nodded and watched Richard adjust his gold cuff links. "I know. I've been working on it almost a year now. Most other investors gave up, thinking he'd never sell the company." Logan's eyes narrowed. "Tommy plays the waiting game. Watches the weak ones crumble. He likes a man with patience, so I just gave him what he wanted."

Richard lifted a brow. "Patience, huh?"

The pen tapped in a steady beat. "The Japanese respect the art of patience. It's Americans who want immediate satisfaction."

"There's nothing wrong with going after your goals."

"Move too fast and you'll lose every time." He paused. "When I go after something, I always win. Because I wait for my opening."

Richard shifted in his chair. Silence filled the room as they both watched each other. Then he gave a short laugh. "Trying to tell me something, boss?"

Primitive male energy hummed through the air. "Stay away from Chandler."

Richard blinked, and then recovered quickly enough to screen his features to attain an element of blandness. "That a direct order?"

Logan leaned back and studied the younger man. "Consider it a warning. You're a hell of a lawyer, Richard. You remind me a lot of myself in my younger days, when I was so hungry I'd do anything for a deal. But I won't watch while Chandler becomes one of your sacrifices."

"What are you talking about?"

"Don't involve her in your games. Something is going on that I haven't figured out yet. I will, though. And if she gets hurt, I'll find the person who did it." He smiled. "Then I'll make him pay."

Electricity pulsed within the silence. Richard cleared his throat. "Point taken. Since we're putting cards on the table, I've got a few truths for you, boss." Ruthlessness gleamed in his brown eyes. "Stay out of my personal life. I'll see Chandler for as long as she's interested." He smirked. "You may have the hots for her, but she wants more than a quick trip to the bedroom. I can give her that. No hidden motives."

Logan knew with a cold certainty the man was lying. He quickly squashed the flicker of disappointment when he realized Richard Thorne needed to be stopped in any way possible. He forced himself to nod. "Every man for himself."

"Guess so." Richard stood up and dropped a handful of papers in front of him. "Look those over. If everything goes well today, we'll be able to draw up the final contracts."

"Fine. Richard?"

"Yeah?"

"A man always deserves one warning."

A flicker of wariness flashed in Richard's eyes, then disappeared. Satisfaction surged within him at the man's unguarded response. Logan thought he'd left until he heard Richard's voice from the doorway.

"I heard what you said about patience. But the Japanese have another code they follow, boss."

"What's that?"

"Don't play the game until you know the rules." Then he walked out.

Logan stared at the closed door for a few moments.

His gut told him time was running out, and he needed answers. He stared thoughtfully at the phone before reaching for the receiver.

Chapter
5

Chandler lay back on the mat in Corpse pose after finishing her class. Palms up, legs slightly open, she enjoyed the benefits of a demanding routine and let her muscles relax. She had an hour free before the intermediate students arrived, and needed to clear her mind. The morning class had been difficult because of her constantly drifting thoughts regarding a certain business executive.

Why did she think she could challenge him?

Logan Grant was, indeed, a master of the game.

She'd been prepared for him to initiate a ruthless game of pursuit and retreat. She expected him to break her down by playing on the weakness of her body's reaction. Throughout the last week she built up her defenses to handle any maneuver thrown at her. When she realized she had no need to fight off his advances, she discovered his subtle manipulations had already begun to work.

When she demonstrated a new stretch, he always seemed to need her personal assistance. As his employees teased him on his inability to copy her movements, she'd be forced to position his muscled arms; come in contact with the bare flesh of his calves; adjust his shoulders so the breath went deeply into his lungs.

He always arrived early to help her set up for class.

He insisted he liked to clear his mind before the other employees arrived. She would have believed him if it hadn't been for the accidental brushes of his fingertips against hers as he reached for the mats; or how he stood behind her, his breath a warm rush against the nape of her neck, his voice murmuring in her ear when he made a comment.

He acted like a gentleman, but every moment they were together, she knew he wanted her, desire showing his speech, his touch, his eyes.

He was driving her insane.

She eased herself to her feet and bent to position both hands on the mat. Her head hung down and released her neck muscles. She discovered many things about the famous CEO by casually questioning his employees. She wasn't surprised to find respect and admiration in most of their statements.

What intrigued her was the warmth expressed by everyone she spoke with. She found he financed a luxurious vacation for an employee recovering from a hospital stay. He set up special tuition reimbursement plans for anyone who wanted to pursue higher education. His open door policy invited workers with a problem to see him personally, and its continued usage proved the effectiveness of such a plan—all surprising actions from a man with a heart of steel.

But did any employee know the inner Logan Grant? Chandler realized his job demanded all of his effort and time, but the sacrifice was evident when she watched him from across the room. Even when surrounded by people, he always stood alone. An invisible barrier stretched around him. Logan had climbed the ladder of success, but he hadn't taken anyone with him. It had been a lonely climb.

She wondered why knowing that about him hurt. Her new feelings were dangerous. She'd been prepared to withstand the aggressive actions of a man who wanted her in his bed. What she hadn't expected was the tender emotions flowering inside of her in response to the onslaught of a warm, summer rain rather than a crashing thunderstorm. But perhaps he knew how she felt. Perhaps it was all part of his game of seduction.

"I think I'm extremely jealous of the men in your classes."

Chandler jerked upward and spun around to face a pair of wicked gray eyes. He towered in the doorway, looking powerful and at ease in his black, conservative, custom tailored suit. He'd taken off the jacket and hooked it over his shoulder. His white starched shirt sleeves were rolled up to his elbows, and a pair of red suspenders molded the fabric to his frame. Black winged tip shoes peeked from underneath his slacks. He cut an intimidating figure. She tried to gather her scattered thoughts. "What do you mean?"

Logan walked towards her. "If that's the view students get during class, sign me up."

She blushed at his pointed gaze, and realized her hips and backside had been raised in the air. "That is not very gentlemanly of you to notice, or comment on, Mr. Grant."

He put his hands to his heart. "I was only trying to protect a lady from future embarrassment. What if I had been an old evil lecher bent on ravishing your body?"

"Aren't you?"

"Aren't I what?"

"Bent on ravishing my body?"

His eyes darkened. One lid dropped in a naughty wink. "Yes, but I draw the line at being called old and evil." He reached out and brushed at a stray tendril of her golden brown hair. "How do I know you didn't strike this pose to drive me insane?"

She fought a smile. "Mr. Grant, I would never deliberately provoke you."

She knew by the look on his face he remembered that night. His voice dropped. "You're doing it right now."

"Doing what?"

"Provoking me."

"I'm not doing anything."

"Each time you call me Mr. Grant in such a proper tone, you challenge me to make you say my first name. I have many pleasurable ideas in mind. Want to hear them?"

"No."

He smiled and tossed his jacket on the coat rack. "Too bad. Anyway, I'm sure you'll be happy to know I've come on business."

Chandler blinked and grabbed for composure. Too

many delicious ideas lingered in her mind. "What kind of business?"

"I'm having dinner with an important client tonight. I gave him some information about your seminar, and he seems interested. I'd like you to come with me."

She hesitated. Having dinner with him could be dangerous on her part. But if she declined she'd miss an important opportunity. After a few moments, she nodded. "Okay. Thank you for speaking with him about the program."

"You're welcome." He glanced around with interest. "This is a beautiful studio." He walked toward the oversized bay windows which overlooked the Hudson River and mountains in the distance. "It's very peaceful. You have to actually strain to hear the sounds of the taxis and factories."

She laughed. "I fell in love with this location the moment I saw it. A fire gutted the building years ago, and it remained vacant. I think the structure was too far off the beaten path for investors to make a profit." A gleam of pride shone in her eyes as she spoke. "I renovated the place and bought it outright."

"You did a wonderful job." His gaze encompassed the bare wood floors and large, airy space. One wall was covered with mirrors, and at the far end the windows were flung open, allowing the late summer breeze to whisper in. Black and white photographs displayed a figure posed in a series of different postures called Sun Salutation. Near the front of the room, small vases filled with fresh daisies and wild flowers graced an elaborate rock garden. Toward the back sat a pottery bowl filled with softly bubbling water. A small Buddha statue sat in the center. The plump, smiling figure radiated peace.

He motioned toward the display. "What's that for?"

"When students first come into the studio they take off their shoes and bow before starting their practice. It's a way of leaving your ego at the door. There's no competition in a yoga class, so we try to come to the practice with humility. Buddha represents enlightenment. Flowers and water represent new life. Rocks represent the earth. We pay our respect to all of these elements."

The beauty of her words struck him full force. He pondered them as he strolled through the room. Logan caught a glimpse of her office in the corner and peeked through the open door. The room held a worn pink sofa, one battered desk, and a variety of papers scattered across the floor. Purple mats and meditation cushions were stacked neatly in the corners. He smiled and breathed in the faint scent of incense. "Did you have a difficult time finding students? Your location is away from the mainstream where business thrives."

"The first year was a struggle," she said. "I invested in some advertising and sponsored workshops for the community, so it helped with new clients and referrals." She shook her head, remembering those months of hard work as she struggled to make a profit on a business she believed in, but others mocked.

"I've reached a point where there seems to be enough demand to increase classes and hire more help. There's so much more I want to do here. When I first decided to develop the Yoga and Arts Center, I knew I wanted a place where people could escape from the hustle and bustle of everyday life. I stumbled upon this building when I visited a meditation retreat close by. I knew immediately this was what I had been looking for."

He watched her from across the room with curiosity. "This was an enormous undertaking for anyone. Did you have help?"

The shutter dropped over her face and closed off all emotion. "No," she said softly. "I did this by myself."

"But now you need me."

Her gaze cut to his. Fire glittered within her eyes, reminding him of emeralds catching the sun. "I needed an opportunity to show how my program could work. If you had declined my proposal, I would've found someone else."

He closed the distance between them. Her head tilted back to look at him with defiance. "But you didn't." Logan ran his finger along the side of her jaw. "You found me. You're mine now. You belong to me."

Raw, sexual energy sizzled in the air. She fought for breath as her fingers curled into tight fists to hold herself back from touching him. She wanted him—his mouth on hers, his hands on her body, his taste against her tongue. All the weeks of abstinence only increased her hunger. Logan growled something under his breath, either a curse or a prayer, and his head lowered toward hers. His arms reached out to snag her and draw her closer and—

"Chandler!"

Her name echoed through the room. He released her, never taking his gaze from her face. Chandler shook herself out of the sensual spell and turned, torn between relief and regret at the interruption.

Harry rushed through the entrance in his usual manner and stopped short when he spotted them. "Oh!" He hesitated. "Sorry, I didn't know you were busy."

She waved him in. "It's okay, we were just finishing up." She made the introductions and watched them shake hands. Logan acted as if he was measuring up a business rival. Poor Harry looked confused. "Logan was just leaving. He doesn't like to be away from the office for too long."

"Oh, I have plenty of time," Logan drawled. "My schedule is clear for the afternoon. So, you're Chandler's lawyer?"

Harry beamed with pride. "Yes, Chandler is my first official client. She was one of the only people who supported me though school. Even after I failed the bar she always believed in me."

"I gather you two are close friends."

Harry nodded. "We've known each other for years. Whenever I'm under pressure she helps me relax. I knew when she decided to open the Yoga and Arts Center she'd become a success. You were lucky to snatch her up before she's in demand."

"She helps you relax with yoga?"

"Sure. She also gives a great massage. She knows all the pressure points."

Chandler almost groaned. She knew her friend's intentions were good, but the look on Logan's face was quite distressing. He looked as if he could cheerfully strangle her friend. "Harry, is there something you needed?" she interrupted.

"Want to have dinner tomorrow night? I need to talk to you about some things happening at work. Anyway, I've been craving Italian lately."

The room fell silent. Chandler dared a look at Logan's face and was sorry she did. He looked ready to strike.

His lean, muscled length coiled tight, as if to hold himself back. His jaw clenched and unclenched. She watched with fascination as his gaze came to rest upon her with clear warning.

A thrill shot through her at his obvious jealousy. It seemed his control over the last week was finally at an end. He thought something was going on between her and Harry, and wanted to put an end to it. He had the same look he always gave Richard when he caught them together.

Chandler bit back the explanations on the tip of her tongue meant to soothe his worries. Logan Grant had started this game the moment he kissed her. Surely, it wouldn't hurt to put him in his place by making him think she could be involved with Harry. Time she taught him a lesson.

Her lips curved in a smile. "Sounds good. Why don't I meet you at seven?"

"Great. We'll talk then. Nice to meet you, Logan." He turned and left. The clock ticked, and she stood her ground as she waited for Logan to finally speak.

"You will not go to dinner with him."

She blinked. "You're joking."

His face set like hard stone. Slowly, he walked towards her with a predatory grace. "Consider your affair with him over. If something was meant to happen between the two of you, it would have occurred years ago."

She took one step backward for each step of his. "You have no right to tell me what to do. You know nothing about the relationship I have with Harry."

"I know you're not in love with him." Arrogance pulsed through his tone. "I know you don't respond to him the way you do to me. I also know he's not right for you. Just like Richard Thorne isn't for you."

"And you are?"

His jaw tightened. "I won't let you go running to your ex-lover because you're scared to death of the way I make you feel. You do the same thing with Thorne. You're with him because he makes you feel safe."

"Safe is good."

"Safe is cowardly."

He advanced a step. She retreated as she said, "Harry is sweet. You're overbearing and insufferable. I won't let you walk all over me."

"You don't belong with him."

"Harry listens to my ideas and supports me. You're domineering and a pigheaded."

"I won't let you do things that will get you into trouble."

Chandler continued backing up from his looming figure. "Harry is patient and understanding. He'd never rush me into bed without being my friend first."

"I won't wait around on the sidelines while you try to compare me to men in your past."

"Harry would never demand something I'm not ready to give."

"I won't let you lie about your feelings."

She caught the gleam of triumph in his eyes too late. Her back slammed against the wall and trapped her from further retreat. She tilted her chin in defiance. He was so close she saw the heat in his eyes, smelled the musk of his cologne. She rallied her crumbling forces and battled for control over her treacherous body. "Harry would never use forceful tactics to get what he wanted."

"Harry will never make love to you the way I will, Chandler."

Her knees went weak and her gasp of outrage was smothered by his mouth over hers. He plundered her lips in a sensual invasion that drove the breath from her lungs. Heat exploded through her as his tongue thrust against hers, diving in and out of her mouth as if to pummel every dark secret, demanding her response, until she grasped his shoulders for balance and hung on. Her nails dug into his hard muscles as the searing kiss went on.

Raw sexual energy crackled between them as Logan slid his hands up her back to rip at the pins holding her hair. He dragged the honeyed strands through his fingers and murmured in pleasure as the heavy waves tumbled down to cloak them in a world of mindless abandonment.

She pressed her body against his, luxuriating in the feel of his hips cradling hers, the lean strength of his thighs, the bold evidence of his arousal. He pulled back, heard her strangled cry of protest, and tilted his head to kiss her deeper. He used his lips and teeth and tongue to push her to the limits of control, until she became helpless beneath the onslaught and surrendered completely.

When he withdrew from her, it took a few moments to register the loss. She blinked in confusion and stared up at him. His eyes were hot and smoky as he gazed at her, but his words fell like icy drops of water and made her stiffen in shock.

"Cancel your dinner appointment with him. If you insist on starting this game, I'll insist on finishing it."

When she finally recovered enough to hurl some choice words at him she was too late.

He was already gone.

• • •

Richard slipped his hand into hers as they walked down the street. The evening was mild, and crowds flowed out of the movie theater in search of a trendy wine bar or gourmet bakery. "Did you enjoy the movie?" he asked.

"Yes. I love foreign films but rarely have anyone to go with." She made a face. "Not many men are too interested in reading subtitles."

"Good thing we found each other. I have the same problem." The words echoed in the air as her black boots clicked on the sidewalk. A shiver of warning trickled down her spine. Dammit, what was wrong with her? They'd enjoyed a perfect date so far, and his interests coincided with hers. He brought her daisies for God's sakes—her favorite flower. And did she fall to her knees in gratitude? Nope. Not her. Instead, she questioned every motive and secretly wished he was Logan.

"Wanna stop at the juice bar before I take you home? They make everything organic."

"Sure." She stomped down on her urge for unhealthy chocolate and followed him into the juice bar. They ordered and settled in the corner. Chandler studied him from under her lashes and wondered what was making her uncomfortable. Maybe it was time to dig deeper. "So, how'd you begin working for Logan?"

He raised a brow. "Hmmm, not my favorite topic for a date but I'm sure you're curious. After law school, I knew I wanted to study business law and a friend of mine recommended Logan's firm. I began at the bottom and worked my way up to be his primary advisor."

She smiled. "You must've worked very hard. Funny, I picture you more as the environmental sort or fighting for lost causes."

He laughed. "Well, I admit I grew up struggling for money and want to lead a comfortable life. Business law is steady with normal hours. But I do offer my time pro bono at various charities."

Another perfect answer.

"How about your family? Are you close?"

He took another sip of his blueberry concoction and tilted his head. "Normal stuff. Sister moved out to California, got married and had two boys. My parents retired—both teachers. I have dinner with them every Sunday."

Her gaze probed those chestnut eyes and wondered why he seemed as if he was reciting from a report rather than sharing. "What do they teach?"

"Mom taught elementary and dad was a history professor."

"Did something happen?"

"What do you mean?"

"You mentioned money problems."

His face tightened, then smoothed out. "Oh, we had the normal struggles a family has in this economy. We always had enough to get by, but I wanted a bit more for my own future and my own children." As if he'd reached the end of his patience with the inquisition, he reached again for her hand and pressed his thumb into her palm. "I'd like to concentrate on the future. And you. It's not often I meet a beautiful woman with the same goals in life."

She forced a smile. "Thank you. I feel the same way about you."

"Good. Because once I see something I want, I don't give up."

She cleared her throat at the subtle warning that somehow sounded so different from Logan's declarations. Logan pissed her off with his macho demands but truth shimmered beneath every vow. With Richard, once again she felt like something was off. "Well, it's getting late, and I have class in the morning."

"I'll take you home."

When he pulled up in front of her apartment, she reached for her purse and turned. "No need to walk me up—it's hell getting a space. Thank you for the wonderful evening, Richard."

She expected a polite good-bye, so when he reached for her with deliberate motions, she stiffened in his arms. He studied her face for a while, stroking back her hair. "Chandler, is something bothering you? Aren't you attracted to me?"

Guilt speared her gut. "Umm, yes, of course. I'm just—taking my time."

A slight smile curved his lips. "Then let's take our time." He lowered his head and his lips closed over hers.

Chandler decided to give herself over to the kiss. Pushing away the disturbing image of his boss, she tentatively wrapped her arms around his shoulders and opened her mouth. His tongue surged and stroked, as his hands caressed her shoulders and moved down to gently cup her breasts. She tried desperately to concentrate on the sensations of her body; of the logical knowledge they were perfect together; of the pleasant taste of berries on his tongue. But nothing helped.

She felt... nothing.

She allowed him to kiss her for a while longer before she couldn't take the deceit and pulled away.

"Next week?" he murmured.

Panic surged. Why oh why couldn't she be attracted to him? She was a horrible, horrible person. "Umm, I think so but my schedule is a bit crazy. I'll talk to you later." Chandler squeezed his hand in reassurance and stumbled out of the car.

By the time she settled herself in her comfy pjs and slippers, her decision became clear.

Perfect or not, she was not attracted to Richard. She'd end up hurting him, and she couldn't live with herself if she led him on.

The phone rang.

Caller ID gave her the warning. She groaned and picked it up.

"Enjoy your date?"

The husky timbre of his voice stroked her between her legs and made her squirm. "Are you following me?" she hissed. "I swear to God, Logan, you better back off."

"It's not you I'm following."

She gasped. "Why are you spying on Richard?

Have you no shame? He's your attorney—I would think he's the only person you trust."

Silence hummed over the line. "Actually, he's the person I distrust the most. Keep your enemies close is the first rule in business, sweetheart."

"Do you trust anyone?" she sneered.

"Yes. I trust you."

The simplicity of the words rang through her, truer than any of Richard's declarations over the evening. Oh, she was a goner. She needed major therapy. "Don't say that," she whispered.

"Why not? I always tell the truth. I want to strangle him for playing games with you. I'm just hoping you eventually figure out he's a phony and only telling you things you want to hear." Logan's warning resonated down to her soul. Her gut screamed in agreement. Logan uttered the words she didn't want to face, because that would mean he was involved in a different game. The thought of such duplicity sickened her. No, she couldn't go through another experience like the one with her ex-fiancé. She might fall apart.

"I don't want to talk about Richard now."

"Good. Neither do I." He paused. "What'd you do?"

She sighed. "A French movie. Juice bar. Any other questions?"

"I hate movies with subtitles. And why the hell would anyone want something healthy after a movie? No wonder you're cranky—you didn't even have a decent dessert."

She laughed, her bad mood suddenly gone. "You are hopeless. I have to get to bed."

"Now that's a topic I'd rather discuss."

"I bet. Good night, Logan."

"Good night, Chandler. Sweet dreams." Goosebumps broke out from the low, sexy murmur. She hung up the phone and groaned.

She was in so much trouble. Chandler buried her face in her hands and wondered what the hell she was going to do.

Chapter
6

The following evening Chandler sipped her wine and gazed at the man who wreaked havoc in her life. Her dinner appointment with Harry had been postponed, replaced with one of Logan's making.

She had picked up the phone a hundred times to cancel on Logan, but always replaced the receiver while she raged at his incredible arrogance. The whole time she dressed she vowed he would not order her around like one of his employees. The only reason she hadn't canceled was the business opportunity for her school.

When he picked her up she acted cool and distant, prepared to ignore any apology or explanation he offered. It only angered her further when he'd taken her lead and treated her with the utmost politeness and kept their conversation on a neutral basis.

She wanted to hit him over the head with a blunt object.

Chandler re-focused her attention on the conversation. "I'm pleased with the final negotiations," Thomas Weatherall said. He glanced lovingly at his wife. "Time to relinquish some responsibilities and give Laura the attention she deserves. She's been patient for too long."

Laura laughed and laid her hand over her husband's. "I knew what I was walking into when I married him, but I admit I'm looking forward to doing some traveling. With the kids grown, we finally have time to do what we want."

Chandler smiled. She liked Thomas and Laura Weatherall the moment she met them. Obviously, the older couple was still in love after many years. They complemented each other nicely. He was a tall man, quiet and reserved, with silver hair and a stately manner. Laura was short and energetic, with red hair and sparkling eyes. Her movements were quick and her laugh was loud. Chandler bet Thomas learned not to take life quite so seriously with his wife around. She applauded Laura's success.

Laura turned to her. "Chandler, I think your idea of a stress workshop is wonderful. I know Tommy's company could use it desperately. All those nice young men and women end up with ulcers and migraines by running themselves into the ground. Have you seen any success yet?"

"I think it's working out rather well. Logan will analyze the results in six months, and hopefully we'll be able to expand." She prayed he wouldn't say something to the contrary. His chuckle took her by surprise.

"We're not halfway through yet and already the employees seek her out with their problems," he said. "I'm afraid if I tried to get rid of her they'd band together and overthrow me as monarch."

Everyone laughed. Chandler glanced at him and caught his wink. She felt guilty at her previous thought to injure him.

"Well, you have to be a miracle worker if you get our 'man of steel' to relax," Tommy said, ignoring Logan's groan at the nickname.

"Yes," Laura chimed in. "I've been telling him for years all he needed was a good woman. Now maybe he'll stop trying to invite himself for dinner every Thursday night."

Chandler arched one brow. "Let me guess. Meatloaf?"

Laura shook her head. "Pork chops. And I have to warn you, I've already found three other women he finagles dinner from on a weekly basis. I think it's all in his master plan."

Logan threw up his hands in defeat. "I admit I'm a lousy cook. I complement you, Laura. No one makes food like you do."

Laura leaned in. "I bet he says that to all the girls."

Chandler stopped smiling when she caught the sensual gleam in his gray eyes. His voice dropped. "Once I find the right one I'd never stray. It's a contract for life."

She clumsily reached for her wine and tried to hold back a blush at the pointed smiles directed at her. Logan made it evident he was interested in more than business, and his clients seemed delighted at the thought.

Tommy pushed back his chair and stood up. "If you'll excuse us, I'm going to take my wife for a spin on the dance floor."

Chandler watched them, hands entwined, as they walked away.

"Are you still angry?"

She looked up. She studied his face, captivated by the slope of his jaw, smoky eyes, black brows. His mouth could have been sculpted by an artist. His lips were finely outlined with just a hint of softness evident in the lower one. The khaki sports jacket he wore hugged the broad line of his shoulders and emphasized the breadth of his torso. She struggled to keep her voice cool. "Of course I'm still angry. Since I've met you, I feel like I've been run over by a steamroller."

Logan chuckled. "Funny, I've felt the same way since you walked into my office."

She snorted in disbelief. "I haven't acted like a bully and ordered you to cancel dinner dates."

"I don't know how else to make you listen. You don't believe me about Thorne, and now you think Weston is harmless. He wants more than friendship."

Chandler let out her breath in disgust. "Harry is harmless. I only tried to make you believe something else was going on because I wanted to teach you a lesson. I'm sorry."

He studied her for a moment, then relaxed. He leaned forward to whisper in her ear. "Did you like making me jealous?"

"No!" she denied hotly. "Of course not, I just wanted to—"

"I think you wanted to see how far you could push me." His fingers slowly stroked the delicate flesh of her wrist and glided up her bare arm. She tried to contain her racing pulse. "Maybe you wanted me to lose my temper, so I'd be forced to show you how good we are together. Hurl you over my shoulder and carry you into the bedroom. Thrust my tongue inside of you over and over—"

"Logan!"

His hand dropped from her arm to her thigh. She fought for breath. "We'll spend hours locked in the bedroom because I have a long list of wants. To feel you melt beneath my fingers. Hear my name on your lips when you beg me to take you, opening yourself to me so—"

"Please!" She placed her fingers over his lips. "You win. I get the picture. You don't—you don't have to go on."

His eyes lit with mischief. "Are you sure? I was just getting to the part when you wrap your legs around my hips and—"

"Logan!"

He chuckled and brought his hand up to touch her cheek, which was now a fiery red. "I can't help it, you blush beautifully."

"You're impossible."

"And you're lovely." A sudden smile touched her lips at his admiration. Her blush clashed with her pale rose dress skimming over her body in the most delightful ways. He wondered if she'd worn her hair down just to tease him. It was clipped away from her face but tumbled down her back. When the candlelight touched her, she shimmered, an ethereal figure of grace and beauty. He was almost afraid to touch her in case she dissolved in a ray of light.

"Thank you." Chandler cleared her throat. The imprint of his hand still burned. "I like Tommy and Laura. Have you known them long?"

He took a swallow of brandy. "We worked together in the same firm for a number of years before I decided to start out on my own. Tommy's been good to me. More like a friend than a business associate. When my mother died years ago he helped me through a rough time."

She reached over and covered his hand with her own. "Logan, I'm sorry, that must have been difficult. Were you close?"

"Yes, she was all I had left." A shutter dropped over his face. "When my mother became pregnant my father was forced to marry her. He hated us both for that. You see, he had great ambitions and living in a shack with a wife and kid wasn't in the picture. So, one day he left to pursue his dream of fame and fortune."

His fingers gripped the snifter. "She fell apart after that. She had to work so hard to try and take care of me, and she tired easily. I never realized she was dying. She kept that from me for a long time. By the time I had built a successful career it was too late. She was already gone."

Her fingers squeezed his. "That must have been so much responsibility for a young boy to take on," she said softly. "Your mother must have been proud of your ambitions."

He didn't speak for a while, as he contemplated the amber liquid in his glass. "It was too late. I became successful too late to save her."

Her heart broke into a million pieces. His matter of fact tone told her he still carried the pain of his mother's death. Even with his achievements, he couldn't erase the guilt, and she felt tears sting her eyes when she thought of the little boy who'd taken the weight of the world on his shoulders. She laid a hand on his hard cheek, and turned his face toward her.

His face steeled for pity, but she gazed at him with only deep understanding. "You gave her the greatest gift a son could. You became everything she always wished you to be."

Something passed between them, a current of emotion so strong she sucked in her breath at the sheer intensity. His hand gripped hers in reaction, and Chandler knew she had learned something intimate about this man no other woman had been told. She was honored by the gift, fearful of the connection forged, and dizzy with the sensations passing through her body. He opened his mouth to speak but Laura interrupted them.

"Logan, take this lovely lady onto the dance floor and show her what you can do. We've already requested Frank Sinatra."

He gave her a questioning look. "Ms. Santell?"

"I'd be honored, Mr. Grant. Tommy must have known that besides chocolate, Frank Sinatra is my other addiction."

He led her through the elegant dining room and paused along the way to greet a few business associates. The restaurant was small and intimate, with carefully placed tables sprinkled throughout the room, tastefully set with fine linen and sparkling china. Waiters dressed in crisp white uniforms glided past their patrons with subtle grace and anticipated every need before fading appropriately into the background. Chandler's heels clicked as they stepped onto the highly polished dance floor. The wood gleamed from the play of light cast from a crystal chandelier.

The lead singer signaled to the band and stepped forward. His low, husky voice poured into the microphone and Logan pulled her gently into his embrace. His arms encircled her waist, and his hand pressed into the small of her back to draw her close. Her breasts teased the hard muscles of his chest. As their bodies swayed, her nipples dragged across his front. She gripped his shoulders in response to the caress and stumbled. He eased her closer.

The lilting strains of the slow, moody ballad drifted in the air. The floaty material of her silk dress brushed against his thighs as they moved. Logan muttered something under his breath.

"What?"

"I said Laura must want to torture me. I should be

arrested for the lecherous thoughts I'm having in a public place."

Chandler hid a smile. "She'd be shocked at your lecherous words, too."

"I think it turned you on."

She gasped. "You're incorrigible."

"So you've said." His gaze dropped to her mouth. "Laura likes you. She thinks you'll be good for me."

"I think she's tired of making pork chops every Thursday."

Logan chuckled. "Smart mouth. From the sweetest of smiles comes the sharpest of barbs."

"Who said that?"

"I did."

"Oh. I thought you were quoting someone."

"I was quoting myself. Why do you look so nervous?"

"You're staring at my mouth like you're starving, and I'm your next meal."

He gave a wolfish grin.

"I'm still trying to convince myself I'm not your prey."

"When you look at me like that, I think I'd chase you to the ends of the earth."

"See, you are a poet. And to think I'd given up on dry, logical businessmen. Maybe there's hope for your lot."

"Dry, logical businessmen can transform if they find the right woman."

Their eyes locked. This time he caught her before she stumbled. His fingers threaded through her hair hanging down her back. He clung to the silky strands.

The faint scent of vanilla drifted up to him. He groaned.

Her face reflected confusion. She blurted out her next words without obvious thought. "Why do you try so hard to chase me?"

"Why do you run so fast?"

Her lower lip trembled. "Because I'm afraid."

The stark admission hung in the air between them. He felt the wall between them start to crumble. Instead of experiencing triumph, he was overcome with the need to protect her, to sooth the wild fear beneath the rubble. "You never have to be afraid of me," he said. "One day I'll prove it."

She relaxed in his arms and allowed her body to mold against his. His hands moved up and down her spine as if asking her to trust him. She shivered.

Smoke filled the room around them, glasses tinkled, laughter rung out. They were all distant sounds and images secondary to her rapid pulse and the fire in her belly. When the music stopped, he set her gently away from him. His gaze raked over her face, as if reading her thoughts. Then he led her back to the table.

His friends beamed, their smiles widening as they fell into easy conversation over a succulent dinner of seafood: lobster dripping with butter, grilled shrimp in scampi sauce, juicy crab legs that snapped crisply between their fingers. The Pinot Grigio was cold and fruity, the bread warm and lightly seasoned with garlic. Chandler dug in with gusto, eliciting some teasing comments, and the evening passed with banter and good humor. While the men settled the check, she turned to Laura with genuine warmth.

"I've had a wonderful time. I'm glad we met."

Laura smiled back. "I feel the same way. You and Logan must come to dinner one night at the house."

Chandler bit her lip, uneasy at what the older woman thought. "I don't want you to get the wrong impression. We're just business partners, even though Logan isn't hiding his desire for more. I'm not sure yet. About him. About anything."

Laura studied her a moment. Her eyes danced. "Do you mind if I speak frankly?" She shook her head. "Logan reminds me of Tommy when I first met him. When we started getting involved I was scared to death. Everyone told me he was a workaholic, and he'd ignore me and the children once we got married. Maybe they could've been right." She paused. "But they weren't. Tommy changed. Oh, sure, he'll always love his work and his company. It's a part of who he is. But I know I came first, and he never let me think otherwise. I believe when the right woman comes along anything is possible."

She patted her hand. "You're probably just as scared as I was. Logan can be a terribly intimidating man. He holds a lot of himself back; but he's more open with you than I've ever seen before. Sometimes a man needs someone who's willing to take a chance on him."

Chandler forced the words out. "I need a man who wants the same things as I do. Who believes in the same things."

The older woman looked thoughtful. "I understand. I felt the same way you did, once. Then Tommy
let me see the inner person, and everything changed."
She hesitated. "If you're ever ready to get a glimpse of
who Logan really is, give me a call. I'll tell you where
to find him on Sundays."

Before Chandler questioned her strange words, the
men came back. They exchanged good-byes and she
waited at the table while Logan got her coat. When he
returned, he smiled. "They enjoyed meeting you."

"I had a good time. Tommy asked to see me in his
office to discuss the program." She fiddled with the
edge of the tablecloth. "Thank you again for recom-
mending my workshop."

"You're welcome. Thanks for being my date tonight."

"You're welcome."

"We must be the two most polite people on earth."

Chandler laughed. They stared at each other for a
few moments. "Well, I guess we should call it a night."

"Yes, I guess we should." He escorted her towards
the door, stopping to complement the maitre d' on the
service, then guided her into the silver Jaguar.
Chandler leaned back into the seat as Logan weaved his
way through the city traffic with the ease of an expert.
She closed her eyes and allowed herself to relax, decid-
ing not to question him when he jumped on the Henry
Hudson Parkway and shot off into the night. It was
awhile before he reached the outskirts of the city and
pulled into a dead end road.

"This isn't my apartment."

"No," Logan agreed. "It's not." She turned to look at him when he cut the engine. "I'd like to show you something."

She gave an unladylike snort. "I think I've heard that line before."

Logan chuckled. "I'm sure you have. Please be assured if I had a different intention my approach would be flawless."

Her lips twitched. "The male ego is incredible."

"I can offer you a killer cognac or a hot cappuccino."

"Sold."

The street was quiet as they walked up the pathway. Chandler squinted in the darkness, but only caught an impression of a stark simplicity to the features of the house. The three story, modern structure seemed to thrust toward the sky, its roof hooking low over the front, sandwiched between two large picture windows. As Logan led her through the heavily carved door, the raw power and elegance that permeated the room struck her.

The color scheme was a relaxing blend of cream and sand tones, set off by soft leather and warm teak. A variety of cactus plants were carefully scattered about. Chandler walked past the large modern marble fireplace and peered up the wide spiral staircase leading to the upstairs.

"Your home is lovely, Logan." Her gaze took in the high ceilings and a massive wall of carved glass. She pictured how the room would look bathed in the light of the morning sun.

"Thank you." He watched in amusement as she studied the pile of books by his desk, neatly alphabetized by author. "I could have bought one of those fancy condos, but somehow the moment I found this place I knew it was home." He handed her a heavily cut glass. "Here, start with a little of this, then I'll put on espresso. It's a Godiva cordial."

"Hmmm, chocolate." She sipped in pleasure. "Do you mind the commute to Manhattan?"

"Not really. I have an apartment close to the office if I need to stay overnight. The quiet and privacy is worth the drive."

"I know what you mean. I grew up in the city and always dreamed of moving upstate. Most of my childhood was spent in my father's office. As luxurious as it was, somehow I think a cottage in the mountains is what I would like my children to remember."

"Not million dollar business deals."

She nodded. "I'm sure you'd disagree."

"Don't you think I want my children to have it better than I did? They'll have a choice whether or not to enter the corporate world. Besides, I always wanted to try horseback riding."

A giggle escaped her lips. "Somehow the image doesn't fit."

"Why not?" he demanded.

"Because, you'd have a hell of a time accepting the horse as boss—you wouldn't be in control."

His voice dropped to a low growl. "I don't have a problem relinquishing control if the reward is worth it."

Sexual tension lit up the room. She gulped her chocolate cordial and gasped as the warm liquid slid down her throat. She searched wildly for something neutral to say to break the silence. "Didn't you want to show me something?"

Logan smiled lazily. "Are you ready to see it?"

Chandler wondered if the alcohol made her hear things differently. There seemed to be a sexual undertone to everything he said. Maybe she shouldn't have had that last glass of wine at dinner. "Yes, I'm ready."

Logan loosened his tie, moving with slow, deliberate motions. The silky material slid through his fingers and gleamed against his tanned hands. The lump in her throat grew. He pulled the tie off and threw it over the back of the chair, never taking his eyes from her face. Easing out of his sports jacket, he tossed it over the chair to join the tie.

Her fingers tightened around the stem of her glass.

He stood in front of her in casual dress slacks which emphasized muscled thighs and lean hips. She couldn't stop her gaze from roving over him, overwhelmed by the sheer power of the male figure before her. She opened her mouth to halt this strip tease which took her very breath away, but his hands moved toward the buttons of his crisp white shirt and slipped them from the buttonholes one at a time. He revealed a line of curling dark hair. Her thoughts turned to wicked, sexual fantasies of popping the rest of the buttons in one sweep, ravishing him on the floor, then pulling off the rest of his clothes by using her teeth. And the things she could do with his belt—

His fingers stopped on the third button.

"It's in the bedroom."

She managed a strangled squeak. "Bedroom?"

"Yes." He paused. "Do you want me to go get it?"

"Get what?"

"The thing I wanted to show you."

She cursed herself the moment her gaze dropped. She hurriedly glanced away. "Yes, that would be fine. Do you want me to come with you?"

One black brow shot up. "Do you want to come with me to the bedroom?"

Chandler reached up to push back her hair. "No, no, I'll wait here." With a relieved sigh she watched him turn and walk up the stairs. She sank into the deep folds of the sofa and groaned. Why did Logan Grant always turn her into a stuttering idiot? The man constantly made her look foolish and she had no other excuse except for her overactive hormones. Why was she on guard with him? Because he declared she would be in his bed one day?

Would that be so terrible?

She rested her head back on the plush leather sofa and studied the ceiling. Laura's words spun through her mind, already foggy from the alcohol. If a man met the right woman, anything was possible.

Was he the right man for her? His kisses made her body burn for more. His quick wit and dry humor challenged her mind—she liked that. And, when he talked about his mother she ached to hold him and take away his pain. Were her emotions all caught up with lust, or could there be something more? Something like love—

Chandler's eyes widened. Love? No, she couldn't be in love with Logan Grant. She needed someone she could trust and depend on. Someone who could love her in the same way she loved him.

Like Richard Thorne.

Obviously, Richard was the type of man to build a future with. Unlike Logan, he worked in the business world but was not controlled by the culture.

Or was he?

She shifted as all of her thoughts finally took root. Something glimmered in those chestnut eyes—something she couldn't seem to trust. Staring at the ceiling the most disappointing revelation came to her—the truth of her feelings.

She would never love a man like Richard Thorne. She was falling in love with Logan.

Chandler shivered with a small sliver of pure, unbridled fear. Could a man who always needed to be in control let go and allow himself to love? Did she really want to take a chance on someone who may never be able to give her what she needed? At least she was happy with her life now. She had peace and stability. She had work. She had friends and students she cared about. She had—

She had no one to come home to at night or wake up with in the morning. She had no one to make her body burn and her heart sing. When Logan took her in his arms she felt like she could fly. Was that wrong?

Maybe she needed to take a chance on life. On Logan.

Logan walked back into the room. He propped a large flat package up on the thick beige carpeting and pulled off the wrapping. The image he revealed made her gasp with pleasure.

It was a painting. Her senses were assaulted by the stark beauty it depicted. An ancient castle rose above the earth, surrounded by rich gardens of flowers that climbed up the walls in an almost desperate attempt to mask it. Gaping windows peeked through wildly clinging leaves, finally breaking free to rise into the sky. The old broken castle stones told a story of time. Struck by the sense of history, Chandler wondered how many wars the castle had stood through, how many births, how much bloodshed or laughter had taken place within its walls.

"What country?"

"Spain. It's one of the oldest castles still intact. I spotted it in a gallery and knew I had to have it." They stared at the painting together for a while, not speaking.

"I was going to hang it over the fireplace."

She nodded. "It's stunning." He studied her face, and nerves tightened again in her belly. Chandler brought the glass to her lips and found it empty. He hid a smile as he carefully re-wrapped the painting and poured her another glass.

"Be careful with this stuff, sweetheart. It's potent."

"I'm fine." She watched him from under her lashes. He filled another glass for himself and walked over to a leather reclining chair, rubbing his temple. A slight frown creased his brow.

"Are you feeling okay?" she asked.

He waved his hand in the air. "I had a long day. Tommy told me one of my executives has to go before we complete the deal. He screwed up and cost us money. We can't afford any other mistakes."

"Who?"

"Jim Chrisetta."

She sat up. "Jimmy? Oh, Logan, you can't fire him, his wife's expecting a baby. Didn't he just get a promotion a few months ago?"

He looked at her in surprise. "How did you know? Wait, don't tell me, you had a heart-to-heart chat about his stress levels."

"Very funny."

"The promotion made this whole damn thing complicated. He did so well in his last position, so I moved him to management. Now those department's figures are down from last quarter. I have no choice."

"Of course you have a choice. Jimmy told me he's been under a lot of pressure with this promotion. He works around the clock and never gets to see his family anymore. You gave him too much responsibility. Management doesn't suit him."

Logan shook his head. "We had a serious discussion before the promotion, and he knew what the job entailed. His old position is already filled. Besides, Tommy was insistent."

Chandler crossed her arms in front of her. "You own the company, and you call the shots. Jimmy doesn't deserve to be fired because he thought he could handle something and made a mistake. This will crush his spirit. You can't fire him."

"Sweetheart, it's business. I can't get emotional."

Her eyes grew sad. "I've heard that explanation before," she said. "So sorry a person has to get hurt in the pursuit for money and glory, Chandler. It's all for the good of the company, Chandler."

His face hardened to stone. "I'm not your father," he stated coldly.

"No," she agreed. "But you are a businessman, aren't you?"

The challenge simmered in the air. She watched him struggle with his temper. He held himself rigid and still in his chair as he fought for control. A surge of adrenaline ran through her. Dizzy from the alcohol, angry at his logic, she recognized the driving need to make him lose his temper. As he pulled himself together, she felt a flash of disappointment she couldn't mask. She stood up and stumbled. "I'd like to go home."

"Sulking?"

She sputtered in indignation. "Sulking! I am not sulking. I think this conversation is over and I want you to take me home."

"This conversation is not going the way you want," he corrected patiently, "and that is why you want to go home. I refuse to let you throw me in league with your father, even though I've never met him. Maybe I'd understand better if you would tell me what happened between you and him."

"I don't want to talk about it." She shifted her feet for better balance.

"Okay, if you don't want to talk about your father, or the reason you left his company, can you do me a favor?"

"What?"

"Can you help me get rid of this headache?"

She studied him with suspicion. He massaged his temple, seemingly annoyed he'd be bothered by pain. He looked harmless enough, but Chandler knew him well. His admission could be part of his master plan to get her into bed. "You have a headache?"

"Yeah. It's been pounding at the back of my head all day. I'm afraid it'll turn into a migraine."

"Maybe you wouldn't have these health problems if you didn't fire Jimmy." He glowered at her. After a few moments she realized he was serious. "You really do have a bad headache, don't you?"

"No, it's all in my master plan to get you in bed." She bit her lip. "Yes, I really have a headache. Didn't you say something in class about pressure points?"

"Yes." She walked over and set to work. "We need to switch positions. I'm going to sit in the chair and you're going to sit, legs outstretched, on the floor with the back of your head between my knees."

"I like this kind of therapy."

He ignored the look she shot him and did as he was told. Chandler leaned over to position his shoulders. Her hair fell forward and brushed against him. He let out his breath in a hiss and jumped.

"Are you okay?"

He muttered something she couldn't catch. "Fine. I just hope I know what I've gotten myself into."

"Relax. Take some of those deep cleansing breaths I've taught you."

His shoulders rose as he drew air deeply into his lungs. The heat of his skin burned against her palms and made the thin fabric of his shirt a flimsy barrier. Slowly, the muscles in his shoulders started to unclench. She kept her voice low and soothing. "Focus on your breathing. Feel the air being drawn in and out, letting your belly expand like a balloon. Allow your muscles to relax while all thoughts float away." Her palms skated lightly over his shoulders and down his upper arms. She kept her tone even and drew him into a hypnotic state.

She pressed her thumbs into the back of his shoulder blades and massaged the muscles. Resistance met each stroke, but she eased her fingers back and forth until he responded to her touch. As she spoke, she worked each muscle in his shoulders and upper back, enjoying the sleek feel of his body. Hard muscles rippled beneath her palms. His steady breath whispered through his lips.

Chandler leaned over the edge of the chair. Her fingers traveled up the nape of his neck to his scalp. Dark crisp strands of hair clung to each fingertip as she massaged his scalp with gentle kneading motions. She turned him to sit and face her as she lingered at his temples and pressed. She caressed his hairline and forehead, smoothed down the line of his brow, and explored the carved features of his face.

A groan escaped his lips as his head bobbed closer to her breasts. "I see why this technique is considered dangerous. I'm your helpless victim."

Chandler smiled and pulled at his ears, moving her thumbs in small circles around the sensitive flesh. "Is some of the pressure lifting?"

"Yeah, most of it was in my right shoulder."

"Hmmm, you have a nice knot there. Stretch out on the floor face down." She moved from the chair to straddle his back as she probed the spot. "Focus your breathing on the area while I work on it a little more."

She kneaded the muscles but still felt resistance. Concentrated on relieving his pain, she slipped her hands beneath his shirt and continued the massage. She squeezed and released, letting her hands glide over his bare skin. Muscles jumped beneath her touch as she explored the hard body beneath her. It felt like steel sheathed in satin.

Electrical currents raced through her. Suddenly, she realized Logan's breathing had turned ragged. His muscles stilled beneath her hands. She stopped and dug her nails into his shoulder as the swirling tension enveloped the room.

She became aware of their positions. Bent forward, her hair fell over his left shoulder and brushed against the bare skin at his neck. Her thighs shifted and rubbed against him as she massaged him. Her nipples hardened against the thin silk of her dress, begging to be touched.

He suddenly rolled onto his back, leaving her still sitting on his torso. His shirt gaped open and revealed his upper shoulders to her hungry gaze. Her legs were spread wide as she straddled him, and one of his hands rested on her upper thigh for support. Those five fingers burned into her skin as he squeezed lightly.

"Chandler?"

His husky question made her heart race. He seemed to fight for control. She knew all she had to do was pull away and proclaim the evening over; she'd be safe for another night.

Chandler decided she was tired of being safe.

Her fingers glided over his face and neck in a caress. She gave in to the pleasure of freely touching him, glorying in his strength and suppleness as a woman now, not as a teacher.

A hiss of air escaped his lips when he realized she wasn't running away. She lay sprawled across the heavy weight of his thighs and looked him straight in the eye.

"You're not running." He pressed his thumb gently against her mouth, waiting for her response.

"I can't," she said simply. "You win."

She watched the emotions flicker over his face, partly surprised that she spotted no gleam of triumph for his victory. In fact, a slight frown marred his brow. With a muttered curse, and one rapid motion, she was on her back, his mouth covering hers. Chandler forgot every thought she ever had except the way Logan Grant bestowed pleasure.

With a single thrust Logan parted her lips and hungrily plundered the honey sweetness he found, over and over again, melding their mouths together in a fusion of desire and need. He became ruthless in his victory, demanding every response she had to give.

Her senses were overpowered by the scent of his breath, the musk and soap from his skin, the dark heady taste of raw male hunger. His teeth tugged gently on her lower lip, then bathed her flesh with his tongue. With a low moan, he reached up and plunged all ten fingers into her sable strands of hair.

One hand shot out to hold her still as he led her in a game of attack and retreat. His tongue led a teasing dance and urged her to play. She gripped his shoulders and tried to drag him closer to her arching body.

He gave a low laugh and dropped tiny kisses along her jaw, down her neck, the hollow of her throat.

"Tell me what you want." His hand cupped her breast and teased her nipple through the thin silk.

She struggled for breath. "I want you to touch me."

"I am touching you," he murmured. His teeth nipped at her shoulder while his fingers plucked at the hard crest.

"No, under my dress. Take it off."

"Yes, ma'am." Deftly, he undid the buttons and pulled it over her shoulders. His eyes burned hotly over the lacy scrap of bra that revealed more than it concealed, before he snapped open the clasp.

Cool air rushed against her skin as she was bared to his sight. Shyness overcame her, but the look in his eyes made her flush with pleasure, knowing he wanted her, knowing she pleased him.

"God, you're lovelier than I remember." He worshiped the creaminess of her skin with his gaze, the silky feel of her with his hands. "You'll see how good it can be, Chandler. Only with me. Then you'll know we were meant to be together." His words made a throbbing need pound between her thighs, and she curled her nails into the hard muscles of his shoulders.

His mouth lowered to one breast, his breath warm on her skin. A whimper caught in her throat as she arched upward and begged for more. His lips rubbed over the hard crest, back and forth, the slight scratchy feel from his five o'clock shadow a delicious contrast to the softness of his lips.

He suckled gently, then scraped his teeth across the hard nub, making her cry out. Liquid heat coursed through her body and her fingers clenched in his hair, urging him on, frantic with need.

She tugged at the buttons of his shirt and tossed it aside. Her hands ran over his broad chest and reveled in the hard, lean muscles rippling under her palms, the crisp dark hairs that swirled in an intriguing pattern and disappeared into the waistband of his slacks. A long stream of words escaped his lips, either a curse or a prayer, and she let her fingers trail down his chest to trace the edge of his slacks.

Slowly, she let her hands drift downward, testing the hardness of his desire, the raw strength and masculine power pulsing beneath her fingers. His stomach muscles clenched under her touch, his entire body hard.

Chandler looked up and watched his face. His eyes were half closed as he fought for control; his gunmetal gray gaze glittered with hot, male need as she wrapped her hands around him.

Carefully, she squeezed.

With a muttered groan, he lifted her off his thighs and turned her so that her back pressed against his chest and his hips cradled her buttocks, spooning her. She reached back and gripped his thighs for balance, and he chuckled when she tried to twist back around.

"Oh, no you don't, you little witch. I haven't waited this long so you could push me over the edge in a few minutes."

"But I want to touch you," she insisted. "I want to make you feel the way I do when you open your mouth on my breasts, and touch my skin."

"And how does that make you feel?" he asked.

"Strange." She sounded thoughtful. "Hot and tingly, like I'm craving something, something I can't reach yet."

Logan stilled, choosing his words with care. "And you never felt like this before?"

"I did once, but not this intensely. And the other time became, well, painful."

He realized then that she'd never had a man fully satisfy her. She probably didn't realize her past lover selfishly took her virginity and ignored her needs. Logan cursed the stupidity of the man. There was an untapped wealth of passion contained in Chandler Santell. The knowledge he'd be the first to give her such an experience affected him in a way he never expected. Overcome by possessiveness, he knew he could make this woman truly belong to him. But it was more than that. He realized he wanted her to surrender not only her body, but her heart. Humbled by the gift she wanted to bestow, he suddenly wanted to be worthy of it.

She needed to trust him completely.

So tonight he couldn't make love to her.

He closed his eyes and fought for control. Then he bent his head and pushed back the heavy mane of hair from her neck. He let his warm breath brush against her ear as he bestowed light kisses down her cheek. "I want you to close your eyes and relax, Chandler. Let me show you what I can do to you."

His voice poured over her like hot caramel and

wrapped her in a cocoon of warmth. His hands moved over her breasts and squeezed. She gripped at his thighs as the tension grew and a low moan of frustration escaped her lips. His fingers ran down her stomach and stroked her legs. She arched upward, demanding more, demanding something, uncertain.

"Oh, sweetheart." He sucked in his breath as he studied her, and she reveled in the blistering heat of his gaze as he took in her half naked body clad only in a scrap of pale pink underwear. Her eyes closed halfway as he traced his thumb along the line of her panties, and the aching emptiness between her thighs throbbed in demand. She gasped and arched upward.

"Logan?"

"I know you feel like you're losing control, but I'm going to show you more pleasure than you've ever known. Let me give you this."

Her breath came out in a ragged pant, but she was too far gone. Her body took on a life of its own and demanded more. His palm settled over her center, and he lightly massaged her tender flesh.

Her hips shot up when his fingers pressed. He rotated his hand, dragging the lacy material back and forth over her, until her heart pounded and her blood roared, and she thought she'd die of pleasure if he kept going.

"Open your legs for me, Chandler," he muttered darkly in her ear. One finger slipped under the elastic, testing her swollen heat, her readiness for him. She gasped at the sensation and wanted more. Her legs opened for him. With a murmur of satisfaction he slipped another finger under the material and touched her intimately.

His teeth nipped at her earlobe as his fingers slid inside. Stretching her wet, pulsing heat, he played gently and circled his thumb over the swollen bud of her desire. With each swipe, she thrashed her head at the exquisite tension. Each muscle tightened as she reached for more. Slowly, he rubbed back and forth, increasing the pressure, until she gave up and gave him everything she had.

She screamed as convulsions wracked her body and pushed her over the edge. For one single moment in time she flew through space in a channel of pure pleasure. As she floated she was aware of the soothing words whispered in her ear, the arm that anchored her against his chest, the hand that now lovingly stroked her thigh. She relaxed into his body, trusting his strength. She enjoyed being held close by this powerful man who taught her things about life she'd never known. After a while she realized he held himself still. His muscles clenched with tension. She felt him hard against her.

"Logan?" she asked hesitantly.

"Hmmm?"

"What about you?"

She heard the smile behind his words when he spoke. "What about me?"

Chandler turned her head. A faint blush rose to her

cheeks. "Well, ummm, I thought we were going to, well, that is I thought you wanted to—" She bit her lip and tried to get the words out.

"Make love to you?" he asked as he turned her body until she was facing him. His lips rubbed over hers, and he slipped his tongue inside to taste her. She welcomed him, their tongues playing with each other until they tired of the game and kissed hungrily. When he pulled away, he tipped her chin up and studied her face. "What I just did to you gave me more pleasure than you'll ever know." His thumb pressed over her swollen lips. "There's nothing I want more than to carry you into the bedroom and make love all night long, until both of us don't know where one begins and the other ends. But I want more. I want you to trust me. I want you to give yourself to me in every possible way, and I won't settle for less. When I take you into bed there will be no Richard Thorne. No doubts. And no more running away."

The stark words hung in the air between them. She realized this was one of the strongest men she'd ever known. A surge of emotion caught her. He was a proud man who stood alone in the world, and a ruthless executive who made million dollar deals without breaking a sweat. Yet he chose to show her tenderness, unlike Michael who had told her he loved her, and then treated her like a plaything for his own pleasure. Her initiation into sex had shown her none of the softer emotions she longed to receive as a woman from a lover.

She decided such bliss mingled with magic existed only in her daydreams.

Logan Grant showed her it was real.

He gave her pleasure while denying himself. He held back when she was vulnerable, and chose to wait until he earned her trust. He gave her fair warning of his intentions, and even if he only wanted an affair, he wanted all of her for that period of time, demanding no less.

Her emotions for Logan went deeper. She was falling in love with him; but if she gave herself tonight, she'd be lost. His emotions had nothing to do with love. When their affair was over, she'd have nothing left. He'd break her heart, and she'd be forced to dissolve their business contract, which would destroy the Yoga and Arts Center. She'd be back in the same position she was four years ago—with nothing.

She wasn't ready to take that kind of risk yet, make that choice.

Logan knew her answer. Confusion shimmered in emerald green eyes, along with wariness, and he told himself to be patient. Things always came with time. Chandler would be his if he waited for her to realize she loved him.

Then he'd have everything.

He smiled. He pulled her against him and held her close. "I didn't tell you any of this to scare you." He stroked her hair. "I wanted you to know where I stand."

"I always knew you were a bully," she muttered into his chest.

Logan chuckled. "And you, my little free spirit, are one of the most stubborn women I've ever met. Now, you'd better get dressed before all my good intentions go straight to hell."

Chandler quickly dressed, smiling when he distracted her to place a tender kiss in the valley of her breasts.

He locked up his house and caught her watching him with a thoughtful expression. "What are you thinking about?"

Chandler grinned. "I've come up with the perfect addition to my stress workshop."

He shook his head as they walked to the car. "Still thinking about work, hmmm? So, what's the new idea?"

As he reached down to unlock the passenger side door she stood on tiptoe to whisper in his ear. "Sex therapy, guaranteed to reduce stress and tension in the most pleasurable of ways."

He was still chuckling when he dropped her off at her door.

Chapter
7

Chandler sipped her herbal tea and glanced around the overcrowded cafe. When Richard called asking to meet Sunday afternoon, she'd thought it was the perfect opportunity to talk about their relationship. She'd woken up with a sense of guilt. Somehow, even though Richard was the perfect mate, she didn't love him. The night spent with Logan proved it. But she needed to tell Richard in person she only wanted friendship. He deserved to know the truth.

"Chandler, how are you?"

She looked up and smiled. He took off his fleece jacket and settled into the overstuffed chair. She admitted he looked as comfortable in the artsy coffee shop as he did in his office. The Hideaway Cafe boasted a large variety of teas, coffees, and desserts, and remained a favorite with the holistic health crowd. Copying from the Village atmosphere, large chairs and tables competed for space among sculptures, paintings, and plants. A popular meditation chant flowed from the speakers and soothed the ears. The menu was strictly vegetarian, and Chandler overheard a lively debate from her left, regarding the benefits of a non-dairy diet. Most of the patrons wore long flowing clothes and even longer hair. She wondered briefly what Logan would think of the place, but quickly pushed the thought out of her mind.

Richard ordered a ginger tea blend and studied her from across the table.

"I've missed you," he said. He reached for her hand and entwined his fingers with hers. She kept a smile on her face, but gently disengaged herself. A frown creased his brow at her action, but he didn't say anything.

"It's good to see you too," she said.

He looked amused. "Hmmm, I get more enthusiasm from my dentist."

Chandler laughed. "I didn't mean it like that." She paused. "Richard, we need to talk."

"You're right. I called because I want to ask you a question, an important question."

She shifted in her seat. "Okay. You go first."

He took her hand again, more firmly this time. "Since we've met I've been doing a lot of thinking. I enjoy your company. Besides having a good time, we have a lot in common. And I have feelings for you." She opened her mouth to say something, but he stopped her. "No, let me finish. I'm getting older. I want to be with a woman who has the same goals, a woman who wants to have children, a family."

"Richard—"

"I want you to marry me."

The sounds of a Chinese flute drifted across the room and filled the sudden silence at the table. Struggling for composure, she took a deep cleansing breath. An odd urge came over her to laugh. The man across the table should be her soul mate. She should be overjoyed at finding someone so right, and accept his proposal. Damn Logan Grant for ruining it. Damn him for making her feel things she shouldn't.

"I'm honored," she said softly. "It's been a long time since I've met a man I can have a friendship with. But it's not enough to base a marriage on."

"Friendship is the strongest foundation a couple has. The rest fades away." He squeezed her hand. "Let me make you happy. I want to build a life with you."

Her lower lip trembled. "I don't love you. I care about you, but not enough to get married. You're my friend, but I—"

"It's Logan Grant."

She pulled back with surprise. "What?"

He let out his breath and turned slightly away from her. "You're having delusions about Grant. The sad part is I've seen this many times before."

A cold chill settled over her. "I don't want to talk about this."

He shook his head. "Don't you get it? He always has an agenda. He seduces women for two reasons, business and sportsmanship. With you, it's probably for both."

She kept her face calm, but her stomach twisted into a knot of fear. "This has nothing to do with Logan."

"Oh, yes, it has everything to do with him. You know something? I'm tired of being the nice guy all the time. I thought you were a woman who could see past all that smoke Grant throws out, but I guess not. Do you think you can trust him?"

"I—"

"Because you can't. The truth is, he personally warned me to stay away from you. When I told him our relationship was none of his business, he threatened my job."

She gasped. "He would never do that. I know he likes to control people, but he lives by a code of ethics."

Richard laughed humorlessly. "Ethics, huh? He doesn't care about truth or ethics unless they can get him what he wants. I'm worried about you. He's after something, and you're the target."

"That's crazy. I don't have anything except a yoga school."

"Then why did he order a dossier on you?"

Iciness crept up her spine. The room swayed but she forced her voice to remain calm. "How do you know he ordered a dossier?"

He sighed. "I went into his office to get something signed and found some papers with your name on it. I was curious, so I asked him. He told me not to worry about it. When he left, I went back and searched his desk. Those papers detailed the story of your life, ordered straight from a private investigator."

The roar in her ears grew, but she fought it back. "Maybe it was just a background check. We do have a business contract."

Richard stared at her with cold eyes. "I do all the background checks. They're one page documents. They don't detail what you ate for breakfast when you were five years old."

The truth slammed through her like a hurtling freight train. Richard was right. Dear God, if Logan had read about her past, that meant he knew about her father, Michael, her father's obsession with marriage.

And his need to marry her off to a businessman.

Goosebumps broke out over her arms. Their past encounter flashed before her mind: Logan's concentration on giving her pleasure, the threats regarding Richard and Harry, his need to be the only man in her life.

Now she knew why. He wanted to marry her to gain her father's business. He was a professional, just like Michael was, and wasn't about to take any chances of her getting involved with another man. Logan didn't want her. He wanted the money.

When she looked back up from the table, Richard regarded her intently. Concern shone in chestnut brown eyes. Anger burned through her, pure and hot and demanding. Last time she'd run away and started a new life. This time she'd track down Logan Grant and make him pay.

"Chandler? Are you okay?"

She forced a nod. "You're a good friend. I know the popular saying about killing the messenger, but I don't blame you for telling me the truth. I needed to hear it, I guess."

"Then let me ask you a question. Now that you know about Grant, will you give me an honest shot?"

Chandler bit her lip. Reality hit full force. No matter what she knew about Logan, she did not love the man across from her. It wasn't right to lead him on and hope her feelings would change.

She gently squeezed his hand. "I'm sorry, Richard. I think we should remain friends. That's all I can handle right now."

For one moment, she thought she caught a glitter of hatred, but it was gone so quickly she figured it was her imagination. He nodded. "Okay. But I'm not giving up. With a little time, you'll see how right we are for each other."

He didn't give her time to answer. He threw some money on the table and leaned over to kiss her on the forehead. Then he was gone.

Chandler sat in the cafe and stared at the table. Someone had carved Nancy loves Ray into the battered wood. The chanting switched to a familiar Bohemian rhythm. Raw emotions rose up inside of her in tune to the pulsing music, and she closed her eyes. It was the same nightmare all over again. A man she was falling for only wanted her for the business. This time she wasn't about to meekly sit around and wait for Fate to decide.

She rose from the table and grabbed her coat. She needed to find him. There were a few things she wanted to say.

Chandler paced her daffodil carpeted floor like a tiger in her cage. She tried the office but nobody knew where he was. She'd called his house and reached his answering service. She'd sent a text, left a message on his Blackberry, and still heard nothing. Dammit, she wasn't about to wait for Monday morning and have a blowout with him at his office. If there was any way she could continue her program, she needed to talk to him in private. He was a millionaire CEO in Manhattan and he refused to answer his phone? Where the hell would a high powered executive be on a Sunday afternoon?

Laura.

She blinked. Laura Weatherall had mentioned something about Logan disappearing on Sundays. She dove for the phone book and dialed her number. Laura's cheerful voice came over the receiver.

"Hi, it's Chandler Santell. Do you remember me? We went out to dinner."

"Oh, of course, Chandler. I'm so glad you called. How are you?"

"I'm fine." She paused. "Actually, I'm not so fine. I need to get a hold of Logan and I can't find him anywhere. Do you know where he is?"

A short silence settled between them. "Yes, I do. Is it an emergency?"

"Yes. It's important."

"You can find him at Greenbriar Home for the Elderly. It's in Westchester. Let me just get the address."

Chandler jotted down the number and thanked her. She locked up the house and jumped in the car. As she made the drive upstate, she tried to imagine why he would be spending his afternoon at an elderly home. Did he have a grandmother there she didn't know about? Friend? Not that it mattered, of course. She just wanted to clear the record between them, and try to keep their relationship on a business level. After telling him exactly what she thought of his rotten, underhanded ways.

The three level building was surrounded by evergreen trees, and gave off a rustic feel. She pulled into the parking lot and made her way up the twisting path, nodding to a few residents as they were maneuvered in wheelchairs along the sidewalks. She stopped at the front desk, where a woman gave her a cheerful smile.

"Can I help you?"

Chandler realized she had no idea where he would be. "Ummm, I'm looking for a particular person. He may be visiting someone but I'm not sure who."

"What's the name?"

"Logan Grant."

The woman's smile grew warmer. "Oh, Mr. Grant. He's in the community room. Second floor. Make the first left out of the elevator."

"Thank you." She walked through the hallways, noting the clean, simple atmosphere of the rooms decorated in soothing blues and greens. Sunlight poured generously through the windows and fell upon cherry wood tables and comfortable cloth chairs. She wondered if the building catered to an exclusive crowd. Most nursing homes she knew gave off the scent of disinfectant and a gloomy glow. When the doors slid open on the second floor, she made a left and followed the frequent bursts of laughter echoing down the hall. She paused in the doorway and studied the scene before her.

A group of eight elderly men and women sat gathered around a large table. Most were in wheelchairs, others sat on high cushioned chairs. The sounds of Frank Sinatra boomed from the speakers and filled the room. Brightly colored chips were stacked up in piles in front of each person, and they all held cards in their hands. Logan sat at the head of the table with a fierce scowl upon his face. Then he threw one of his cards in the pile.

"I'm taking one card," he announced to the group.

A woman on his right giggled. "I think you're bluffing, babe. And I'm raising you five bucks to prove it."

She threw her chip into the circle with a confident air. The man next to her chewed on a toothpick and squinted at his cards. "Evelyn, you're a lousy player. You think everyone bluffs. That's why you've lost every hand."

"Well, one day someone's gonna bluff, and I'm gonna win."

The man snorted with disgust. "You shouldn't even be allowed to play for a theory like that. Women."

Another woman threw her chip in. Chandler noticed she had two glasses full of water in front of her. One of the cups held her teeth. She gave a toothless grin and cackled. "Come on, Jim, you're pissed 'cause you lost the last three deals. Women have been beating your butt for years, and you can't handle it."

Jim chewed harder on his toothpick. "Hey, Shirley,

I noticed you checking out that new guy in room 212. Pretty hot, huh?"

Shirley blushed and reached for her teeth. "I didn't notice."

Jim laughed. "Didn't notice, huh? Is that why I caught you staring when he leaned over to grab a soda in the cafeteria?"

"Shut up and play!"

"Fine, I'm in."

The rest of the group threw in their chips. Chandler watched Logan fight the smile on his lips, but his eyes lost the battle. For one moment, she caught him completely unguarded. Genuine affection warmed his gray eyes and turned them to smoke. His face softened into a playful expression, as he contemplated his cards and put on a show, pretending he had a hand that would blow them away. He teased them back, played the role of peacemaker when they fought, and made them laugh. Then his gaze slid up and locked with hers.

She held her breath. He stared at her for what seemed like hours, until she felt like prey in his trap. She waited for his carved features to settle back into stone, but his expression didn't change. For those few seconds, he let her in and allowed her to see a part of him he kept hidden. Her stomach dipped and plunged. She glimpsed a man who experienced laughter and pain and caring.

A man who experienced love.

Then the moment was gone.

He rose from the table and motioned her over. "I fold." A combined groan echoed from the group. Jim called him a wimp. Logan chuckled. "You're mad 'cause you want more of my money. This is a ruthless crowd. Sure you guys don't want to come work for me?"

"Nah, you don't pay enough," Jim grumbled. Everyone cackled with laughter.

"Minimum wage, Jim. Just give me the word."

"I make more with Social Security."

Logan winked at her. "Actually, I'm excusing myself because this lovely lady will break my concentration. Chandler Santell, let me introduce you to the poker club."

He rattled off the list of names, and she was greeted with a warm enthusiasm from everyone except for Jim. He looked as if he was sizing her up to see if she was worthy of Logan's company. The realization that the elderly man was protective of the city's most ruthless businessman inspired a spark of tenderness.

Logan called over one of the nurses. "Lucy, take my place, and don't let them intimidate you."

Jim snorted. "Yeah, and why don't you change the music while you're at it. Sinatra's old news. Put on Lady GaGa."

Logan shook his head and guided her out of the room. They didn't speak as he led her toward a lounge marked PRIVATE QUARTERS. She watched while he stopped before the window and stared out at the lake.

Old faded Levis clung to his thighs and muscled calves. He wore a navy short sleeve Ralph Lauren polo shirt which showed off corded arms sprinkled with dark hair. A gold Rolex shimmered around his wrist. He stood with legs slightly apart, hands on hips, his powerful shoulders thrown back with an unconscious male arrogance. She shivered as she recognized her body's instant reaction. The man was a pure sex symbol, but she refused to let her mind be weak any longer. He was also a liar.

And dangerous.

"How did you find me?"

His tone was mellow. His deep voice stroked her like a velvet glove. Chandler cleared her throat. "I called Laura. I told her it was an emergency."

He nodded, then turned. She was struck full force by his presence, and the raw masculinity that filled the room. "Is it an emergency?"

Her eyes narrowed with bitterness. "Probably not for you. But when someone lies to me, I like to know the reason why."

One brow lifted. "Sounds serious."

She waited for more but he stood there, staring at her. The anger came back, hot and demanding. "Serious for people who believe in the truth. Not so serious for people who don't care who they hurt to get what they want."

"Do you regret last night?"

Color flooded her cheeks. She shifted her feet for

better position. "Last night never should have happened. It won't again."

"Won't it?" he murmured.

Temper exploded within her. She reminded herself to breathe calmly. "No, it won't. I don't sleep with men who treat me like a plaything."

"I thought I treated you like the passionate woman you are."

"Why did you order a dossier on me?"

He stepped back as if struck. Surprise glimmered in his eyes, then quickly turned to regret. He cursed under his breath. "How did you know?"

She clenched her fists. "That's the question? No denial? No explanation? Oh, but of course, that's a businessman's answer, isn't it? Fine, this is my answer—it doesn't matter. You admitted the truth. Consider our contract null and void."

She turned to walk out the door. In seconds, his hand shot out and clasped her upper arm.

"Don't be stupid, Chandler. Don't throw your entire school away because of your temper. Think for a minute."

She did. Her words had been impulsive, but pride kept her silent. He turned her gently around and tipped her chin up, forcing her to meet his gaze. "I did order the dossier. And you're right, it doesn't matter how you found out. I'm asking for one thing."

"You have no right to ask for anything." She practically spit out the words.

"I know. I'm asking anyway. Hear me out. If you want to leave after I'm done, I won't stop you."

She told herself to walk out the door without a glance back. Her mind directed her to act. Her heart told her to stay, at least for a little while longer.

"Fine. You've got five minutes."

He nodded and settled down in one of the chairs. "It's been a long time since I've wanted to trust somebody. I told you before, I won't make any excuses about how I've lived in the past. I did what I had to do. But when you walked into my life, I wanted something else. For the first time, I wanted to know what it would be like to trust a woman. Have a relationship."

He let out a humorless laugh. "But I'm still a businessman. Your father called my office to set up a meeting to discuss a huge merger. I've been trying to get him for years, and he never made a move. You walk into my life, and suddenly I get this phone call. Something didn't add up, so I hired a PI to check your background."

Dizziness swept over her, so she grabbed the chair opposite Logan. He spoke in a factual manner. "When the dossier got delivered to my office, I started to read it. Dry details about your childhood. How your mom died. Then I stopped."

"Why?"

"It wasn't enough." He laid his palms flat out on the table and leaned over. "I wanted to learn about you, but not through a statistic report. I want you to tell me what happened with your father, and who hurt you in the past and what made you the woman you are. I knew if I read it, you'd never forgive me. I knew we wouldn't have a chance."

His jaw clenched with resolve. "So, I threw it away. I went with my gut and decided to take a shot. I'm going to trust you. I'm going to trust you're not in league with your father, and you don't know what's going on either."

The fight went out of her. Alexander Santell was trying to control her life again. She had to make a decision. She could trust Logan to stand up to her father and make his own choices. Or she could flee like she did before.

"You lied to me," she whispered.

He shook his head. "No, Chandler. I'd never lie to you. Ask me a direct question and I'll give you the answer. Telling you I ordered a dossier and threw it out didn't seem to be something you needed to know. I never lied about my feelings for you."

"What about Richard?"

"What about him?"

"Did you threaten him?" she asked.

His face tightened. "I warned him. Told him I knew he was playing games and to stay away from you."

"Did you threaten his job?"

"No. That would be stupid. He's an excellent lawyer. But something is going on, and I haven't been able to figure it out. I don't want you involved with his power plays."

She made herself ask the next question. "Do you think he's involved with my father?"

"I don't know. I'll find out, but in the meantime he needs to keep his distance."

"You had no right to get involved in my relationship with Richard."

A smile touched his lips. "I had every right. You let me show you things no man has before. You gave me part of yourself, and I'm not about to stand back and let another man try to hurt you."

She closed her eyes and searched for the answer. She had to choose which man to believe. Either way, she wasn't ready to admit the whole truth about her father to anyone. Her past pained her, and she needed to explore her emotions before she made another leap of faith. This time she needed to be sure of who she could trust.

"I don't know you." She opened her eyes, and knew he could see the raw fear reflected there. "I'm not sure how much I can trust you."

He nodded. "I know. I won't ask about your past. You can tell me when the time is right."

"What do you want?"

"An honest chance. Stop fighting me and yourself. And I'll try to give you what you need." He shook his head in mock humor. "Not that I know how good I am with this. I'm more the Type A personality. Not your normal sensitive millennium man."

She laughed. "It's okay. I realized that immediately."

"Do you believe me about the dossier?"

She looked him in the eye. Chandler was amazed at the simple answer she uttered automatically. "Yes." Her gut told her he spoke the truth. All he asked for was time. She'd never experienced such complicated emotions with a man before, and if she walked away she'd always regret. She'd learned long ago not to live life with regrets. "Yes, I believe you," she repeated.

A gentle smile curved his lips, the one she'd seen when he spoke with the elderly residents. "Good. Now we can get down to business."

"What business?"

"Getting to know me." He settled back in the chair. "Ask your questions."

She bit her lip to stop from laughing at his efficient demeanor. "Hmmm, somehow I didn't think getting to know each other would feel like a business meeting."

"Best way to learn about a person—direct questions and answers. What do you want to know?"

She smothered a giggle. The opportunity to ask anything was too tempting to ignore so she tried to pick a good one. "Are you into sports?"

He snorted as if disgusted with such an easy question. "Racquetball and skiing. Hate football. And I'm not afraid to admit I'm a Mets fan. Gotta love the underdogs, even if they haven't won a World Series since 1986. Next?"

She wrinkled her nose and thought hard. "First girlfriend. Tell me about her."

"Sally Demarco. Went to the junior prom together. Dumped me for a football player."

"Is that why you hate football?"

"Very cute. Next question."

"Favorite color?"

"Blue. Not too loud and not too fashionable."

"Interesting. Favorite meal?"

"Anything I don't have to cook. Come on, ask me a real question."

"Why do you come here every Sunday?"

That threw him for a moment. Then he grinned like he was proud of her. "Good one. I like to visit with older people. It's amazing how much you learn by listening to their stories."

She waited for more but he seemed to be finished. Slowly, she reached out and took his hand. Startled, he watched her interlace all five fingers with his. She smiled. The warmth of her flesh against his made his entire body shudder. "Now tell me the truth," she said softly.

Chandler watched the demons dance within the depths of his eyes, fighting to get out. "When my mother got sick, I didn't have enough money to take care of her. We had no insurance. Private care centers were too expensive, and I couldn't spend all day with her. She had nowhere to go except for the state nursing home."

She winced when she imagined the horrors of a little boy trying to make the right decisions for his mother. "You had no other family to help?"

"Nope. Mom was an only child. My father had taken off years ago and wouldn't have helped anyway."

"What happened?"

"She died there. I was at school. I went to visit her in the afternoon and her bed was already occupied by someone else. They never even called the school, just let me find out when I got there. Told me it was some kind of mix up and they were truly sorry." He shook his head as if to clear the memory. "Anyway, the place was a horror. I decided I'd make a safe home for people with no money to go. Like a private institution, but with no pressure of funding."

She blinked. "Logan, did you build this?"

"Yes. This is what I couldn't do for my mother when she was around. But every time I see a person here smile, or thank me, or meet one of their families, it's all worth it."

Sudden tears burned behind her eyelids. "You didn't name it after yourself?"

He shrugged. "I hate that stuff. I don't want to be a picture on the wall as founder, and my mother wouldn't want that either. I want to be involved with every person here." He looked disgusted with himself. "Oh, hell, now I sound like a wimp. Just like Jim said."

She laughed and lowered her forehead to their clasped hands. One tear ran down her cheek and splashed against his wrist. His fingers tightened around hers. "You make me crazy, Logan Grant," she muttered. "Before you know it, we're going to discover behind that Type A personality lies a streak of sensitivity."

"Don't let the rumor get around." She raised her head and smiled. He smiled back. "Want a complete tour?"

"I'd love it."

"Just watch out when I introduce you to Mr. Baxter. He likes to pinch ladies' backsides."

"That's okay. Men deserve a thrill now and then."

"Not that kind of thrill. One look at your butt, and he'll drop dead of a heart attack."

She laughed. "Thanks."

He leaned down and dropped a quick kiss on her lips. One finger trailed down her cheek. "Thanks for giving me a shot."

Electricity crackled between them. Sexual awareness burned hot, taking away her breath. He sensed the connection and dropped his hand to allow her the space. Chandler fought for composure, fought the need to hurl herself into his arms and let him take her for another ride of pure pleasure. She regained control and nodded.

Logan smiled as if he knew her thoughts. Then he led her outside.

Chapter
8

"Hi."

"Hi."

"Why are you—?"

"I tried to—"

They both stopped at once and laughed together. Logan moved further into the conference room. Chandler shifted her feet. Her eyes roved over his figure, and she knew a silly grin tugged at her lips. She'd tossed and turned most of the night, haunted by erotic images dancing behind her closed eyelids that kept her from sleep. Now, with him standing before her, she felt like a teenager seeing her boyfriend after a night of heavy necking. "What were you going to say?" She fought the impulse to pull his head toward her for a long, passionate kiss.

His gaze focused on her mouth. "No, I interrupted you. Ladies first."

The musky scent of his aftershave drifted in the air and teased her senses. "Why are you here so early? I thought you had a big meeting."

He took a step forward and reached out to grasp a stray tendril of hair. Slowly, he wrapped the silky strand around his finger. "The meeting was rescheduled. I can't make class tonight."

She fought to keep the disappointment from showing and nodded her head. "Oh, sure, I understand."

He released the lock of hair and trailed his fingers down the line of her jaw toward the wildly beating pulse at her neck. "I tried to call you this morning but I got your voice mail."

"I had an early class. I didn't sleep well, so I decided I might as well get up and do some work." The moment the lack of sleep admission left her lips Chandler felt heat rush to her cheeks. Logan pounced.

"Didn't sleep?" He gave a lazy smile. "Any particular reason?"

She cursed his sexy good looks and his damn confidence. Yesterday had been perfect. They played a rousing poker game, ate lunch with the residents, and took a stroll around the lake. He showed her a different side to his personality, a softness, and when the day ended he walked her to the car with a polite kiss good-bye.

His eyes told her he wanted to strip her naked and make love to her right there in the parking lot. His body told her he remembered every intimate detail and would claim her soon—when the time was right. Somehow, his polite kiss only made her fire burn hotter.

She wondered how many "morning-afters" he had gone through in his life. Was he used to putting a woman at ease and setting her up for the next time? Was it all just a bunch of bedroom games after all? He was way out of her league. Women probably threw themselves at him on a daily basis, all of them sexually experienced and quite capable of clever repartee after an encounter.

"No particular reason." She tried to look unconcerned by the hand gliding down her throat to hover at the top of her breasts. Already, her body began to melt under his touch. Her nipples thrust toward the material of her sweat suit in bold demand. "I got caught up in an old movie. It ended after midnight."

He laughed. "Liar," he taunted. "You were up all night imagining what it would have been like if I made love to you." He leaned over. His warm breath rushed over her lips. "You wondered what it would be like if I thrust deeply inside your body, over and over, until you were part of me."

Chandler trembled. She wanted everything he described. "Yes," she said, halfway terrified of the intense feelings she had.

Satisfaction carved out his features. He cupped her face with his hands and lowered his mouth. "Then kiss me. Let me show you how much I want the same thing."

His lips covered hers. He sipped from her mouth lovingly, and slid his tongue between her lips to touch hers, imitating the merging their bodies would do. With a low moan, she opened and invited him in, shaken by the sweetness of the kiss.

He pulled away and smiled down at her. "Can we have dinner after my meeting?" he asked.

"I can't. I'm meeting Harry for dinner."

"Cancel."

She sighed at his dark scowl. "No."

"Why not?"

"Because I'm not going to let you bully me! I told you Harry is a friend and nothing more. He needs to talk, and I can't let him down."

He studied the stubborn tilt to her chin. "Is he gay?"

"No!"

"Girlfriend? Wife?"

"No."

"Then I don't trust him. He wants to be more than your friend. I know how men work."

She took a deep breath. "Most of the conversation tonight will center around the woman he's had a crush on for months. He hasn't been able to get up the nerve to ask her out yet."

"Who is she?"

She tried to keep the smile from her voice. "Her name is Rachael. She's a stenographer who does a lot of work for McKenzie & Tetenbaum. Harry's had a crush on her since she started, but he's afraid she isn't interested."

He digested that, his face stony. "I still don't like it."

"I'm going, Logan. You're going to have to trust me."

For awhile he didn't speak. Then he reached for her. He dragged her against him and kissed her with combined frustration and hunger. Chandler surrendered, recognizing his need to assert control over the situation.

Breathless, she waited for his response when the embrace ended. A shutter dropped over his face. His hands clenched into tight fists. Knowing he had no choice but to accept her decision, Chandler waited for him to admit his uneasy feelings but concede defeat.

"I'll call you tonight at nine thirty. That should give you two plenty of time to catch up and return home." His tone held a firm warning. "Be waiting for my call or take the consequences." He turned and strode out of the room and left her gaping at his back. By the time she recovered her power of speech, he was gone.

So much for compromise.

Cursing fluently under her breath, she stomped over to the easel and dragged it to the front of the room to set up her display of nutritional charts. The man was impossible. As soon as she started to think he could learn to be fair and open-minded in a relationship, he pulled a stunt like this. Demanding she be available for his call? Caveman tactics like that should be extinct. He actually thought every woman he met would meekly accept the ground rules he threw out, grateful for the honor of being involved with the mighty Logan Grant.

Well, this yoga instructor would teach him a lesson or two.

"Chandler?"

She shook off her thoughts and turned at the sound of a voice in the doorway. Jim Chrisetta hovered in the entrance of the conference room, a tall, lanky figure with dark hair and serious brown eyes. He always seemed to be the most somber in the group, taking her instructions as intensely as he did his financial sheets. They had spoken a few times, and she'd been impressed with the responsibility he felt toward his wife and daughter. But Chandler knew responsibility sometimes took a drain on one's own energy and left a person vulnerable to the stresses of life. She only hoped Logan recognized the sensitivity in Jim and saved his job.

With a bright smile, she waved him in. "Come on over, I was just setting up for class. Boy, do you have an exciting night ahead. By the time you leave, you'll know everything about the fat contained in food, the benefits of vegetables, and how to discipline yourself not to have that second piece of chocolate cake."

He smiled back and took a tentative step toward her. "I wondered if you had a minute to talk. I know I'm early, and I don't want to take time away from your preparation."

She dropped the charts on the table and walked over. "Don't be silly, I have this stuff memorized." She studied him for a few moments, noticing the slight droop to his shoulders and the deep worry in his eyes. She dropped down on the mat and eased herself into Lotus position. "Come and sit down. Relax for a few minutes."

He looked down at his business suit and then at her. He seemed to think it over, wondering if he dare wrinkle his freshly pressed slacks. Then with one determined motion he sat down on the mat. Chandler bit her lip at the satisfied look on his face from the tiny act of rebellion. "What's up?"

"I'm going to be fired."

She managed to keep her expression neutral. Had Logan spoken with him already? Were there rumors floating around? She kept her tone calm and even. "What makes you say that, Jimmy?"

"I don't know if you're familiar with the deal Logan's working on with Thomas Weatherall. Tommy has a pretty healthy investment business, and the merger between them is friendly. We won't have to set up new management, so Tommy will remain on top with Logan overseeing the whole project. Anyway, Tommy gave us an important tip about a small computer company called Vicomdata that he wanted to acquire. Saw great potential in the creative staff. Vicomdata wanted nothing to do with a merger and wanted to remain independent. Logan was able to finagle placing one of his people into the company to get information about a specific loan. Once confirmation was received, Logan would be able to buy the loan out and force the company's hand."

"He used a corporate spy?"

He looked uncomfortable with the term but nodded. "Yeah. We all got a confidential fax regarding the status, and were warned not to leak any information. Well, the guy at Vicomdata used to work with me, and is actually a friend. Name is Charlie. Rumor must have gotten to someone over there—God knows how, and one night I got a call."

He shook his head in disgust. "I was working overtime to catch up on some paperwork. I had at least three deadlines due by morning, and was still getting my feet wet in my new position, so needless to say I wasn't thinking too clearly. I spoke with a manager at Vicomdata who pretended to know Charlie well, and basically got me to confirm that he's one of Logan's employees. It happened so fast I didn't even realize I had slipped up. The next morning, Charlie was fired from Vicomdata and back here without the information. Needless to say, Logan wasn't too pleased. We lost the edge on the deal and a large future profit."

Chandler let the story sift through her mind. "Jimmy, do you like your new position in management?"

He shrugged. "It's okay. I enjoyed my old job better. I'm not crazy about telling people what to do and always calling the shots. But when Logan offered me a management opportunity I realized it was more money and prestige. This is the first promotion I ever got. My wife was really proud."

She smiled. "When someone offers you a promotion it confirms you're doing a good job."

"Exactly."

"But if your reward is to be locked into a position which makes you unhappy, do you think it's worth it?"

He frowned. "I don't know. I never thought about it. A promotion is supposed to be for the better."

"Yes, that's the idea. But sometimes a person doesn't realize a simple raise would have done just as nicely."

Jimmy nodded. "That's what I wanted. But I couldn't let Logan down. He was trying to help me."

"How do you know you'll be fired?"

"Logan will have no choice. Tommy was mad as hell

about the screw up, so he'll probably order Logan to fire me. Logan wants the merger so he'll have to listen. And my old job is already filled, which leaves me out."

Chandler almost winced at the correct assumption. She searched for a way out of the mess he was in. She couldn't promise he wouldn't be fired, no matter how much she wished she could. She needed to show him he'd be able to handle the situation.

"Okay, so you made a mistake. You were caught off-guard, and this manager used your friendship with Charlie to get information. Quite unethical in my eyes, but I know business is business."

His shoulders sagged. "Yeah."

"Do you really think you should be fired because of one screw up in the last—?"

"Four years."

"Four years?" she continued.

"It was a big mistake. I probably deserve it."

She thought about his remark. "Be honest with me. You're a person who worries a lot, right?"

He grinned sheepishly. "That's what my wife says. Yeah, I like to make sure all my responsibilities are taken care of."

"When you get up in the morning, what thought is always in the back of your mind? What is your greatest fear, the thing you worry about on a daily basis?"

"Well, I guess that would be what just happened. Or what's going to happen. Being fired."

"Exactly. What scares you the most about being fired?"

He looked puzzled by the question. "I was afraid of not being able to support my family, of being called a failure, feeling like a failure."

"Do you feel like a failure?"

"No. I messed up, but I don't think that negates the last four years of doing well."

"Exactly." She leaned forward. "Do you realize you're finally free? Your worst fear is about to be confirmed. You're going to get fired. And you're still okay with yourself. They can't take away your own inner core. You can get another job. You can follow a dream you've always had. You can march into Logan's office, free of your fear, and tell him why he'll be making the biggest mistake of his life if he fires you. From now on, any job you hold won't have a hold on you. Your family is what's most important. Now you'll be able to give them more of yourself, because your work won't be holding all the cards."

Jimmy stared down at the mat. She held her breath and hoped he understood what she said. She wanted him to be free of all the fear and stress he held close to his heart. If he was able to realize there was a whole other world out there, then losing a job shouldn't destroy his self respect. In fact, it could open up a new realm of possibilities. If he could only see . . .

Jimmy looked up. He smiled. Her heart lifted at the look on his face. He understood. The deep lines of worry that normally creased his brow disappeared. A determined glint shone in his serious brown eyes. She'd gotten through to him.

She smiled back. "Okay?"

Jimmy nodded. "Okay." He got up from the mat, swiping at the wrinkles in his slacks, straightening his jacket and tie. "You know, Logan is usually a fair guy. He'd probably give me a good referral. Or I could even go back to school. I always wanted to finish up my Masters degree."

"Anything is possible." She watched him walk to the door, his shoulders set in a determined line. "Jimmy?"

"Yeah?"

"Do me a favor. Don't forget about the deep breathing I taught you. Always focus. Never take life too seriously. And I promise to send you copies of the nutritional charts in the mail."

He laughed. "Thanks. My biggest screw-up was not listening to you in the first place. If I'd just taken a couple of deep breaths to calm down, I probably wouldn't have slipped. Next time I won't make that mistake."

She watched him walk out the door. After a few moments she eased herself up from the mat. There was no way she would let Jimmy lose his job without a fight.

She needed to think of a plan.

• • •

"Mr. Grant?"

Logan swivelled around in his leather chair. A tall

man with silver hair stood in the door way dressed impeccably in a black suit and red silk tie. Green eyes stared back at Logan with an openly assessing gaze. The man's shoes were polished to perfection, and a gleaming gold Rolex flashed from his wrist. Everything about the man shimmered with raw energy.

For a moment Logan felt thrown by the striking resemblance Alexander Santell bore to his daughter. Logan carefully screened his expression to attain an element of blandness. Santell was a powerful adversary if crossed, and until Logan knew what game the man was playing it would be wise not to show any other thoughts that crossed his mind.

"Mr. Santell, please come in. I wasn't expecting you until six." Logan stood to welcome the man.

Santell strode across the room in long, graceful strides and reached out to grasp Logan's hand in greeting. "I was able to wrap up my last meeting very quickly, and I thought it would be nice to talk to you alone before my lawyer and associate arrive for our conference."

Logan nodded, but couldn't help but be struck by the powerful aura the man projected. "I see. Please, take a seat. Would you like coffee, brandy?"

"No, thank you. Damn doctors are constantly on my case to cut my intake of caffeine and alcohol. I say if you can't live the way you want why bother tacking on a couple of years?"

Logan smiled, and sat back in his chair, settling himself comfortably. "I agree with you. There seems to be problems with everything we eat and drink today. I'm just waiting until they tell us the air we breathe has been poisoned for the last decade."

Alexander Santell let out a rich, booming laugh. They studied each other for a few moments, making mental notes. "So, have you thought about my offer?"

Logan nodded and kept his expression bland. "I must admit I'm curious. My employees and I have been trying to secure a meeting with you for a while, but you've insisted you want nothing to do with a merger. Then, suddenly, the offer of a lifetime drops in my lap. Naturally, I've been interested in your change of heart."

Santell's eyes narrowed. "And well you should. I don't want my company merged with someone who trusts every offer thrown at him. I need someone who has the ruthlessness and business sense I've had since I was young. All the trade journals and even my fellow associates say you're the man of steel. I know quite well how you received your nickname. The real story, that is."

Logan's tone held a faint warning. "I don't discuss my past, Santell, neither with my friends nor my enemies. As you don't fit in either category yet, I advise you to limit the topic to business."

Santell gave another booming laugh. "Yes, I'm sure you would. But what if this business contract happens to involve my daughter?"

The mention of Chandler threw Logan for a few moments, before he quickly gathered his composure. A lazy smile curved his lips. "I had a feeling she'd be mentioned in this little chat. I assume you know we're working together?"

"Hell, yes, I knew the moment she walked into your office. What surprised me was the reason you accepted her offer. Every other company in the city laughed her out of the building. Yet, you agreed to the proposal. Your actions made me start wondering. Do you mind if I smoke?"

Logan waved for him to continue as he reached for an ashtray he kept in the top drawer. The older man opened his jacket and pulled out a cigar. He clipped the tip, lit it, and drew the smoke into his mouth, sighing with pleasure.

"God, the Cubans sure know how to make a cigar." He paused, enjoying his smoke while Logan waited. "I wondered about the real reason you accepted her offer. Knowing your business savvy, I doubted it was for the classes. So, it came down to two choices. Either you were interested in becoming involved with my daughter personally, or you decided it would be good to have her working for you as leverage."

"Leverage?" Logan tapped the pen absently against the edge of the desk. "What kind of leverage?"

The older man grinned. "You're a smart man. The moment she walked into your office you must have known she was my daughter, once worked for me, and that we haven't spoken on an intimate level in years. You must also know how desperately I want her to marry the right man. Hell, I worry about her constantly. Ever since she started this crazy yoga business I hoped one day she'd come to her senses. She needs someone to show her she belongs in my company. But since she won't talk to me, let alone run it, my second option is to give it to the man she marries and hope she takes her rightful place. I have a feeling the man could be you."

Logan's expression never changed. The steady tap-tap-tap of the pen was the only sound in the room. He gazed at the older man across the desk as the pieces of the puzzle finally fit together. Alexander Santell had made his first mistake by assuming he knew all the details of Chandler's past. His more deadly mistake, was assuming he could manipulate Logan as he did his former business executive—namely Michael Worthington. The thought of the man who was once Chandler's fiancé turned Logan's stomach and made his gut wrench.

"What if I don't want to marry her?" Logan asked.

A glitter of triumph lit moss green eyes. "Oh, I think the idea appeals to you immensely. Besides getting my company, you'd get my daughter. From my detective's report the other night, it seems the two of you are on more intimate terms."

Logan dropped his casual demeanor. He leaned over the desk, every muscle drawn with tension. His fist clenched over the pen he held, and he lowered his voice to a silky pitch. "Listen to me and listen well, Santell. If you ever send another person to track me or your daughter, I'll destroy you. If you know me half as well as you think you do, you'll realize I don't make threats. I make promises."

The older man smoked his cigar. Slowly, he nodded, a thoughtful expression on his face. "Point taken. It seems you're more involved than I originally thought, which is another reason to think about my offer. I miss my little girl, and I worry about her. I think you'd be a very good match."

"As good as the last one?"

Alexander waved the question away. "That was a mistake from the beginning. Worthington wasn't strong enough for her, and I regret the episode. He ended up ruining my entire relationship with my daughter. I admit I made a mistake. When the deal of a lifetime was dropped in my lap, I needed to get my daughter married fast. I thought Worthington would be perfect for her. It didn't seem like a bad idea at the time, since Chandler started to stray. I figured a marriage would help her settle down and focus." He shrugged massive shoulders in an innocent gesture. "It would have worked if Worthington had been the right man." Alexander pointed his cigar at him. "But I have a gut instinct about you, Grant. I think beneath your cool exterior, you have real feelings for Chandler. And I know you'll make my company profitable."

Santell stood up and stamped out his cigar in the ashtray. "The flock should be here in a few minutes to go over the details. If you agree, I'll deliver on my promise when the ring is on her finger."

Logan caught the triumphant expression on the man's face and knew Santell thought the game was over. As an experienced player, Santell had recognized his hunger, and offered to feed it. Logan smothered a groan and cursed himself for letting his emotions about Chandler show so clearly. He'd gain a lucrative contract that would put L&G Brokerage on top. And he'd finally possess Chandler, body and soul.

All he had to do was agree to the deal.

The swirling emotions ripped at his gut as he gazed at her father. Logan knew if he accepted the proposal, Alexander Santell would control him. If Chandler ever found out their marriage was based on her father's business deals, he'd lose his chance at gaining her heart.

"And if I don't agree?" Logan asked.

Disappointment glimmered briefly in Santell's eyes. He shrugged again. "Then you don't get the contract. And, because of my displeasure I may have to encourage my suppliers and business associates to put a little pressure on you. The contract with Weatherall was superb, by the way, but nothing like what I can do for you." He turned to go, but stopped at the door. "Oh, I also forgot to mention that Chandler is quite sensitive to any ruthless dealings in business. It would be a shame to have to tell her all the details of your past, wouldn't it?"

Logan chuckled. "I heard you like to play hardball. Again, I warn you not to involve her in your little games. You'll regret it."

Santell nodded. "Thank you for listening to my proposal."

"It was enlightening. Did you ever stop to think about what Chandler might want?" Logan ground out. "Or does that even matter to you?"

Santell laughed. "Her welfare is what is most important. I've been taking care of her since she was a little girl, and I know what's best. She may not realize it, but this will make her happy."

"You're a real son of a bitch, Santell."

Logan heard the older man's laughter as he walked out of the office. Swivelling back around in his chair, he stared blindly out the window and watched the hazy colors of sunset settle over the smog infested city. He raked his fingers through his hair and cursed under his breath. Things were becoming more and more complicated ever since Chandler Santell walked into his life.

What the hell was he going to do?

He groaned and replayed the confrontation. He'd learned a few interesting things about his adversary. First, in his own twisted way he loved his daughter. Second, the prime motivation driving him was the fear he was getting older and had no one to leave his legacy to. Evidently, he'd been taught that bullying the people he loved was a good way to control them, but that had ended up pushing everyone away.

Including Chandler.

Logan considered his options. A few years ago there would have been no doubt about his actions. A contract with Santell's finance company would put him at the top for a very long time. He would have achieved everything he'd set out to do. He'd make his mark on the world. But now, there was Chandler to consider and her reaction if she knew her father was trying to buy her another husband, one who happened to be another corporate executive.

Logan had a pretty good idea her reaction would not be favorable. Towards him or her father.

A sudden thought danced before his mind, and he paused before the window. Her father wanted to marry her off to a businessman, and he was the perfect target. But Alexander Santell was a smart man. He'd have a back-up plan to cover his gamble.

Richard Thorne.

Logan muttered an oath under his breath as the final piece fell into place. That was the reason his attorney was interested in Chandler. He'd bet his entire company Thorne had been approached with a nice fat carrot. Marry the daughter and gain the company. Prove yourself and get a prize. The old man was playing both of them at once, and whoever came out on top would win.

He shook his head with disgust. Now Chandler was in the middle of a war she knew nothing about. Somehow, there had to be a way to get everything, without hurting Chandler.

Logan rose from his chair and buzzed his secretary to bring in a pot of strong coffee. It was going to be a long night. And he didn't want to even think about Chandler meeting Harry for dinner this evening.

He wondered how a simple yoga teacher could wreak such havoc in his once logical, orderly life.

Chapter
9

"Why did you want me to change the reservation time?" Harry asked as Chandler dove into her pasta primavera with her normal gusto.

"I'm trying to teach someone a valuable lesson." She closed her eyes in delight as the first mouthful passed her lips. Crunchy broccoli drizzled with olive oil and parmesan cheese.

Was there anything more perfect than al dente pasta with fresh vegetables? "One hour later is perfect. It's for someone who, you'll agree, deserves a good lesson."

Harry put down the fork and stared at her. "Okay, what's going on? You don't sound like yourself. You always say accept a person the way he or she is. Don't punish someone or have false expectations. Has something changed?"

She sighed. "Thanks a lot, Harry. There's nothing worse than hearing your own words come back to haunt you, especially when it's from one of your students."

"You know I hate it when you call me a student," he grumbled. "I'm your friend and equal, remember? Are you ever going to get over the fact you were two years ahead of me throughout school?"

"Sorry." She laughed. "Sometimes I forget you decided to quit my yoga classes."

Harry glowered at her. "That's because you were constantly on my case giving me lectures on nutrition, on stress, on exercise. During class you always embarrassed me by correcting my postures in front of the other students. I had to quit. Class was damaging our friendship."

She fought back a giggle and took a sip of wine. "I apologize. I was concerned with your well being. I guess I was so used to tutoring you in school that I got carried away when you joined the Yoga and Arts Center. Lord knows, I shouldn't lecture on nutrition. My love of food always makes me put my foot in my mouth when I preach about a healthy diet."

"Yeah, you do eat a lot."

She raised an eyebrow. "I only have a big dinner. The rest of the day I exist on fruit and vegetables."

He snorted.

She shot him a glare and stabbed her fork into a crisp red pepper. "Well, getting back to our previous subject, I admit it's not my usual style to teach someone a lesson but I feel there's no choice."

"Who is it?"

"Logan Grant."

Silverware clattered as it hit the plate. "The man who has the power to send you packing and put you in the poorhouse in six months?"

"That's the one."

He studied her with suspicious eyes. "There's something going on you're not telling me. When I met him, I felt like he was ready to cut my head off. Why would he take an instant disliking to me? Unless of course . . ." he trailed off.

"What?"

"No. You wouldn't."

Chandler focused on her plate. She had a feeling she was in for a lecture.

Harry's mouth dropped open. "You did. You're sleeping with him."

"No!"

"Then you're thinking about it!"

She decided not to answer and continued shoving pasta in her mouth.

"I knew it." He muttered under his breath and shook his head. "I knew you'd snap one day because of all that meditation."

"You think I'm crazy, don't you?"

"Yes, I think you're crazy. For years you've insisted you'd never get involved with another corporate mogul. Then you pick the most ruthless executive in the city that just happens to have the future of the Yoga and Arts Center in the palm of his hand. He could wipe you out with one clean swoop. Yes, I think you're crazy." He picked up his fork and stabbed his swordfish.

She sighed. "I know, I know. I never asked for this to happen. But don't you think a person can change? If there's a good reason?"

"What kind of reason? People don't usually change overnight."

"If one person fell in love with another, don't you think it's possible?"

She watched as Harry gently placed his fork down. "You didn't."

"What?"

"You fell in love with him!"

She looked away. "I never said that."

"You didn't have to, I know you too well." He paused. "Oh, Chandler, what have you done?"

She met his gaze. Confusion muddled her thoughts. "I've never felt like this before. At first, I fought him so hard I never gave myself an opportunity to explore my feelings. But little by little, he showed me signs."

"What kind of signs?"

"Signs that he wants more in life than just money and prestige. Maybe he wants a wife and family and a home in the country." She pushed back her heavy mane of hair. "Something about him draws me. He's so alone. I feel like in some crazy way he needs me."

Harry groaned. "Logan Grant is not some stray puppy you can bring home. He's not a lost man who showed up in your yoga class looking for inner peace. He's a ruthless business executive who could hurt you. Anyway, what happened to the lawyer guy? Thorne, right?"

She sighed. "I like him as a friend."

"I thought you said he was perfect for you."

"He is."

"Hmmm, do women not want perfect now?"

She laughed. "I just don't love him. On the outside

he seems to be everything I'm looking for. But my gut tells me he's a liar. Isn't that weird?"

"This whole conversation is weird."

She lowered her voice. "I'm tired of being afraid to trust, to love. I think Logan wants a relationship, not a one night stand. I'd like to give him a shot. After I teach him a lesson, of course."

"What kind of lesson?"

"He ordered me to cancel dinner reservations with you. When I refused, he commanded me to wait for his call at nine thirty. Then he practically threatened me not to disobey him."

"You changed our reservations to eight. We won't be home before ten."

She smiled. "I know."

"I guess he'll just call you on your cell."

She tried not to look guilty. "I left it at home."

He reached for his vodka and tonic and took a long swallow. "Why do I feel like I'm going to be caught in the middle?"

"I'm sorry, I don't want to drag you into this. But you have to admit I'm right. Ordering me to be available for his call? Can you blame me?"

"Actually, I agree with the guy."

"What!"

He nodded. "He's right. If my current lover—"

"I'm not his lover!"

"Okay, if my 'lover to be' decided to go out with some man I didn't know, who said he was an old friend, I'd be nervous. I'm surprised he let you go in the first place. Cut the guy some slack."

Chandler buried her face in her hands. "I can't believe this. Men always stick up for each other. I just don't get it."

"I can't believe you're pushing him this far."

"I only want to prove a point."

"As long as I'm nowhere in the vicinity when nine thirty comes and you're not there to pick up the phone, I'll be safe. Logan strikes me as a dangerous man to cross."

A shiver ran down her spine. "Stop trying to scare me, Harry," she said. "His nickname doesn't give him the power to fly or bend steel. Besides, I intend on calling him when I get home. It may not be nine thirty, which will prove my point, but it'll still give him the reassurance he needs in this relationship."

Harry looked doubtful. "Okay. If you're sure you know what you're doing, then I won't rain on your parade." They ate for a few moments in silence. "You're really in love with him?"

"I could be making the biggest mistake of my life, but yes, I think I'm in love with him." She gave a humorless laugh. "My father would be basking in his glory if he knew."

"You still haven't spoken to him?"

"No. He calls on a regular basis and talks to my machine. I don't know if we'll ever be able to patch up our relationship after what happened with Michael."

"Are you going to tell Logan about your past?"

She dipped her bread in the sauce and bit into the hard crust. "He knows a little, but I'm not ready to reveal all yet. Besides, I don't know what will happen between us. I'm going to grab today and not worry so much about the future." She pointed her fork at him. "You should do the same and ask Rachael out."

Harry groaned. "I've been practicing my speech for months but every time I get close my mind goes blank."

"Slip her a note with your phone number on it."

"I'll have an anxiety attack."

"Harry, she's going to say yes. I bet she has the hots for you and just wants you to make the first move."

"Yeah, maybe."

She smiled at his glum tone. "Come on buddy. Dessert is on me. How about the chocolate mousse?"

He raised an eyebrow and glanced at her tiny waist. "How can you lecture on nutrition and still keep a straight face?"

"I will ignore that remark and chalk it up to negative feelings regarding your inability to take a chance on life."

Harry snorted.

After a rich dessert, they paid the bill and walked out of the restaurant. It was a cool, summer evening which brought hints of the fall to come. The breeze lifted her hair and caressed her skin. The night sounds swarmed around them as they made their way to their cars, the click of her high heels echoing in the smoggy city air.

Chandler thrived on the nighttime activity in Manhattan, enjoying the atmosphere without getting drawn into the tension and stress of everyday life. Taxis hurtled down the streets; brakes screeched when traffic lights had the nerve to turn red. Swarms of people walked in unison and ignored DON'T WALK signs, jumping around buses and screaming at drivers without a glance back. Vendors urged pedestrians to stop and buy their wares, from Coach purses to 14 karat gold necklaces, all at fifty percent off and so hot the merchandise burned your fingers immediately. Vagrants begged to wash the windshields of passing motorists, and called out for spare change. Chandler threw quarters and dollar bills into the cups of the homeless who held signs ranging from I AM BLIND to I HAVE NO LEGS, and never wondered about the truth of the statements.

She knew Harry shook his head at her gullibility. Native New Yorkers were supposed to be hardened to people who lived on the streets, but she slept better at night believing the money helped. Every winter she bought a number of coats and gave them out to the homeless. She volunteered for soup kitchen duties around the holidays, especially since her rift with her father. Her community may be filled with a variety of con artists, but it was her home, and she needed to give back something to one of the most diverse melting pots in the US.

Harry stopped beside her ancient red Chevy and

waited for her to unlock the door. "Well, I wish you luck. You are now exactly one hour late for Grant's call."

Chandler glowered at him as she fished around in her purse for her car keys. "Thanks for the support. Tonight was a real blast."

He laughed. "I hope it was worth it. What's the matter?"

She dug frantically through the leather compartments. "Dammit, I can't find my keys."

"Did you leave them in the restaurant?"

"No, I clearly remember getting out of the car, reaching for my purse, and—uh, oh." He followed her pointed stare. The car keys dangled neatly from the ignition. The car was locked up, safe and sound.

"You have an extra key, don't you?"

She closed her eyes in despair. "You know, I always told myself I should get an extra key made. I never seemed to get around to it."

"This car is older than dirt. The new ones make it impossible to lock your keys inside."

"I don't have money for a new car, Harry."

"Why'd you buy American? You can't lock yourself out of the imported cars."

Chandler glowered. They stood together and looked through the closed window. "Well, we have a couple of options," Harry said.

"Do tell."

"We can call the police and wait for the next couple of hours, and hope they come amidst the calls for robbery, rape and murder."

"Next option."

"We can break your window to get to the keys."

"Keep going."

"Are you a member of any auto club?" he asked hopefully. Chandler shook her head. "Then I'll take you home, and we'll call a locksmith in the morning."

"I won't be able to get into my apartment."

"Wait, let me guess. You never did get around to making an extra set of keys for your apartment."

"Give the man a gold star."

"Then you'll have to come home with me and crash at my place."

Chandler bit her lip. "Sounds like a logical solution. There's just one teeny, tiny glitch."

"Logan Grant."

She groaned and leaned her forehead against the roof of the car. "He's going to kill me, Harry. Besides not being there when he calls, I'm going to be at your place all night. I left my cell in my locked up apartment. He'll never trust me again."

"Hmm, mine's dead, we're a pair. Savvy New Yorkers with no cells. Just call him from my place and explain the situation. If he freaks out, he can pick you up at my apartment."

She picked up her head. "That could work."

"Right now it's our only choice." He tugged at her hand and led her over to his car.

It was a half hour ride to his place. Harry lived in one of the fancy condo duplexes Logan passed on, complete with health club, cafe, swimming pool, and other amenities. Harry made a pot of coffee while she rang Logan's home phone. This time she'd apologize to him. Four rings. Five rings. Six. Seven. Eight.

Where was he?

She heard the click of the answering machine— Logan's deep voice instructing the person to leave a message at the beep. She stared at the phone in her hand as if it held all the answers. Then she replaced the receiver.

"What's the matter?"

"He's not home." She stared at him in amazement. "Logan isn't even home."

"Maybe he's in the shower. Or screening his calls. Leave a message on the machine and maybe he'll pick up. Or call his blackberry, he's attached to it twenty four seven."

"Maybe. But he specifically wanted me home for his call. I assume he's not working a deal this late." She frowned. "You don't think he purposefully left the house because he knew I'd be home waiting for his call?"

"Hell, I don't know. Are you two playing these games with each other for a reason?"

She didn't answer. She kicked off her shoes and relaxed on the sofa for the next ten minutes, then picked up the phone again.

No answer.

She spoke into the machine and told him to pick up if he was there.

No answer.

Her temper surged. She forced herself to take long deep breaths. It was after ten o'clock and Logan Grant wasn't home, which probably meant he hadn't been home when he was supposed to have called. He could be out at this very moment, satisfied he'd taught her a lesson, laughing at the idea that she had hurried home to wait for a call which would never come.

She was going to kill him.

He was going to strangle her.

Logan sat in his car and gripped the steering wheel as he fought to control the rage coursing through his body. It was after ten, and she wasn't home. He'd called and texted her twice and still no response. So after patiently waiting another half hour and only getting her cheery voice telling him to leave a message, he'd decided to drive to her apartment and wait.

And she still wasn't home.

He took a deep breath and tried to think the situation over. He'd been nice enough to allow her to go to dinner with a man who may be trying to coax her into bed at this very moment. He tried to give her the benefit of the doubt when she asked for his trust, knowing how important that was to her in a relationship. He decided to try to be the man she wanted him to be: patient and understanding, kind and generous, trusting and open-minded. A man like Richard Thorne pretended to be. He played by her rules, thinking with enough time she'd come to him on her own. Admit she loved him. Then he could finally drag her into his bed where she belonged.

Now she could be doing that with another man she insisted was only a friend.

His stomach coiled at the thought. He stared out the windshield at the deserted parking lot and listened to the eerie silence. His fingers tapped absently against the steering wheel as he went over his options. He'd made a mistake. He allowed his feelings to get in the way, and now she was taking advantage of the situation. He almost laughed out loud when he suddenly realized the sad picture he made. The mighty "man of steel" was really a poor chump sitting in the parking lot of a woman's apartment building, waiting for her to show up from a date with another man.

Shards of ice ripped at his heart as he reigned in his emotions and took control. This was the last time his lady would make a fool out of him. He'd been going easy on her, allowing her to play the game by a different set of rules so she felt safe.

Now they'd play by his rules.

He pushed the uneasy thought out of his mind that she was really in cahoots with her father. Could she be using him? Could she be so clever that even he had been fooled? As he gunned the engine and pulled out of the lot in a roar of screeching tires, he realized how much he wanted to believe in her innocence.

His first action was to find out where Harrison Edward Weston III lived.

And God help the man if Chandler was there.

Chapter
10

Chandler's eyes flew open when she heard the pounding on the door.

She groaned and buried her head deeper into the cushions on the sofa. The tired springs creaked under her shifting weight and warned her that accommodating strangers for the night was something it was usually not required to do. She'd already fallen off the couch twice, finally discovering a comfortable position around dawn, and felt like she only grabbed fifteen minutes of precious sleep before the pounding had begun. Or maybe it was her head.

For a moment there was silence. She breathed a sigh of relief and tried to drift back, but the door suddenly vibrated under the insistent pounding of a fist. She struggled to open her eyes and glanced at the clock on the mantle. 6:00 AM. Saturday morning.

Someone was insane.

She muttered under her breath about Harry's rude friends and fell off the couch for the third time. Tugging down the hem of the Giants T-shirt she borrowed, she padded barefoot to the door. The banging grew more intense, and she saw the wildly shaking door trying to withstand the power of the person behind it. She unlocked the chain and threw the door open, glaring behind tousled waves of hair, and collided with a pair of icy gray eyes.

His gaze roamed over her figure, taking in her shirt and bare feet, her sleep rumbled hair and the surprise on her face. He stepped inside and shut the door gently behind him. The click of the latch echoed in the silence. Fighting the urge to run like hell and not look back, she blurted out, "How did you find me?"

She hadn't thought it was possible but he managed to look even more terrifying after her question. His voice was soft when he spoke, contradicting the hardness in his eyes. "I called in a few favors to get Weston's address. I'm sure you thought you were safe since his number is unlisted. Then again, you don't know me as well as you thought, do you, Chandler?"

Her response was never heard. At that moment a door banged open and Harry stepped in the hallway dressed in a pair of boxer shorts. One hand rubbed his head as he stared at them through sleepy eyes. He looked from Logan's tightly coiled figure to Chandler's defensively crossed arms and made his way toward the kitchen. "Oh, good, you're finally here." He reached for the coffee pot. "I see you found me earlier than I expected. Now maybe I can get some sleep."

Chandler nervously glanced at her tower of testosterone and winced. He was going to attack Harry and it was all her fault for playing games. "Logan." She laid her hand on his arm. His muscles jumped beneath her touch. "Please listen to me. Nothing happened here last night. In fact, the whole story is really bizarre if you'd just listen to me for a few moments."

She heard the splash of water as Harry filled the coffee pot. His cheerful voice echoed through the hallway. "I love Chandler to death, but I have to admit she can be a handful at times. She was so upset last night we didn't get to bed until after one."

Logan took a step toward him. Chandler threw herself in front of his towering figure in order to save the life of her friend. Harry's cheerful words continued drifting in the air amidst the sound of bubbling coffee. "She's never spent hours analyzing another man's actions before. When she found out you weren't home last night, I thought she would have your head on a platter."

Harry ignored Chandler's strangled words of protest at his discussing her private feelings in front of the cause of her distress. "Now, my guess is you showed up at her apartment to wait for her and therefore missed her call. Of course, she didn't believe me, and chose to rant and rave about the games you insist on playing in this relationship. A call on your Blackberry may have saved the situation, but she needed to prove a point. She only called your home number."

Logan's brow shot up.

Hot color rushed to her cheeks as she glared at the spot where Harry's voice drifted from the kitchen.

Harry continued. "So, I surmise you assumed she tried to con you while she had an affair with me. I assure you, this is not true. She gives me enough trouble as a friend, let alone a lover."

Chandler opened her mouth to yell, but promptly closed it at Logan's threatening stare.

"She spent the night on the sofa, and I slept in the bedroom. She locked her keys in the car at the restaurant last night, so she bunked here. When she called and found you weren't home, she assumed you were trying to teach her a lesson by making her wait for a call that would never come. Of course, she wouldn't have made it home by nine thirty anyway. She pushed our reservations back by an hour."

Chandler closed her eyes in defeat. Her best friend had sold her out. She was going to kill him.

The cabinet door banged. Mugs clunked on the table. "You're welcome to join me for a cup of coffee before I get myself together, but I'd probably advise you to go somewhere and talk. I'm sure both of you learned your lesson about challenging each other, and I really hope I never have to find myself in this situation again; awaiting the arrival of a man whose only ambition is to tear me limb from limb."

Harry stepped from the kitchen so he was in full view. The two men studied each other for a while. Harry waited. Logan assessed. Chandler held her breath and berated herself for getting involved in such a primitive male encounter. She felt like prey between two predators.

"I can firmly assure you, Weston, that you'll never be put in this kind of position again."

Harry nodded. A twinkle of amusement lit brown eyes. "I'm glad to hear it."

Chandler looked from one to the other and shook her head in disgust. "The two of you are acting ridiculous," she said. "You're both speaking as if I'm not in the room and I resent it."

"Go get dressed," Logan ordered. His eyes narrowed at her current attire.

"But I want to explain—"

"You have exactly two minutes to get some clothes on. Any time after that I will consider an invitation to dress you myself."

Her mouth fell open. Then quickly shut at his expression. She turned and left the room, cursing her meekness as she tugged on the black jeans she had worn the night before, and the gold silk blouse. She used mouthwash, splashed some water on her face, ran her fingers through her long wild waves, and was back out the door with seconds to spare. When she re-entered the living room, Logan firmly took her hand and pulled her out the door, barely giving her time to call her goodbye to Harry.

She settled herself in the seat and fastened her seat belt. "Do you know where my car is parked?"

"We're not going to pick up your car." He threw the clutch into gear and shot away from the curb. "I'm taking you to my house."

She digested the statement, then nodded. "I think that's a good idea. We need to talk. One of the most important parts of a relationship is communication, and we need to make sure our signals won't get crossed again."

Logan didn't answer. She tried to say something else, but thought better of it. She couldn't seem to judge his mood, and didn't want to set off his temper. She decided to wait until they reached his house.

She leaned back and watched him through heavy lidded eyes, intrigued by his appearance. He wore faded old Levis that clung to his muscular thighs, a white t-shirt, and a black leather jacket. With his dark hair blowing in the wind, the easy way he threw the clutch into gear, and the hard, sensual lines of his face, he looked less like an executive and more like he should ride a Harley Davidson and charm young girls out of their clothes. She hid a smile at the thought.

He finally swung up to the house and got out of the car. In silence, he escorted her inside, turning to shut the door behind him and lock it. Once again, the click of the latch made shivers run down her spine.

She pushed away her silly thoughts and faced him. "Logan, I think last night proved that ultimatums do not work in a relationship. When you told me to be home by a certain hour, I felt threatened, so I tried to do something to reassert my independence. But my plan backfired, and only ended up getting us confused and dragged poor Harry into our mess. I think this whole episode showed we're having problems facing our emotions."

She stopped for a moment to judge his reaction. He shrugged out of his leather jacket and stood before her in his t-shirt and jeans, hands on hips. The thin cotton material stretched lovingly over his muscular chest. He seemed to listen to what she said, even though he had an oddly determined expression on his face. Knowing she had a bad habit of chattering when she was nervous, she paced the room and tried to find the right words.

"Perhaps this is a sign for us to slow things down. Trust and communication are essential to a successful relationship. Maybe we need to get to know each other a little better. Maybe we should get used to the idea of compromise."

She pushed back her heavy mane of hair and sighed. "I admit to my fault in this, and I'm sure you're sorry for the way you barged into Harry's apartment to assume the worst. Maybe we can turn this episode into something of a learning experience. What do you think?"

He reminded her of a warrior. He stood by the door, his legs apart, thumbs hooked in his pockets as he waited. His eyes narrowed, an unreadable expression on his face that made her more nervous than his testosterone temper tantrum had. Waves of energy and tension emanated from his figure and pulled her to him in a way she recognized all too well. She fought the physical attraction that raged between them and awaited his response.

"Are you finished?"

"Yes. I've told you how I feel. Now, I think you should explain your feelings and maybe we can work something out that would be agreeable to both of us."

Suddenly, his mouth curved into a lazy smile and displayed a set of perfectly straight, white teeth. He wore a purely devilish smile that promised retribution, and promised it slowly. Her stomach twisted in response at the predatory look on his face. With ease he closed the distance between them. His hands reached out to settle on her shoulders and he ran his palms down her arms in a caress. His voice poured over her like warm, sticky molasses.

"Chandler, in a couple of hours everything will be clear. You'll know me in every way imaginable, and I'll know you. There will be no more communication problems, no more games, and no more lies. I'm taking you to bed, and there's not a damn thing you can do about it."

In one swift movement his hands glided down to grasp her hips. He leaned down and swung her up and over his shoulder, one hand easily holding down her legs to keep her from kicking. For an instant Chandler could have sworn she misunderstood him, until she found herself upside down, being carried confidently up the spiral staircase.

"You can't do this!" She fought for breath as her stomach bounced against his shoulder. "Logan, men don't treat women like this anymore. It's, it's primitive!"

The rumble of his low chuckle drifted to her ears. "Things were a hell of a lot simpler then, sweetheart. I wanted you to trust me, but I only ended up giving you enough space so you could re-build your defenses. By tomorrow, you won't have any doubts left."

She caught a flash of cream carpeting, the sound of a door being flung open and closed, the scent of musk and lemon permeating the air. "Put me down!" she shrieked. "I refuse to be treated in this heavy handed manner."

"Yes, ma'am."

The world shifted as she was dumped into the middle of a four poster bed. She sank into the luxurious mattress and tried to regain her balance. Inching her way to the edge, she tried to make a jump for freedom when a gentle push at her shoulders reversed her direction and caused her to fall back again. This time there was no chance of getting back up.

Logan pinned her under him, his hard muscles pressed against every curve of her body. Her chest heaved and her breasts strained against her silk blouse. Her long hair fell wildly around her, the tawny strands blending with the desert tones of the comforter. His fingers interlaced with hers and held them beside her head.

She stuck out her chin with pure stubbornness. "I won't let you make love to me because you have some twisted motivation to make me surrender."

His lips curved into a sensual smile. "I'm going to make love to you because I've never wanted another woman like this before in my life. You invade my thoughts and haunt my dreams. I need you to fill a hole inside of me I didn't know existed before I met you. Those are my motivations, Chandler."

Sexual energy crackled between them like a burst of summer lightning. She closed her eyes. Dear God, she ached for him desperately, ached to believe his words but the fear was still there. The fear a man could deceive her and break her heart. Confusion and desire and anger twisted inside of her, and when she opened her eyes, she let him see it all. "Don't lie to me." Her voice shook. "Damn you, Logan, don't you lie to me."

His grip gentled. "I won't." He lowered his mouth so his breath mingled with hers. "I swear I'll never hurt you. Let me make love to you and show how my body could never lie."

His mouth closed over hers. He let his tongue plunder its dark, silken depths and possess her completely. Fire ignited in his blood as his tongue tangled with hers, tasting her, giving in to her, demanding a response until her body thrust against him. Her body trembled under his weight. He rubbed his mouth back and forth over hers. The dark stubble on his jaw and chin rasped against her sensitive lips. She shuddered. His hands untangled from hers to stroke downward, and he felt the tips of her breasts push against the material of her blouse, and the unconscious invitation of her hips lifting against his.

With a low groan, he tore his mouth from hers and eased the buttons of her blouse open. He unclasped the delicate lace of her bra so her upper body was bared to his hungry gaze. His eyes feasted on the glory of her heavy breasts, creamy against the tan skin of his hands. Rosy peaks thrust toward him begging to be touched. He dragged his palms over her soft flesh and stopped at the edge of her jeans, caressing the dip of her belly button, the slenderness of her hips, the flatness of her stomach.

Chandler gripped his shoulders and whispered his name in urgency. She tugged at the edge of his t-shirt with jerky, desperate movements and heard the low rumbling of laughter from him. Then he pulled briefly away to pull it over his head and toss the material on the floor. He was gloriously naked to the waist, and her eyes adored the muscled planes of his chest. Lovingly, she ran her hands over his skin and enjoyed the crisp feel of his hair beneath her palms.

He dragged her upward to press her breasts against his chest and his hands caressed the waves of hair at the nape of her neck. He kissed her with open-mouthed abandonment, and a low moan rose from her chest.

"Feel how much I want you." He guided her hands to the evidence of his desire. "There are no games or lies between us now. Just give yourself to me and I'll show you how to fly."

She smiled against his lips and dropped butterfly kisses along the line of his jaw. "I only have one problem with that proposal."

He removed her blouse and bra then traced the sensitive line of her naked spine with his fingertips and stopped at the curve of her jean-clad buttocks. "What?"

"I don't want to fly alone this time."

He laughed low. "I'll be with you every step of the way."

With one quick tug at her hair, he exposed the delicate line of her throat and tilted her breasts upward. His mouth lowered to one peak, his tongue making teasing patterns around her nipples. Her nails bit into his shoulders. Carefully, he tugged at the hard crest with his teeth, and then his lips opened and he took her breast into his mouth.

His tongue tasted her, drinking in the scent of roses and vanilla that drifted from her skin, sucking gently at the hard nub. Her whimpered cries echoed through the air as she thrust her fingers into the dark strands of his hair, holding his head to her breast. He moved his mouth, wanting more and treated her other breast to the same pleasure as the first.

"Logan, please." She arched upward to get closer to the sweet torture.

"Please, what?" He rubbed his lips over one crest knowing the motion would make her shudder with pleasure. "Please this, Logan?" His tongue licked gently, flicking over the hard nub again and again. "Or please this, Logan?" He took her breast fully in his mouth, suckling, while his hand stroked the skin of her belly. She cried his name.

"Or maybe it was please do this, Logan?" His hands eased down to the snap of her jeans and unfastened them. The rasping sound of the zipper being lowered cut through the air. His fingers slipped into the opening, and the heat of her response burned against the material of her panties. His breath hissed between his teeth as she arched upward.

Chandler was slowly going out of her mind. Liquid heat coursed through her body and pounded between her thighs. She melted into a trembling mass of nerves and responded to every touch, every kiss, every look from him, always aching for something she knew would ease the raw desire throbbing within.

Needing to touch him, she tried to release the buckle of his jeans but her trembling fingers refused to cooperate. A low moan of frustration escaped her lips. "Logan, you're torturing me."

"I'm torturing myself." He groaned. "And to think I had intentions of slowly seducing you. Lady, I've never had such a problem trying to control myself before."

"The man of steel?" She stroked him through the material of his jeans and felt his hard strength. "I don't believe it."

"I'll have to make you pay for that remark."

With a low mutter of impatience, he tugged off her jeans and black lace panties with one swoop, tossing them to the floor to join the pile of clothing. He got up from the bed and stripped off the rest of his clothes, standing before her naked.

Chandler sucked in her breath at the raw power of the man, his lean strength and grace evident in his carriage and quiet dignity. His arms and legs were corded with muscles, his stomach flat, his chest and shoulders broad. "You're beautiful," she whispered.

He joined her on the bed and stretched over her. "And you're exquisite," he whispered back. "Your body fits to mine like we were made for each other." His lips played with hers, slipping his tongue inside her mouth to taste her sweetness. He ran his hand down her thigh, then back up. His palm settled over her. He felt the heat of her core, and used his knee to ease her legs apart, opening her for his touch. His fingers slipped inside and parted her swollen flesh. She gasped into his mouth and her nails dug into his upper arms.

Fierce satisfaction burned through him at the liquid warmth of her response. His thumb plucked at her hidden nub. He gently guided one finger inside, then gentleness fled replaced by his need to make her soar.

"Logan!" Her cries of pleasure ripped away the steel around his heart. The rippling tension tightened, and he felt her body scream for release just beyond reach. He sipped from her lips and swallowed every moan as his fingers pushed her to the edge of ecstasy.

He reached over for the packet beside the bed, taking the necessary actions to protect her. Reveling in her freedom and fierce response, he fought for control over his body, his muscles tight with tension. Taking hard, ragged breaths he eased her legs further apart to settle between them. "God, Chandler, you're so ready for me I can't wait anymore."

"Please, I need you now, I need you…"

He paused at the barrier. Her slick dampness made a path for him. "Open your eyes."

She obeyed, staring into twin burning embers of smoky steel, his face tight with tension.

"I want to see your face when I make you mine."

She shuddered as much from his words as from the slow movement of his body as he filled her, inch by inch. She gripped his shoulders hard, her eyes widening, and her breath driven out of her lungs by the sheer size of him possessing her. Her body clenched around him in a tight fist. He buried himself deep inside of her, and then paused.

"Hold on, sweetheart. This is going to be a wild ride."

He moved. The sexual tension escalated to a rapid rhythm as he slowly withdrew all the way and then drove back inside, again and again. Her body arched upward, and she held on hard as the pace quickened, faster and faster. His name broke from her lips as she rode a wild wave of desire that filled her up inside to a point where she felt her body about to explode. And still he continued, driving in and out of her wet, clinging heat, her body welcoming him, embracing him, holding him until the orgasm hit hard, and she was suddenly pitched into a world of glittering pleasure. Her soul broke out of her body and soared high above as she exploded into a million pieces of pleasure and flew beneath the stars.

She heard Logan's fierce cry, felt his body shudder, and her arms clasped around him tighter and held him close. As she drifted back downwards in a shimmer of foggy pleasure, she whispered the words that refused to be caged any longer.

"Logan, I love you, I love you."

Chapter
11

Chandler opened her eyes and the full force of the sun struck her face as it streamed through the open windows. Her gaze settled on the figure next to her. Amidst a tangle of luxurious white sheets she followed the line of a muscular calf and thigh, dusted with dark hair, up to a broad chest which rose and fell with each breath, to the slope of an arrogant jaw, hard cheekbones, and fierce black brows. One arm was anchored firmly across her waist, holding her close. She watched him for a few moments, enjoying the sensual lines of his face, the masculine power he radiated even in sleep, the relaxed pose of his lips. The thought of the pleasure those lips bestowed made a faint blush rise to her cheeks, even as her breath quickened at the enticing thought.

After many hours spent learning every intimate secret about each other, they'd finally fallen into an exhausted sleep. She had thought it would be impossible for her body to crave anymore, but just the thought of his mouth on her sensitive flesh had the power to make her stir once again.

Maybe he'd created a monster.

"Keep looking at me like that, lady, and you're going to get yourself into a hell of a lot of trouble."

Startled, her gaze flew back to his face. An amused

glint sparked in gunmetal eyes, and his mouth curved in a hint of a smile. Her blush deepened. "I thought you were asleep."

He rolled over and reached up to push away the heavy waves of hair from her face. "How could I sleep when I felt your hungry gaze on my poor, defenseless body?"

She closed her eyes in embarrassment. "I'm sorry. I know it's crazy, when we spent practically all morning, well, together. I thought it would be impossible to keep wanting you and I'm sure there's only a certain number of times a man can, well, can—oh!"

His mouth covered hers and stopped the flow of words. His tongue dove in and out of her mouth as he leaned over and pressed his body into hers. The bold evidence of his desire pulsed against her thigh. When he finally pulled away, she gasped for breath.

Fierce satisfaction rippled through him. He'd never met a woman who so welcomed his touch on her body; demanded and reveled in the pleasure of lovemaking to such an extent. He'd felt as if he never had a woman give all of herself to him before.

Throughout hours of intense pleasure, she cried out her love to him. The words were like sweet music, ripping at his control.

Chandler Santell was finally his.

"Don't look so surprised," he said teasingly. "I made plans to be strong and give you time to recover. If I'd known you were having the same thoughts I would have woken you up hours ago."

Chandler laughed and ran her fingers through his dark hair. "You've turned me into a nympho. I was supposed to teach a yoga class this morning. Linda will probably be wondering where I am."

He trailed tiny kisses down her neck. "Hmmm, I have hours of paperwork I'm supposed to catch up on today. But I have a feeling it'll have to wait until Monday."

"That's two days away. Surely, you'll be able to get into the office by tomorrow."

He chuckled. "A day and a half. We kept ourselves occupied all morning. It's now officially afternoon." Her breath caught as he gently bit her ear lobe, and his tongue explored the delicate shell of her ear. "I have plans for us the entire weekend. Work is not involved."

"What? A business tycoon who refuses to work on the weekend?" She laughed as his teeth punished her. "What could possibly be more important than the Weatherall contract?"

"Our contract. We haven't had our three month review yet." He blew in her ear. Her body shot up in an unconscious, erotic reaction which he watched with interest. "I'm now ready to give you my full attention."

His mouth closed over one breast and drew the tip between his lips. She gasped. "We have a lot of financial figures to analyze," he said. Her nails scraped down his muscled back. "We should go over each case one by one in order to track the full benefit of the program." He eased her legs apart, his fingers playing gently, bringing forth the warm liquid response.

Chandler fought for breath. "How much energy are you willing to devote to this review, Mr. Grant?"

His fingers drove inside of her, wringing his name from her lips. He settled over her and drew her body close to his.

Logan smiled. "I assure you, Ms. Santell, I will give you every inch of my attention."

And he did.

"We should eat."

"Hmmm?"

She lay against him, her long hair fanned out around his stomach and thighs. He was propped up against the headboard. His fingers rippled through the honey colored strands and arranged each wave at a certain angle.

The sun had sunk low on the horizon and threw shadows against the wall of the bedroom. A cool breeze drifted through the open windows. The cream colored curtains billowed outward, then smacked gently back against the panes of glass. The phone rang constantly, and as the answering machine picked up, a variety of voices filled the tape, demanding a call back. He'd turned his Blackberry to vibrate. The phone shook with anger as it buzzed insistently on his cherry wood dresser. They both ignored it.

Chandler sighed with contentment. "You know, food. Energy. We haven't eaten all day and I'm starving."

"I knew you'd be a demanding woman."

She laughed and stretched luxuriously. "If you want

me to keep up with you, I need to be fed. You have more muscle, and therefore, more energy than me. It's not fair."

"My aim is to keep you weak and defenseless, chained up in my bedroom for the purpose of pleasuring me."

She punched him in the arm. "I have to break you of these terrible medieval ideas. The first chore to help you confront your narrow-mindedness is to cook me dinner."

One black brow shot up. "Cook?"

"Yes, you know, to make, prepare food. Cook." She twisted around to study him with suspicion. "You do know how to cook, don't you?"

"I made hamburgers on the grill once."

Chandler closed her eyes and groaned. "Wonderful. No wonder you have so many employees working for you. You can go to a different house each night without anyone becoming suspicious." She rose from the bed, glanced around the room, and plucked his white shirt from the back of a chair. He watched her with a wolfish grin. She tossed him a threatening glare and buttoned the shirt all the way to the neck. The hem fell almost to her knees. She rolled up the cuffs, pushed back her hair, and walked out of the bedroom.

"Where are you going?" he called out, admiring the way her derriere swung enchantingly when she walked.

"To see what you have in the house to make dinner."

Smiling, she found her way into the kitchen. Chandler knew immediately Logan barely used the room. New copper pots dangled above an old-world Spanish custom cabinetry island. Smooth earth-toned marbled counter-tops graced the room. The elegant off-white ceramic tile floor shone with a high gleam, and all the stainless steel appliances looked to be the latest gourmet's delight.

Sighing, she opened the sub-zero refrigerator and made a mental list: hamburger meat, a piece of chicken, one head of iceberg lettuce, bread, cheese, milk, bacon, two eggs, and various containers half-filled with concoctions she barely recognized. She checked the rest of the compartments in horror.

A pair of strong arms circled her waist from behind. "Find anything interesting?" He splayed his palms wide over her belly.

"You have no vegetables."

"You say that like I've committed a crime."

She turned to face him with concern. "Logan, from the looks of this refrigerator, I'd say you eat a lot of take-out or strictly red meat."

"So?"

She shook her head and worried her lip between her teeth. His eyes watched the action with interest. "Vegetables are the key to a healthy diet. They supply you with all the nutrition needed on a daily basis. If you want to keep up this hectic pace, your body needs them desperately."

"I know what else it needs desperately," he growled against her ear.

"Logan, I'm serious. Don't you have someone to cook for you?"

He shrugged. "Nah. I use a cleaning service for the house, but I don't like the idea of a stranger in my kitchen. I prefer my solitude."

"There are professional chefs who could prepare something healthy for you."

"I work late into the night, sweetheart. I'm lucky if I can grab a home cooked meal once a month." He studied her face for a few moments. "Are you really worried about me?"

"Yes. You have to start changing your habits. Tonight."

He watched her stalk up the stairs and back into the bedroom. Hiding a smile, he felt a rush of pleasure from her obvious concern with his diet. He couldn't remember the last time a woman cared about what he ate or how hard he worked. Her worry caused a heady feeling he was actually starting to enjoy. He followed her. "What are you doing?"

She picked through the pile of clothes on the carpet. "I'm getting dressed to go to the store. I want to pick up a supply of vegetables so we can cook tonight. Do you have a Wok?"

"Hmmm, somewhere in the cabinets, I've never used it. You're not going anywhere."

"What?"

He watched in amusement as she tumbled back on the bed, one leg stuck in her jeans. "I'll go to the store, just give me a list. You don't have your car back, remember?"

She stopped struggling into the tight material. "I forgot. Are you sure you can handle it?"

"Just give me a description of what each vegetable looks like and I'll be fine."

"You're kidding."

"Yes, I'm kidding." He walked to the edge of the bed and eased her one leg out of the jeans. Kneeling down, he slid his palms up over her thighs and parted them gently. Her breath caught in her throat, and incredibly, her body quickened. His lips curved into a sensual smile as he watched her reaction to his touch.

"Oh no, not again."

A low rumble of laughter rose from his chest. He pushed her down on the bed, his fingers deftly unbuttoning the shirt, displaying her naked body to his hungry gaze. He kissed the tops of her thighs, nipping at the tender flesh, working his way inward. "Oh, yes, Chandler, again. I'll never tire of loving you."

His mouth found the inner core of her desire, and her sweet wild cries echoed through the air, as Logan taught her a new way to fly.

Chandler hummed the words with Frank Sinatra as she uncorked the bottle of Pinot Grigio she discovered in the wine rack. Pouring the golden liquid into two glasses, she sipped from hers as she cut up the chicken into neat squares and waited for Logan to return. After he left, she'd taken a hot shower, letting the stinging jets of water soothe each muscle and smiling when she thought over their last encounter. The way he kissed her, touched her. Shown her ecstasy she'd never known existed.

And here she was, in a man's house, dressed in his robe, cooking him dinner, doing nothing but making mad, passionate love for the entire day, and never feeling more happy or alive than she had in her life.

She was totally in love with Logan Grant.

Now he knew it.

She squeezed a little lemon on each piece of chicken and wondered how he really felt about her confession. He'd wrung the words from her lips countless times, and each time he kissed her fiercely, as if she'd said the words he wished to hear. But he never responded with his own feelings. Never told her what he wanted from the relationship. Never said the words back.

Because he wasn't in love with her.

Using her forearm to push her hair away from her face, she attacked the lone head of lettuce and shredded each piece with total concentration. She didn't want to think of any negative thoughts this weekend, but it was something she had to face. Logan may never allow himself to fall in love with a woman, choosing instead to give everything to his business. How long could she go on, waiting to see if his feelings would evolve into love? How long could she wait on the sidelines, hoping one day he'd change?

Then there was the Yoga and Arts Center. The six month trial period would be up soon, and she'd be faced with a decision. The outcome of their contract decided the whole future of her business. If Logan made a practical decision to terminate the arrangement, would she be able to accept it? Could she be involved with a man who never let his emotional entanglements interfere with business? And if he did decide to sign the long term contract, would she always wonder if it was pity and responsibility toward her that made him accept the offer?

The door slammed and interrupted her thoughts. Logan entered the kitchen. Rivulets of water streamed down his face and hair, sopping into the brown paper bag he carried under one arm. "It's raining?" she asked in surprise.

"Just started on the way back." He threw his jacket over the chair and studied her. He seemed to enjoy the picture she made wrapped up in his floor length terry robe. "You took a shower."

"Yes, I didn't think you'd mind."

"The only thing I mind is that you didn't wait for me." He raked his wet hair back with his fingers and shook off the excess water. His t-shirt clung to him, damp from the moisture, and outlined his broad chest.

Chandler stared at him for a few moments, loving the way his eyes crinkled slightly when he smiled, the full sensual line of his mouth, the lean muscled grace when he moved. At that moment she didn't care about the problems between them. She only knew being with him fulfilled her in a way she'd never experienced before, and she would take each moment he gave her as a precious gift, greedily storing up as many memories as she could.

Emotion struck her full force. She closed the distance between them and hurled herself into his arms. She sunk all ten fingers into the midnight depth of his hair and urged his mouth down on hers. Her tongue thrust between his lips savoring his unique taste. They kissed each other hungrily, Logan's hands gliding down her back, pulling her hips into his as their tongues battled in an intimate game, until, breathless, she pulled away.

He groaned. "If that's the way I'm greeted every time I walk in the door, I'll be sure to do it often."

Chandler laughed. "I'm happy." She interlaced her fingers with his and brought it up between them admiring the size and strength of his hand in hers.

He smiled down at her and opened her palm to place a tender kiss. "I'm just as happy." His gaze wandered over her face as if searching for something. She caught a familiar, wicked gleam in charcoal eyes that made her suddenly wary.

"Why are you looking at me like that?"

"I was thinking about all the benefits of vegetables."

She didn't trust the lazy smile that curved his lips. "You agree vegetables are the key to a healthy diet?"

"Not exactly." He crouched down and tossed her over his shoulder, chuckling at her outraged cry of protest. With determined strides, he started back to the bedroom. "I'm just grateful they can be eaten raw. This way, we won't have to worry about our meal getting cold. I've suddenly decided to work up a better appetite."

She tried to keep her tone dignified as he carried her upstairs, but a giggle escaped. "Next time I'll introduce you to the benefits of fruit."

Logan chuckled and kicked the bedroom door closed.

The living room was shrouded in darkness, illuminated by the last few crackling embers burning in the fireplace. Flashes of lightning exploded outside. The only sound to break the peaceful silence was the steady pounding of the rain as it beat against the windows and the distant rumble of thunder. Chandler's head rested comfortably against Logan's chest as they sat wrapped in each other arms on the sofa. Her fingers played with the fringe on the soft blanket cocooning them.

"What are you thinking about?" he asked.

Chandler lowered her voice to match his husky tone. "I was thinking about my mother."

"What was she like?"

She smiled, and her face glowed with memories. "Like an angel. She had long golden hair and a smile that lit up the room. She laughed all the time and tried to fill each moment with happiness."

"Tell me what happened." His hands stroked her hair.

"She died when I was nine. She had cancer. When she was confined to bedrest, we'd make a tent in her room and pretend it was a fort. We'd eat together and play games." Chandler paused, thinking back. "I know my father loved her, but he never had time for her. There was always the business to run, and the bigger the company grew the more time he needed to spend there. It finally got to a point where he was never home, and the fights would start late at night, angry whispers I heard through the walls." She sighed. "I think my father feels guilty about her death even to this day. After she died, it only made things worse. I couldn't seem to reach him. He practically lived at the office, and then he started to send me there after school." She laughed shortly. "While everyone else practiced for cheerleading tryouts, I became best friends with the secretaries outside his office."

"So one day you decided to leave."

She heard the question in his voice. She knew she should share the details of her past with him but the humiliation of the event still hurt; the anger that her own father could use her as a commodity to further his business dealings. She hesitated for a moment, torn between not wanting to have any secrets between them and wanting to keep it buried for a while longer. She didn't want to spoil their time together sharing hurtful memories. Vowing to tell him the whole story at a later time, she repeated, "Yes, so one day I decided to leave."

The driving rhythm of the rain filled the silence. "Do you ever see your father?" he asked.

"Not really. We speak occasionally on the phone but it always ends up in an argument. He thinks I should be married by now."

Logan stiffened. His hand stilled on her thigh. "And you disagree with him?"

"Let's just say I disagree with the type of man he wants me to marry. Marriage is another business arrangement to my father, and I refuse to be involved with one of his deals."

He caught the bitter tone in her voice and almost groaned. Half of him longed to tell her the whole truth; her father had approached him with the business deal of a lifetime, all in exchange for marrying his daughter. Logan had learned Alexander Santell had also offered the same deal to Thorne. If Logan had any doubt of the way Chandler felt about his attorney, he could sever any lingering emotions she may harbor for Thorne by telling her the attorney was courting her because of her father's deal. The other half of him resisted, buying more time until he could figure out what action to take. Something inside him balked at exposing her father's dirty dealings. Instinctively, he knew Chandler still held a tiny thread of hope that one day she'd be able to patch up the relationship with her father. Logan needed to find another way out of this mess. He decided to change the subject. Fast.

"What made you decide to open the Yoga and Arts Center?"

Her legs wrapped around his as she snuggled closer to his body. "I studied yoga and meditation for two years and became certified as an instructor. I worked a couple of different jobs to support myself before I decided to buy my own building and set up my business. Harry had a friend at the bank that helped me with a loan. But then I got to a point where even though my clients were expanding, my bills seemed to be tripling. I struggled more and more to meet those monthly payments. Something had to break. I couldn't get another loan to keep me afloat, so I needed to come up with an idea."

"It was an excellent idea." He trailed one finger up the sensitive flesh of her inner thigh. "Except for that crazy escape clause you threw in."

"The escape clause made you sign the contract," she retorted, letting one hand explore below his waist. His breath hissed through his teeth. "Logan, what are we going to do?"

"I'm coming up with a few ideas."

"No, about our working relationship. The contract." Her eyebrows lowered in a slight frown. "There could be complications."

With one swift movement he lifted her up and on top of his body, positioning her so her knees straddled his hips. Her hair fell in glorious waves down her back and brushed against his skin. Her flesh glowed like burnished gold against the dying embers of the fire. Their figures threw shadows against the wall, mirroring their images.

"I'm going to take care of everything, Chandler." His hands cupped her heavy breasts. He watched her emerald eyes glitter with desire. "We'll work it out. The only complication we need to worry about right now is how I'm going to slake this hunger I have for you day and night."

A sensual smile curved her mouth. She tossed her hair with a shake and laughed. It was a low husky growl, a sexy sound that made his gut clench. At that moment, she reminded him of an ancient pagan goddess; a free spirit who let her body guide her in her pleasures, whose eyes mirrored the wildness in her soul. She leaned over him. Her hands ran teasingly down his chest in a light caress.

"Then we should do something about that complication, shouldn't we?"

She lowered her mouth to his, her tongue tracing the outline of his lips, slipping between them in a slow, sensual rhythm that made his breath catch in his throat and a low moan rumble from his chest. His hips were held captive by her legs as she moved her mouth down his body. She nibbled on his neck, her teeth scraped the muscles in his shoulders, and she playfully bit and licked at his masculine nipples that tightened in response to her touch. Her hands explored the carved flatness of his stomach and roamed lower, tickling the hairs on his inner thighs. She moved inward, cupping his shaft that throbbed and grew even harder beneath her fingers. Logan fought for control when she squeezed him lightly, stroking him, whispering hot words of what she wanted to do to him, with him.

The living room windows shook beneath the driving onslaught of wind, rain and thunder. Trees bent and danced in the storm, casting dark shadows on the wall.

She continued the teasing, sensual torment, moving

her mouth down his body, her breath warm and moist against his skin as he waited in anguish, torn between ordering her to stop and begging her to continue.

"I want to do everything you've done to me," she whispered against him. "I want to drive you to the ends of pleasure and pull you back again, until the only thing you can think about is how deeply you can get inside of me, over and over again."

Logan felt the first touch of her mouth on his core, felt her taste him tentatively, then with more boldness as she drove him to the edge of his control. His hands clenched into tight fists at his side, and a steady stream of both curses and prayers escaped his lips. He pulled her back up the length of his body and covered her mouth with his.

This time she was the one to pull away to reach for the wrapped packet, taking the necessary precautions. Then she took him inside of her with one single motion.

A flash of lightning lit the room. The house shook with a crack of thunder. The shadows on the wall joined together in an ancient steady rhythm, Chandler's head thrown back in ecstasy, Logan's hands grasping her hips, holding her in place while the plunging motions melded them into one. They arched together as another explosion of thunder ripped through the air, the sound overpowering their passionate cries as they came together. Then Chandler slumped over Logan, his hands holding her tightly to him, their breathing mingling together as the storm raged outside, and they drifted into sleep, clasped in one another's arms.

Chapter
12

"Do you think it's time?"

She worried her bottom lip between her teeth, unsure. They both stared at the two objects on the table as they tried to decide what to do. "If we don't do it now you may never have the courage."

"Which button should I press first?"

"Answering machine first, then Blackberry," she said.

They both took a deep breath. Logan reached out and tapped the blinking red light. After a series of strange clicking noises, the answering machine rapidly beat out the messages accumulated over the two day period. Logan wrote them out on a notepad while she eased back on the couch, her head settled in his lap.

The thunderstorm had tapered off during the night and left the morning cool and damp. After a leisurely shower and breakfast, Logan dedicated himself to finding a locksmith willing to work on Sunday. After much cash passed hands and Chandler was safely in her car, she drove home and picked up a change of clothes, then headed back to his house.

Still wrapped up in each other, they continued to ignore the real world until the sun sank low on the horizon. With her head resting comfortably against his thighs, she'd just convinced herself to check her own messages when a deep familiar voice boomed over the speaker. Logan's pen stilled in mid-air. Chandler winced.

"Logan, I don't know where the hell you are, but we need to discuss something about Jim Chrisetta. That lovely lady of yours has been causing some trouble around here, and we'd better get to the bottom of it. You know the number. Call me back."

The machine clicked.

When she looked at Logan's face she decided to ease herself out of his lap, both for convenience and safety purposes. He frowned. Gray eyes held a deep warning. She quickly gathered her courage and reminded herself they were lovers. She had no reason to fear him.

"Chandler, is there something you forgot to mention this weekend?"

She swallowed hard and cursed her unruly hormones for making her forget to tell him about her little encounter with Thomas Weatherall. "Well, actually, something did slip my mind."

"Do you know who that was?"

She nodded. He remained silent and put the pad down on the coffee table. She fought the surge of irritation that flooded through her when she realized how fast he reverted back to the cool, logical businessman who had first greeted her. She realized then how much she loved the man who spent the weekend with her.

"Are you going to tell me what happened?"

"If you'd stop acting like my sixth grade teacher

who discovered I didn't do my homework, maybe I'd feel more comfortable."

One black brow shot up. "This must be pretty bad."

She rose from the sofa. Words bubbled out as she paced the room and tried to search for a way to describe the situation. "Of course, you know how upset I was when you told me you were going to fire Jimmy. I was going to leave the entire situation up to you, until Jimmy came to me on Friday and said he was going to be fired."

"How would he know that? Tommy and I spoke privately."

"He's a smart man. He knew his screw up was pretty bad, and he could see how Tommy may want to get rid of him before completing the merger. He figured your hands would be tied."

"So he came to cry on your shoulder?"

Chandler stopped pacing to shoot him a warning look. "He needed to talk to someone, and I'm honored he felt he could trust me. He couldn't discuss the matter with his wife because he was terrified of not being able to provide for his family."

"Okay, so you told him to talk to me, and he went on his merry way."

She pushed the hair away from her face. "Well, not exactly."

"What did you tell him?"

"I told him he was finally free of his insecurities. I told him he could do what he wanted, explore his options, make a new career for himself. I showed him that working for your company was not what his entire life was about."

Logan swore. "Why didn't you tell him to come see me? You had no right to get involved with this."

"I had every right the moment he came to me for help. And he understood what I was talking about. He actually agreed with me!"

He groaned and rubbed his temple. "Okay, so you encouraged him to quit the business entirely and he agreed. Then what happened?"

Not liking the way he described her advice, she paced more furiously. "Well, then I realized I'd have to do something to help him get his old job back. I knew he wasn't suited to the one you promoted him to, so I went down to personnel and asked some questions about his old job."

"Theresa gave you this information?" he asked in amazement.

"Of course. She told me she's going to start taking classes at the Yoga and Arts Center." Logan rubbed his temple harder. "I found out there was another position similar to the one he had so I knew we had a shot." She paused, knowing this was the delicate part of the story. "I decided to talk to Tommy Weatherall."

He stiffened. Every part of his body grew tense. His nostrils flared slightly. Chandler rushed on and tried to explain before the explosion.

"You have to understand I thought this was the

best way. You told me you didn't have a choice in the matter. I figured if I went to talk to the source of the problem, I'd have a shot at explaining the situation and get him to understand."

His voice dropped. "Do you realize you could have caused problems in the merger by going behind my back?"

She stood her ground, glaring at him, hands on hips. "A human being is more important than any business deal. You told me not to get emotional when I tried to explain how I felt about the situation."

Logan struggled with his temper. "I assume you tried to convince Tommy not to insist I fire Chrisetta?"

She nodded. "Yes. I explained the problem and told him about Jimmy's dedication to his family and the baby on the way. I told him it would be a mistake to let him go."

"And he agreed to let him stay?"

She paused. "Not exactly."

Logan let out an impatient breath. "What exactly did he say?"

"He said he understood my position but he'd have to stay with his original decision."

"So, you left."

"No." His eyes narrowed. "I told him most of your employees were very loyal and always stuck together. I explained that once they discovered the real reason Jimmy was fired, they could become very difficult to work with when the merger was completed. I told him the error Jimmy made shouldn't be counted against him, because the Vicomdata manager used Jimmy's feelings of friendship and loyalty against him. The man tricked him. Once the other employees discover those circumstances, they'll back Jimmy up."

Silence descended. Logan tapped the pen he held against the edge of the coffee table. The rat-a-tat-tat seemed loud and nerve wrangling against the deadly quiet. "You threatened him."

"No, of course not! I gave him a picture of what the future could hold if he made the wrong decision."

"You threatened the man who could dissolve this merger for the sake of one employee. This merger will actually create new business and new jobs for many more workers. But worse, you jeopardized my standing in my own company by sneaking behind my back, giving Thomas Weatherall the impression I don't know how to run my business."

"No, I didn't mean—I didn't want to give him that impression at all. Why can't you understand?" she cried out. "Dammit, you used a corporate spy! You were totally unethical, and it's not fair to punish Jimmy because he was acting like a human being!"

The temperature in the room dropped a few degrees. "I don't involve myself in unethical or illegal activities. I planted Charlie there for certain reasons, and Jimmy was well advised ahead of time. You may not like it, but there are things I need to do for the sake of my company."

"Why do you always have to be so damn rational and cold-hearted about every decision you make? Why do you have to be such a, such a—businessman?!"

With one swift movement he rose from the couch and closed the distance between them. Dragging her against his body, he lowered his head and kissed her fiercely, parting her lips with a single thrust, conquering and invading her mouth with all the hot passion he showed her throughout the weekend. Her body melted against his, and she responded just as fiercely to the kiss.

When he pulled away she gasped for breath. Logan's eyes burned like twin flames of smoke. "Do you think my actions around you are rational and cold-hearted?" He pressed his thumb over her swollen lips. "Do you think when I take you in my arms I'm making the logical decisions you always accuse me of? Lady, from the moment you walked into my office you've thrown my life into chaos. Invading my thoughts and dreams was bad enough, but now you're taking over my business piece by piece."

He bent toward her. "I'm angry because you didn't come to me first. You knew how I felt about the situation but you still couldn't resist trying to save yet another human being from the big, bad world of corporate America. Dammit, do you really think I'm the type of person to make a decision about firing one of my employees without thinking it through? After the time we've spent together, in bed and out, I thought you'd at least trust me."

Chandler looked deep into his eyes and searched for her own answers. Slowly, her instincts grew sharper, and she realized she'd made a mistake. This weekend had shown her the depth of the man who many believed had no soul; who possessed a heart of steel. He may be ruthless in the corporate climate, but her heart told her he was a man who made her laugh, a man who made her spirit soar while he brought her endless pleasure. A man like that would not make a decision to hurt someone unless he was positive it was justified or his only recourse.

She needed to trust Logan regarding Jim Chrisetta.

"No," she answered softly. "I don't think you're that type of person at all."

His arms tightened around her. "Do you trust me?" he asked. "I need to know you have complete trust in me, Chandler. I can't settle for anything less."

She slid her arms around his neck. "I have complete trust in you." She spoke the words against his lips. "I'd never do anything to hurt you. I'm so used to operating on my own instincts and fighting my own battles that I never stopped to think how this would affect you." She pressed her mouth to his and rubbed back and forth in a light caress. "I love you."

With a low groan, he pulled her toward him and deepened the kiss. His tongue swept through her mouth as if to collect each sweet word she uttered and pull it deep inside of him.

"Don't think you'll win every argument like this," he growled against her neck as he lowered her to the floor.

Her fingers worked deftly at the buttons on his shirt.

"I'll have to come up with a better way to punish you."

"I'll look forward to it."

Clothes were removed rapidly as the familiar hunger took hold. It was awhile before they realized the phone was ringing insistently. He dragged his mouth from hers and stared into her eyes.

"We should probably answer it."

"Yep." His hand moved across her naked breasts and down her soft belly.

Chandler fought for breath. "You answered every message that machine threw at you. It would be criminal to let it keep ringing."

"You're right." His palm settled over the apex of her thighs. Slowly, he pressed. His fingers invaded her core, and he watched with interest her emerald eyes cloud over in a sensuous haze.

"It could be a client," she gasped as his thumb massaged her.

"It could be Tommy."

"Let it ring." They laughed as he covered his body with hers.

• • •

"I should have known the problem would involve a woman." Thomas Weatherall let out his breath in disgust.

Logan laughed as he shut the door to his office and

walked behind his desk. "You always were a smart man, Tommy."

"And you look pathetic. You have a sparkle in your eye, and my sources say you came into the office late this morning. You didn't answer my message until late this afternoon. And I left a 911 message on your cell."

"I was busy."

"I'll bet." A half smile touched Tommy's lips. "Okay, dammit, I like Chandler Santell, she's a hell of a woman. Hell of a lot of trouble too, from the last confrontation I had with her."

"I'll never be bored." Logan tossed the final proposal on the polished wood and leaned back in his chair. The leather creaked gently under the shift of weight. "I assume these are the papers you were waiting for."

Tommy picked up the contract and gave it a cursory glance. "I'm sure everything is in order, just as we discussed."

Logan lifted his coffee mug and took a swallow of the strong brew. His gaze cut to the man across the desk. "Jim Chrisetta stays."

Tommy waited a beat, then chuckled. "You can't be serious. I've already told you his screw up cost us too much money. There's no way I'm going to open the door for more mistakes."

"I was the one who made a mistake by offering him the management promotion. I should have realized it wasn't suitable to his working style. I want to move him back to a similar position recently vacated."

Tommy studied him thoughtfully. "Hmmm, so Chandler already said. Are you telling me you agree with her?"

"She has nothing to do with this. She made some points I thought were worth considering, but my decision is my own and it's final. I don't cut employees for one mistake in four years. I've also taken into account the nature of his mistake. He got caught off guard, Tommy. Vicomdata got wind of it and was looking for confirmation. Jimmy thought he was talking to someone who was a friend of Charles. Unfortunately, he cost us money, but not enough to let him go."

"Profit is profit. I don't make deals where I can't be guaranteed efficiency in all operations."

"Profit can easily be guaranteed and you know it. Good employees are hard to find. Jim is loyal, and he's a good worker. You're being a stubborn hard ass, Tommy, and I think you know it."

Tommy shook his head in amazement. "Hell man, you can't afford to walk away from a deal like this for one employee. Give him a good reference, and he'll find something else. Don't let your emotions screw up one of the best deals you'll ever make. Now let's stop haggling and get down to it. If he doesn't go, I don't sign the contract."

"Then we don't sign the contract." He reached over and buzzed his secretary. "Connie, will you please call Tommy's lawyers and cancel the 4 o'clock meeting," he said. "Then push up my next appointment so

I can be out of here early tonight." The red light on the phone went out. Logan studied Tommy, his jaw tight with determination.

Tommy cursed. "You're bluffing."

"You know me better than that."

Tension swirled in the room between them as Logan waited for an answer. After a few moments Tommy let out a short laugh and shook his head. "You're a real son of a bitch."

Logan smiled. "I know. Do we have a deal?"

Weatherall reached for the papers and slipped them into his briefcase. "Do I have a choice?" They shook hands. "Reschedule the lawyers. Let's do this before I get pissed and change my mind."

Tommy moved toward the door. "And to think I was worried you could be getting soft on me," he said in disgust. "By the way, can I tell Laura to stop making pork chops on Thursdays?"

Logan chuckled. "Tell her I'll be calling for the recipe. I have a feeling my body can't take too many vegetables all at once. I'll go into shock."

"Yeah, but think of the other benefits your body is getting." With a laugh, Tommy let himself out of the office.

Logan walked to the window and stared out at the view of the Hudson River. He knew for the first time in his life he had made a business decision not wholly based on clear-headed logic. For the first time, he felt an instinct in his gut that told him it had been the right decision.

Tommy was right. Chandler Santell was a hell of a lot of trouble.

Drumming his pen absently against the windowsill, he admitted his plan to seduce Chandler had been perfectly executed except for one tiny detail. By luring her so carefully into his trap, he had ended up in the same cage.

He was in love with her.

"Logan, I need to speak to you. Immediately." He turned his head at the intrusion, surprised when he saw Jim Chrisetta standing in his office with a determined look on his face. With an inward sigh he resigned himself to smooth the ruffled feathers of the employee he had just rescued from termination. He had a feeling Chandler's advice was going to make his job more difficult.

As he waved the younger man into his office and motioned for him to shut the door, he made a mental note to exact punishment from his lover for putting him through a day of hell.

• • •

"Tell me what happened." Chandler practically pulled him into her apartment.

Logan ignored her demanding words and hauled her into his arms for a long, hungry kiss. After the first muffle of protest, she melted against him and responded with equal fervor. When a satisfying length of time passed, he eased the pressure of his mouth and nibbled gently at her lower lip. "Somehow I'd hoped for a different type of greeting." He slid his hands up and down the length of her spine.

Chandler shivered. "We practiced that type of greeting for two days and nights."

"Sometimes it takes years to achieve perfection."

Laughing, she stepped out of his arms and led him into the living room. "You're early. Dinner won't be ready for an hour. Now tell me what happened." She settled herself on the sofa and looked at him with expectation.

Logan's lips curved in a smile. "I sold Tommy my business and decided to start teaching yoga classes with you. We'll make an unbeatable team."

"Logan!"

He laughed and walked to the cabinet to pour a glass of cognac. "After my meeting with Tommy, I had an interesting chat with Chrisetta. It seems he'll be staying on after all." He sat beside her, taking a long healthy swallow of the amber liquid. "Also seems one of his important reasons for staying had to do with you. He wanted to make sure the stress management classes would continue under your instruction."

Chandler's eyes widened. "Jimmy really asked about my contract with you? Do you realize this means I've gotten through to your employees? They're finally learning to handle their stress and want to continue their training."

"I think half of the male work force I employ is in

love with you. The female portion admires the way you yell at me in class if my mind wanders or if I do the positions wrong."

"I don't yell. I have to be firm, since you always insist on arguing with me. You hate to be corrected."

"I mess up on purpose so I can feel your hands all over my body," he said wickedly, giving her a naughty wink.

She fought a smile. "Was Tommy angry with you about your decision?"

"He disagreed, but after I persuaded him to see my point of view, he decided to sign. He felt I was basing my business decisions on pleasing my new lover. I quickly discouraged him of that thought."

"You must have threatened to ditch the whole deal!"

Logan nodded. "He knew me well enough to realize I don't bluff."

A dazzling smile lit up her face. He was fascinated by the transformation of her features and the sparkle in her eyes, and thought briefly that he had never seen her look so radiantly beautiful. "You decided not to fire Jimmy even if it meant not signing the contract?"

He shrugged. "I'm not a monster. I thought about it and made a decision I could live with."

"You chose a person over money."

He looked puzzled by her tone. "I guess I did."

A surge of joy raced through Chandler and filled her with an energy that made her feel like she could conquer the world. Logan had made the right decision.

When she left her father and her old life four years

ago, the only thing she knew was the kind of person she desired to be, and the type of man she wanted to share her life with. Logan had seemed to be the opposite of everything she demanded, but now, suddenly, she realized he was everything she ever wanted. He was a man with enough strength to fight for what he believed in, no matter what the cost. Even if that cost was a major deal to profit his business. Her father couldn't have walked away from such a temptation.

But Logan had.

He watched her with an odd expression, probably wondering why she looked like she stumbled upon some truth that was about to change her life.

"Chandler? What are you thinking?"

She opened her mouth to tell him she was madly in love with him; that she saw the future in his eyes; that she trusted him with her whole heart and soul. The sound of the doorbell cut off her response.

With a hint of annoyance, Logan rose from the sofa. "Why do I think this is going to be another one of your strays seeking comfort? I think it's time I inform them your shelter is now full." He grasped the knob and hurled it open.

Harry rushed through in his usual manner. "Hey, Logan, how are you? Chandler, guess what? I had a big legal dispute to handle at McKenzie & Tetenbaum, and when I walked into the conference room Rachael was waiting for me. So, naturally, I was excited to see her and decided to finally ask her out."

"And?" Chandler asked.

"Then the most incredible thing happened. She asked me out for coffee. Do you believe it? Maybe she's been interested all this time but was waiting for me to make the first move."

She laughed in delight at Harry's excitement. "I told you! I want to hear the whole story, why don't you stay for dinner?"

"Sure, I'll—"

"Excuse me." Logan tapped Harry's shoulder. Harry turned. Pure masculine irritation bristled from Logan's figure. "I think we have a problem."

Immediately, Harry backed towards the door and grinned. "Oops, I knew I should have called first. Guess I'm still getting used to the idea that Chandler isn't alone anymore, waiting for news about my life." He ignored her protests and paused on the threshold. "Sorry about the inconvenience. Maybe we can all meet for a drink one night. Talk to you later." Harry rushed out as fast as he had rushed in.

The room fell silent.

Chandler crossed her arms in front of her and glared at the man who leaned against the couch in a relaxed stance. He shrugged his massive shoulders and walked into the kitchen. "What are those heavenly smells coming out of the oven?" He breathed in deeply. "It doesn't smell like tofu is in this recipe."

"Logan, how could you?"

"Well, we still have some time left. I think I'll get a refill on that cognac. Want one?"

Chandler followed in his footsteps as he made his way toward the liquor cabinet. "You can't continue treating my friends like this. I thought you understood my relationship with Harry, yet you practically tossed him out the door."

"All I said is that we have a problem." He refilled his glass calmly.

"It was the way you said it and the way you looked when you said it."

"I refuse to give up an evening with you so I can listen to another man's woes. From now on, they can all look for another woman to nurture them."

"You're doing it again!" Frustration vibrated through her body. "You're trying to order me around and give me rules to follow. Just because I'm sleeping with you doesn't mean I'll do everything you say."

He took in her defiant stance and lowered his voice to a silky drawl. "You seemed to be pretty responsive to my instructions last night."

Heat rushed to her cheeks at the mention of that wildly erotic evening in his arms. "I won't let you bully me by using seduction." Her chin lifted. "Why were you rude to Harry when he told you he's interested in another woman? He specifically came over here to tell me he had a date."

"I knew the moment I set up the date he'd rush over to tell you, and I was right. Harry needs to learn I'm first in your life now."

"That's ridiculous, he's always in a rush to tell me things. And of course you'll always be first in my life, I don't think that's even a—what did you say?" She broke off and glanced at him with suspicion. "Did you say you set up their date?"

Logan propped one hand against the side of the easy chair and crossed his ankles like a lazy jungle cat taking a break. "Yep."

She stared at him with horror. "You're the one who persuaded Rachael to ask him out?" Logan nodded in satisfaction. "How did you do it?"

"One of my employees does a lot of business with McKenzie & Tetenbaum. I had him make a few phone calls to track down this woman Rachael, and then I paid her a visit. I mentioned Harry did a little work for my company, and he thought she was an interesting person. My job got easier from there because she immediately lit up and told me she thought he was one of the nicest men she'd ever met. After a brief discussion, I convinced her to ask him for coffee, and guaranteed he'd say yes. The rest is up to them."

Chandler opened her mouth to protest, then quickly shut it. She turned on her heel and marched into the kitchen, muttering under her breath as she went to check the pasta and broccoli casserole. Logan followed. After slamming the oven door closed, she threw the hot mitts on the table and faced him. "How could you manipulate poor Harry like that?" she demanded. "If he had any idea you did this, he'd be humiliated."

"If I didn't step in, those two would never get together. I did them a favor."

"You did this so you could get Harry out of the way." She glared at him. "You used a person's weakness to get what you wanted."

"Don't push it, lady. This was the right thing for everyone. Harry has to stop depending on you."

She threw up her hands. "You make me crazy, Logan Grant! I am usually a calm, focused person. I practice yoga and meditation so I can get in touch with my feelings and approach life with total peace. You are wrecking my concentration! You're jealous and demanding and stubborn and—don't even think about it." She put her hands out in front to ward him off as he started moving toward her. "We will not solve this problem with sex."

He didn't listen. She backed away and circled around the sofa to put an object safely between them.

"Come here," he commanded softly. "When you get into these emotional outbursts there's only one way to reason with you."

"Don't come near me." She stumbled over the coffee table in a hasty retreat. "You can't control me like you do your employees."

"If you were one of my employees you'd be fired for disobeying a direct order. I'm not trying to control you, Chandler, I'm trying to show all your strays that you won't have the time to nurture them on a full-time basis anymore. Now stop moving away from me and come here."

With one swift lunge he tackled her down on the sofa and pinned his body over hers. He grasped both her wrists and held them above her head with one hand. Her chest heaved, and she let out a sigh. She glared at him as his gaze roamed over her flushed features.

"I won't let you seduce me," she said stubbornly. "You manipulated Harry, you're bullying me, and I have to think about what effect this will have on our relationship."

"Dammit woman, if I didn't love you so much I'd put you over my knee instead of doing this!" His mouth took hers in a frustrated assault of emotion, hot and demanding. She melted helplessly beneath him, her lips opening to the thrusting motion of his tongue against hers. His hand released her wrists to peel open her blouse, his palms cupping and squeezing the weight of her breasts, teasing the hard crests. Heat exploded through her as she arched upwards. His mouth moved down her neck, and the words he had spoken suddenly flashed through her mind.

"Logan, what did you just say?"

"Forget anything I said." His teeth bit at the sensitive curve behind her ear and a shudder ripped through her. "Actions speak louder than words. I'm taking you to bed."

He scooped her up and walked into the bedroom. She fought the sensual lethargy that clouded her mind. "No, you said something very important."

He dropped her on the rose comforter and stood over her sprawled body like a warrior with his captive.

"About putting you over my knee?" He unbuttoned his shirt and stripped it off his body.

"No, before that." Her eyes were helplessly drawn to the lean-muscled strength of his chest.

He placed one knee on the bed and leaned over her. His thumb gently stroked her lips, dragging across the tender flesh as she opened her mouth. Her teeth lightly scraped the pad of his thumb. A low groan rumbled his chest. "I told you I loved you. But surely you knew that already."

A surge of joy raced through her. She reached up and pulled his head toward her, kissing him hungrily.

He felt her blossom beneath him, all sweetness and light and passion, her emotions reaching out to touch him in an almost visible caress. "I didn't know," she whispered. Emerald eyes filled with naked longing. "I hoped in time you'd love me, but I wasn't sure. All weekend you never said a word."

His knee slid between her legs and opened her for his more intimate touch. "I showed you how I felt every time I took you in my arms and entered your body." His hands cupped her face. He let her see every emotion he'd been too afraid to let go of—every feeling he never uttered in words. "Each time I cried your name I told you I loved you."

She clung to him and wrapped her legs around his. "I needed to hear the words."

"Never doubt the way I feel for you. I'll have to show you on a more regular basis."

She laughed with happiness and urged him closer. "Maybe some actions are better than words."

He moved over her and joined his body with hers. This time, they both cried out the words as they reached the peak together, and drifted back down as one.

Moonlight beamed through the open window creating shadowy patterns against the dusty rose sheets, throwing Chandler's features into a hazy glow.

Logan stood beside the bed, naked, watching her. She slept with a deep peacefulness that made a smile touch his lips. She was curled up in the fetal position, one hand tucked under her cheek. Her glorious hair fanned out over the pillow, and the rippling moonlight made the strands seem like a halo.

He had to tell Chandler about her father.

Logan turned away and walked to the window to gaze out at the dots of light sprinkling the night skyline. He rubbed his brow at the thought. The woman he wanted to spend the rest of his life with pursued a path of honesty and truth—it was a part of her inner core. He was awed by such qualities, and knew that because he respected her, he must tell her everything—the deal her father had offered him, the offer of marriage, Thorne.

Everything.

It was not something he looked forward to.

He sighed as he tapped his fingers against the windowsill in thought. His life was on the brink of change, and the woman lying in bed was the cause.

Suddenly, a contract worth millions of dollars was not very important.

He'd never been more satisfied with his life. Being with Chandler softened something inside of him, soothed his emotions, made him want to give all of himself to another person and receive the same in return. For the first time in his life he was in love, and he wasn't going to screw it up.

She stirred and murmured in her sleep. Logan turned from the window and made his decision. Tomorrow night he'd tell her the truth. Then he'd tell her father to go to hell, along with his million dollar contract.

He slipped under the covers, pulling her close to his body. She snuggled against him immediately.

Logan closed his eyes and let sleep wrap its misty fringes around him, until he was lured into a world of blackness.

Chapter
13

Chandler grabbed her bottle of water, stuffed it in her purple duffel bag, and glanced at her watch. She'd be late for class again, but Linda could take over for the warm-ups. She smiled. Ever since Logan Grant had been keeping her up at night, she'd been late almost every morning.

Of course, it was worth it.

The doorbell rang as she reached for the doorknob. She flung it open and stepped back in surprise. "Richard, what are you doing here?"

Dressed in a black suit and brilliant multi-hued silk tie, he stood in her doorway with a concerned look on his face. "I need to talk to you. Can you give me a few minutes?"

She hesitated. "I'm already late for my morning class. Can we catch lunch later?"

He shook his head. "I thought about this for a long time, and I can't wait any longer. Please, Chandler."

"Sure. Come on in."

She threw her bag back on the floor and settled comfortably into the sofa. He took a seat beside her. "I haven't heard from you since our last talk. You're involved with Logan, aren't you?"

She fidgeted. "I'm sorry. I told you we could be friends, but yes, I am involved with him now."

"He's lying to you."

A trickle of ice ran down her spine. "I know. He told me about his threats toward you, and I apologize for that. I promise it won't happen again. He also admitted the truth about the dossier."

Richard pulled back looking surprised but quickly recovered. "Well, I'm glad about that, but this is more serious. I was going to keep my mouth shut. It's really none of my business, but I love you and I won't stand around while Grant screws you over."

"What are you talking about?"

"He's meeting with your father at nine this morning. They're signing a contract that will merge your father's company with L&G Brokerage. The biggest coup the industry has seen in years."

The knowledge started to sink in, but she fought to remain calm. In a way, she still refused to believe it. "I'm surprised Daddy would ever give up his company, it's his life." She paused, not wanting to ask. Knowing she had to. "Do you know the terms of the agreement?"

Everything seemed too quiet as she waited for him to say the words she already knew.

"A ring on your finger. He gains the company if he marries you."

This time the room didn't sway. This time she didn't feel as if she'd break into a thousand jagged pieces. A blessed numbness took hold as she stared at Richard and realized he spoke the truth. Logan Grant had scored the deal of the century. The man was so damn good she'd believed he loved her. Just like Michael. Because the bottom line with a good businessman was always money.

And she'd been a fool to forget it.

"Chandler? Are you okay?"

She gathered the last of her strength and nodded. "I'm fine. In fact, this doesn't really surprise me. I just have to decide what to do."

He reached for her hand. Her fingers felt like ice linked within his. "You may not believe this, but I'm sorry I had to tell you. I never wanted to hurt you, even though I'm glad you know the truth about Grant."

"How did you know?"

He shrugged. "I am his attorney. I found the contracts, and when I started seeing meetings with your father turn up on the sly, I got suspicious."

She managed to nod again. "Thank you for telling me. I'm sorry I didn't believe you before but I—"

"Doesn't matter. I know how Grant cons women." He reached into his pocket with his other hand and pulled out a small, black velvet box. "This is the lousiest timing a man can have, and later I'll probably kill myself for being so stupid. But I can't wait any longer." He snapped open the lid. A perfect marquise diamond glittered in the rays of streaming sunlight. "I want you to marry me. I want to show you what a relationship based on truth is like. I want to grow old with you, raise a family, and give you everything you've ever dreamed of. Give me a chance."

She stared at the diamond, a brilliant stone sparkling against the blackest velvet, a symbol of marriage, love, commitment, trust. Then she stared at the man who swore he could give her it all, even though she loved a man who had betrayed her.

The doubt reared up and she tore her gaze away from the ring and studied the man before her. Odd, he seemed to know everything about Logan and her father. Even stranger how insistent he was on getting married when they'd only had two dates, and she'd been vocal regarding her lack of interest.

He stared back, his expression hopeful. Perhaps too hopeful? Why did he want to marry her so badly? A man like Richard would never take second best.

Unless...

The full scenario crashed through her and ripped away her breath. She closed her eyes as she fought for composure. The last piece of the puzzle slipped neatly into place.

He was also working for her father.

Richard Thorne wanted the grand prize: her. Marry her, gain her father's company. Their past conversations and dates whirred behind her closed eyes. He created a persona that never existed, and that's why she always doubted him. In a way, she hated him more than Logan in that instant, because he pretended to be a mirage, just like Michael. Logan may be a bastard but he always remained truthful to his identity. The man of steel.

Chandler opened her eyes. A slight smile played upon her lips as she leaned close, their lips a breath away. Triumph glinted in chestnut eyes as victory neared.

"Never in a million years," she whispered harshly. "Crawl back to Daddy and send him my regards. I wouldn't marry you for anything." Her lips twisted in a cruel taunt. "Not even for a million dollars."

He jerked back. Fury spit from each pore as he stood before her. "You bitch. The only way any man would want you is if your father paid him. Remember that."

He slammed the door behind him.

Chandler sat for a while in her living room and watched the rays of light pour through the window. Grief and rage clamped her in a merciless grip. It was happening all over again. She could sit here while her future was played out in a corporate office, or she could get her butt down there and confront some very old demons.

Chandler grabbed her purse and walked out the door.

"I'm sorry, Chandler, he's in a business meeting now. Do you want to take a seat?"

She flashed her warmest smile at the secretary. "No, I told him I'd drop by, Connie. If you look in the book, you'll see he's meeting with my father, Alexander Santell."

One manicured nail stopped at his nine o'clock appointment. "Oh, my goodness, I never realized you both had the same last name. Sure, honey, go right in. I'm sure they won't mind. Are you okay? You look a little pale."

"I'll be fine. I just have to handle a few things and

then everything will go back to normal. Thanks." Turning from the secretary's puzzled look, Chandler walked toward Logan's office. Her hand paused on the doorknob as she experienced a flash of deja vu. With a deep breath, she opened the door and walked in.

A thick cloud of smoke drifted in the air. She took in the scene before her. Time melted away and kept her a prisoner of the past. Her father stood over Logan's desk, puffing furiously on his cigar, his face set in a determined, stubborn way which many people said she inherited. Logan sat in his chair, relaxed and at ease as he listened to her father's bellowing voice. As the door shut gently behind her, both men turned at the sound.

A deadly quiet settled over the room as they stared at her. Her gaze cut immediately to the man behind the desk, searching his eyes, seeing shards of ice reflected in their depths. A tight fist squeezed her heart, but she showed only a deep calm that mocked her raging emotions.

"Hello, Father."

"What are you—?"

"Chandler, I need to—"

She cut them both off with one swift wave of her hand as she made her way towards them. She glanced at the papers sprawled across Logan's desk, which spelled out exactly what her new husband would inherit the moment she married him. Using their stunned silence to her advantage, she picked up the papers and scanned through them with interest, then tossed the contract back on the desk. A brilliant smile curved her lips but she knew her eyes glittered with a mixture of rioting emotions.

"Congratulations to both of you. It seems I've underestimated you, Father, on your determination to finally pick the right man to head your financial empire." She turned to Logan and bowed. "And you deserve an Oscar for such a riveting performance. You make Michael look like a bumbling acting student against your—how should I put it—experience?"

"Don't." Logan shot up from his chair. The word echoed like a gunshot.

"Now listen here, young lady," Alexander Santell bellowed out to his daughter. "I've been trying to look out for your best interests from the beginning. For the last four years, you've barely even taken my phone calls, but now I want you to listen to what I have to say."

Chandler laughed, the sound brittle and cold to her ears. She pushed back her heavy mane of hair. "I don't have to hear a word you say, Father. You don't own me anymore. I have my own life and my own business and my own money. I can even find my own men, which I will prove to you one day. Of course, I'm sure none of them will be as eager to please me as Logan. You see, he at least had the motivation of a million dollar empire."

Logan's voice was like a whiplash. "Don't say another word. You'll only regret it. And this time my retribution won't be so easy to overlook."

She stared at him in amazement. "Don't you realize

the game is over? As a rational businessman you should have learned when to cut your losses."

His cold icy gaze suddenly turned hot and burned into her. A smile touched his lips. "As a smart businessman, I also know when the other party is bluffing. Game's not over 'till all parties throw in their cards. You may be angry as hell right now, but you can't deny what happened between us and you know it."

Her hands clenched in rage and frustration at his knowing look. She had to force herself to take long, deep breaths so she would ignore the temptation to hurl the nearest paperweight at his smug face. Even when Michael betrayed her, she hadn't felt this enraged. With Michael an icy shell had hardened her heart, and protected her from the swirling emotions now waiting to overwhelm her.

Her body still trembled just at the sound of Logan's voice, the look in his eyes. The anger seething inside of her was on the edge of sexual desire, and she knew it could be turned with just a touch. The knowledge that this man had such great power over her even after she discovered the truth made her want to run from him as fast as she could. Where would she be safe?

But this time there was nowhere to run.

She drew on the deep well of control and discipline she learned throughout the years. "Nothing happened between us," she stated calmly. "It was all based on lies. Therefore, it meant nothing to me." Her eyes hardened with determination even though her lower lip trembled. "I never want to see you again, Logan Grant." Chandler paused. "Ever."

Tension and frustration coiled around his figure. "That's impossible. We have a contract."

Chandler gave a short laugh. "No problem. Funny, how the escape clause works both ways. I never thought I'd be using it in this capacity, but if you check with Harry I'm sure you'll see it's perfectly legal. I'm pulling my services from L&G Brokerage. Effective immediately."

She turned on her heel and paused briefly in front of her father. She stared at the man who raised her, his elegant, stately figure, his mane of silver hair, his green eyes so like her own. For a moment she fought back tears, and then once again, she was back in control.

"You never did understand what I wanted. Power and money don't mean a thing to me. Marrying a man who only wants to get his hands on the company you've built would be a negation of everything you worked to accomplish. All I ever wanted was for you to just be my father."

Chandler walked out of the office with her head held high, leaving the two men staring after her in silence.

• • •

He would be coming for her soon.

Chandler stared out the window in her living room and tried to gather the last shreds of her self control for the confrontation ahead. After she left the office she headed straight home, knowing Logan would soon follow. She knew her lover well. He was going to do everything in his power to convince her he was innocent in the whole mess, and try to repair the damage. He would use whatever skills he could, and focus on every weakness to further his goal—mainly the traitorous response of her body.

And, of course, the knowledge that she still loved him.

She sighed and walked to the clear square space in the corner of her room. She knelt on the thick carpet and let her head hang down, rotating her neck in a clockwise, circular motion to release the tension. Focusing completely on her body and breath, she moved with grace and strength into each yoga posture, clearing her mind.

Four years ago, she'd left everything she'd known and started a new life. But now she was twenty six years old, an adult who was responsible for her own decisions, and she knew there was no running away from the problem. She would have to face Logan one last time and convince him it was over between them.

She only hoped she had the strength.

Chandler heard the door open behind her. She rose from the carpet and turned around. Logan watched her from across the room, his gaze hotly roaming her body, his jaw clenched with determination. Slowly, he removed his suit jacket and tossed it over the side of the chair. He moved with the lean, easy grace that was a part of who he was. Chandler stood her ground.

"I'm glad you realized there was nowhere you could run where I wouldn't find you."

"I realized there was no reason to run this time." Her eyes moved over the hard, sensual lines of his face. "I'm not the same girl I was four years ago. This time I'm stronger."

"You were always strong, Chandler. I knew that the moment you walked into my office."

"You knew a lot more about me than I realized. For instance, you knew all about my father and my past. You saw an opportunity to further your company and you took it. How could I blame you? After all, it was just business."

A variety of emotions flickered across his face. Black brows lowered in a fierce frown. "I knew nothing about your father until he approached me weeks later. He made an appointment to talk to me about a contract that would give me full control of his company. Under certain conditions, namely that the papers would be signed, sealed and delivered the moment I put a ring on your finger."

"So you knew nothing about me until my father approached you with his offer?" she asked in disbelief. "No idea about my past or my disaster with Michael Worthington?"

A muscle worked in his jaw and his hands reached out to grasp her shoulders. "I told you about the dossier, and I told you I never finished reading it. I learned everything when your father finally met with me." He paused. "I also learned he offered the same type of deal to Richard Thorne."

Chandler closed her eyes. "I know. Seems like most of the men in my life think I'm either stupid or desperate."

His voice was whisper soft. "You're neither. What did you do?"

"I threw him out. How did he find out about my father? Another dossier?"

"No, he knew Michael Worthington years ago. I did some research and found they ran in the same circles. Both wanted money and power, and didn't mind marrying to get it. Hell, woman, he never loved you the way I do. He's the one who would choose the money every time."

"You're not still trying to convince me that you love me, are you?" she asked, amazed at his arrogance. "I'm not one of your bimbos, Logan Grant, and once I learn a hard lesson I try never to repeat it. I will never become involved with a man who lies to me. You did. I'll never give you another chance."

"Oh, but you will. You don't have a choice in the matter. You can't pretend everything that's happened between us is null and void just because you want it to be. You lay in my bed and cried my name and took my body deep inside of yours. You gave me your heart and your mind and every inch of that delectable body."

He lowered his head. His breath rushed hot against

her lips. The hard length of his body pressed against hers, the heat from his skin radiated in waves, overpowering her senses with the scent of musk, lemon, and soap.

In that moment she hated him as much as she hated her own traitorous body, already trembling, her breasts swollen and aching, the liquid throbbing heat pulsing between her thighs. She hated wanting him, needing him, loving him still, even though she knew it was all a lie.

"I will never give you anything willingly," she said fiercely. Her nails dug into his upper arms in response to the raging emotions coursing through her. "My body may want sex, but my mind and heart will hate you."

His mouth came down on hers, hard, demanding, his tongue plundering the dark recesses of her mouth with all the raw, seething sexual energy burning between them. She fought him just as hard, but his body slammed against hers, his hands pulled her toward him, forcing her thighs to open so she could feel his desire. His tongue thrust into her mouth over and over again, until she gave him everything he asked for. Her hands gripped his neck, and she opened her mouth fully to accept every dark, stroking motion of his tongue.

Her senses whirled out of control; she became a creature of feeling, each movement of his hand stoked the flames hotter and hotter, until nothing seemed to matter except to slake the hungry, empty space inside of her. His hands dragged across her breasts and rubbed the tight nipples, eliciting a low, animal groan. He bit at her lower lip, then slipped his tongue back into her mouth to taste her again, bending her backward over one arm as the kiss went on and on and on—

Suddenly, she was out of his arms. Her breath came in deep, ragged gulps, and she fought the dizzying sensation of being dragged away from his body. His gunmetal gaze drilled into hers, and his hand trembled slightly as he reached up to push the hair away from her face. The silence stretched between them as the sexual electricity sizzled through the air.

"I never wanted the damn contract," Logan said. "This morning I told your father to go to hell, that I wasn't involved with you to achieve the big prize. You were the prize. After everything we shared together, do you still believe I would choose money over you? And I never lied. I told you when we first made love that my body could never lie. Before you came into my life, I believed what everyone said about me. That I had no heart, and if it did exist, it had turned to steel over the years." He paused. "But you looked into my eyes and showed me they were wrong. You made me whole. What you gave me is worth more than any damn business deal your father can offer. But I guess you don't believe that either, do you, Chandler? I guess it's still easier to believe a man who pretends to tell you what you want to hear. A man who's safe."

The words were like hard stone dropping between

them. She struggled for control and stared at him. Her heart wanted to believe him, but her mind told her she needed to walk away from this man before he took everything she had and completely destroyed her.

"I don't believe you. I don't think I'll ever believe you again."

With a muttered curse, his whole body shook. Raw emotion shimmered in smoke gray eyes. She held her breath in fear as she waited, and then he turned on his heel and walked away.

"So be it. I won't bother you again."

Chapter
14

"You look like hell."

Chandler laughed at Harry's concerned look and continued dragging over the mats for the start of her next class. "Thanks, buddy. I needed a little cheering up."

"No, I mean it. I'm worried about you."

She faced her friend. "I'm okay. Just a little tired. I've been working some extra hours."

He grabbed her hand and led her into the office. Pushing her gently into the worn cushions of the sofa, he stared at her hard. She knew his gaze took in the circles under her eyes and the pale tone to her skin. Then he went over to the tea pot to pour her a mug of the steaming herbal brew. She sipped at it gratefully and prepared herself for one of Harry's lectures.

"We need to talk."

"How did I know this was coming?" The hot liquid trickled down her throat and warmed her belly.

"You can't keep this type of schedule. Linda told me you doubled your class load, and you're busy from six in the morning to late at night. You don't eat. You don't sleep. And Linda caught you the other day chugging coffee when you thought no one was looking. You're falling apart and the main reason is Logan Grant."

Chandler winced at the sound of his name. Three weeks. Somehow it seemed like another lifetime, but at the same time, it felt like just last night she had woken up in his arms, snuggled against his warm body. Then she reminded herself sharply that she'd made the right decision. She'd been strong, and now she needed to rebuild her life.

The Yoga and Arts Center had become her most important goal. Knowing she needed to come up with a drastic plan in order to make up for the capital and time she lost, she dedicated herself to forming as many new classes as she could handle, while she and Linda worked around the clock to survive. Ironically, she was becoming a workaholic and the type of person she normally counseled about reducing stress. She reminded herself it was only for a temporary period, until she got her school back on profitable footing.

And, of course, until she exorcised the ghost of Logan Grant.

"Harry, I don't have a choice right now. We're sinking fast and I have to do everything possible to make sure I don't lose this place."

"Linda said Logan wants to hire you on a permanent contract with his company." He studied her face. "You refused to even consider it. Two other corporations have contacted you about setting up a workshop, and you haven't even pursued a meeting. That would save the Yoga and Arts Center without putting you in an early grave."

"I don't need his charity." Temper surged within her. "The only reason he wants to finish this contract is because he feels sorry for me and guilty for everything he's done. He's probably contacted those other companies for the same reason. I can do this on my own."

Harry didn't say anything for a while. "Hmmm, interesting. Besides giving up your health you've acquired the trait of pride, which you always told me was a sin. You used to always say that accepting help from other people is sometimes the greatest form of strength."

Chandler glowered at him. "I don't need Logan Grant's help."

"I think he's in love with you."

Her mouth dropped open at her friend's stark words. "That's crazy. It was all a big game to him, he never loved me."

"I think he messed up by not telling you about the meeting with your father and obviously regrets it. I think he's the type of man to know what and who he wants without being influenced by your father's money and power. I also think you're terrified of believing him, because then you wouldn't have an easy out of the relationship. I think you're running away from love."

"Did you two bond over a beer or something?"

Harry smiled. "Have you talked to your father?"

"No. I refuse to take his calls or see him."

"Your father would be able to tell you the truth, if you're ready."

"Why are you on Logan's side?" she demanded.

"My whole nightmare came true all over again. It was a replay of four years ago."

He sat beside her and spoke in a gentle voice. "I know you went through hell. But Logan isn't Michael, and I think you could get past it if you wanted to, unless you're not in love with him. Are you?"

Did she still breathe and think and feel? Every part of her body ached for him. She had focused all her energy into work and hoped to drive away the urgent need to go to him. Even after everything he'd done, she still loved him. Nothing could take that away, not even working herself into the ground. A tiny part deep inside wondered if Harry could be right. Maybe Logan had decided to decline the contract. Maybe he had never lied when he spoke about his feelings.

Maybe she had made a terrible mistake and misjudged him.

Her mind went over the time they spent together. In the beginning, she had felt like it was all a game, but then something had connected them. She'd glimpsed a tenderness such an isolated man, the "man of steel" should never have shown. He had made love to her and sworn his body wouldn't lie. He'd sworn she could trust him.

He'd tried to convince her he told the truth, but she was so caught up in her own emotions, she hadn't listened. And she hadn't believed him.

Her mind swirled with a dizzying flow of thoughts. "Do you love him?" Harry asked again.

She nodded.

"Then what are you going to do about it?"

She turned to face her friend in surprise. "What do you mean?"

"You've always fought for what you wanted. When you make a mistake you apologize, fix it, and keep going. If you want him back, you have to take the first step."

"What if I judged him wrong?" she asked. Her lower lip trembled slightly.

Harry smiled. "What have you got to lose?"

A life of loneliness, years of regrets, nights spent alone in bed, wondering if she had made a mistake for giving up so easily. Suddenly, a blinding flash of realization coursed through her. She had to give it a shot. She needed to talk to her father about what happened. She had already wasted three weeks of self pity while she mourned her unhappy, unlucky existence.

She was damn tired of it.

She sprang up from the sofa and slammed the mug down. "Will you call Linda for me and have her take over my next class? I'm going to see my father."

"Sure, no problem." He watched her race out the door. After a moment, she peeked her head back in.

"Thanks, Harry."

He laughed. "Anytime, buddy. Anytime."

The modern high-rise building in the heart of Manhattan thrust toward the sky in rivalry with newer skyscrapers. Tracing the path she had followed since her youth, she waited patiently for the elevator to stop

at the top floor, and then walked through a long hallway filled with a string of secretaries. Her father had
trained them well, as they all questioned her destina-
tion, and she'd been almost tackled by the older
woman standing by the water fountain. The woman's
voice dripped icicles, and her eyes gazed behind thick,
gray glasses. She liked Connie at Logan's office much
better, Chandler thought to herself absently.

The inside of his office was the same. The thick ori-
ental carpet set off the rich wood paneling and cherry
wood desk. Ceiling to wall windows tempted the
onlooker to dream of money and power as he gazed
over the city. Plush chairs scattered around heavily
carved tables to relax clients, and a fully stocked bar
took up one side of the room. The smell of cigar smoke
still drifted in the air, and stacks of paperwork filled
the room, bursting from every spare inch of space.

Alexander Santell looked amazed to see Chandler
storm into his office. She hadn't bothered to change,
thinking her old sweat pants, faded t-shirt declaring
the Yoga and Arts Center, and a pair of worn Reeboks
represented her true identity best. She'd caught up her
honey brown hair in a pony tail high on her head, and
she knew her eyes shone with exhaustion. But a determined spark flamed within her and she directed it
against him.

"Good God, daughter, what have you done with
yourself?" He dropped a leather binder back on his desk.

Chandler looked around the office as the memories

rushed back. Four years ago she had stood in front of her father in his own personal kingdom, an office where she grew up. Now, it didn't seem to be as intimidating as she remembered.

Neither did her father.

He stood behind his desk. His figure emanated waves of raw energy. His silver hair was still thick and distinguished, marking him as an experienced adversary to the younger generation.

But something felt different. For the first time, she saw her father for who he really was: a human being who had lost his wife and only daughter, a man still fighting a losing battle to get what he wanted. She never really noticed before.

Alexander Santell was lonely.

She settled herself down on the smooth leather chair opposite his desk. "I want to know everything that happened between you and Logan Grant." She crossed her arms in front of her chest.

He puffed on his cigar while he studied her. "Why do you always insist on wearing those old clothes?" he asked gruffly. "You always looked so nice in those wool business suits."

"I'm allergic to wool, father. And I happen to like my old clothes; they're more conducive to teaching yoga."

"Ah, yes, yoga. I thought you had lost your mind when you started teaching those courses, but I have to admit you may have started a new craze in the business world. I saw the figures from Logan's report. Besides having every employee up in arms about your departure, you were able to show some results. Employee satisfaction increased. Quality of work improved. And morale went through the roof. Therefore, you made the company money. Nice job."

Her mouth fell open. Chandler wondered if she was hallucinating. "You spoke with Logan about my program?"

"Sure. Maybe you can do your old man a favor and start classes here. I always like to be ahead of the competition, even though there's no way in hell I'll roll around the floor to relieve stress."

Chandler laughed. They studied each other for a few moments. "Tell me what happened with Logan."

Alexander gave a deep sigh. "I was worried about you. You're pushing thirty and I still don't have any grandchildren. I heard you started working with Grant, and you seemed to get along. I decided I'd give him a little incentive by offering him the business. He was perfect for you."

"You thought Michael was perfect for me."

He snorted. "Big mistake. He was a wimp. Logan has character. He passed the real test."

"What real test?" Chandler asked suspiciously.

Her father laughed. "He told me to go to hell. Said he needed no help with you, he had everything under control. Said he had enough power with the Weatherall contract and didn't need my company. Then he gave me a lecture on the way I treated you."

Chandler watched him in disbelief. "He didn't want the contract, didn't want your company?"

He shook his head. "He wanted no part of it. So, naturally, I got pissed because he was disobeying a direct order from his future father-in-law, so I started yelling. Then you walked in."

"I didn't believe him." Her heart filled with horror. "Oh God, I told him to get out and that I wanted nothing more to do with him."

"Hmmm, I figured you did. You always were stubborn." He ignored his daughter's glare and puffed furiously. "But you had your reasons. The man is completely crazy about you. He's a smart businessman, too. You did well, girl."

"You did the same thing with Richard Thorne."

A thunderous expression crossed her father's face. "He wanted the money. I approached him before Logan, thought the kid might have some character. A little competition is good for the soul."

She shook her head in disgust. "You wanted them both fighting over me like I was some sort of prize?"

"No. I wanted to see which one would choose you. And I got my answer. Now stop back-talking. I did it for your own good."

Despair shot through her at his confirmation. Logan was innocent. Chandler squeezed her eyes shut. Somehow, she had to find a way to make it up to Logan.

"I have to fix it." Her chin tilted upward in determination. "I have to find a way to give Logan what he wanted. This time with no strings attached."

"What are you talking about?"

She stared at her father and felt a degree of ruthlessness surge in her. Her father looked at her warily. "You're going to give Logan your company, with no conditions. He doesn't have to marry me, he never has to see me again if he doesn't want to. But he can have his contract."

"Are you crazy?" he shouted. His voice rumbled and crashed through the office. He stood up from the desk and waved his hands in the air. A ferocious frown marred his features. Chandler never moved, never blinked, knowing this was part of her father's normal temper tantrum when he couldn't control the situation. "There's no way in hell I'm going to give my company away lock, stock, and barrel with no guarantee it will be kept in the family! That yoga and meditation has warped your mind, girl!"

She fought a smile and eased back in the chair. "Oh, yes, Dad, you will do this. I never wanted the company to begin with. At least Logan will take good care of it and make sure your profits skyrocket. You can't do much better. But there's one more reason you're going to get Logan to sign those contracts."

"And what's that?" he bellowed ominously.

Chandler smiled. "Because you owe me."

Silence descended. Alexander cursed fluently under his breath. His fingers raked back the silver strands of his hair. He glared at her with glittering green eyes that matched her own.

"Oh, hell."

"Do we have a deal?"

He reached again for his cigar and drew the smoke into his mouth. "Do I have a choice?"

"No."

"Then we have a deal."

She rose from the chair. "Pleasure doing business with you, Dad. Oh, by the way, don't tell him I had anything to do with this. I don't want him coming back to me out of a misplaced feeling of guilt. I can handle my own personal life."

"Then where are my grandchildren?"

She ignored his last remark and walked toward the door. When she turned to face him again there was a softness in her tone and in her eyes she had not felt since the day she walked out of his office four years ago. "You weren't to blame for Mom's death. I never thought that. She just got sick."

His eyes echoed a deep grief he rarely expressed. Slowly, he nodded. "I loved her. I loved you both."

Their eyes met and locked, and she felt a frisson of understanding connecting them, the start of something that could be more in the future.

Now all she had to do was get the man she loved to forgive her for not believing in him.

• • •

Logan replaced the receiver and swivelled his chair around. Darkness had settled over the city. Twinkling lights of the skyscrapers glittered against the dark moonless background.

Alexander Santell's remark played in his mind like a mantra, and the full impact of the older man's speech slammed through him.

The contract was his.

Santell was signing his company over to Logan for nothing. Zero. Nada. Logan didn't have to do a thing except sign on the dotted line.

That's when he knew Chandler was behind the whole thing.

He half closed his eyes and for the first time in three weeks, let himself really feel. After he lost her, he'd reverted to the same son of a bitch he'd been before. Except this time it was different. She had taught him how to be alive, how to love and trust. And when she walked out of his life, she taught him about real pain. Logan realized she'd changed him. He was no longer safe from emotion, and he didn't know what to do.

The knowledge he'd lost her twisted in his gut like a knife, keeping him from eating or sleeping, driving him to ignore the pain by working. But nothing helped. She had sworn to never believe in him again. Now her father was signing over his company.

Logan's hands trembled slightly as he reached for his pen and tapped it against the arm of his chair. Santell must have told her the truth, and she had listened. This was her way of showing him she was wrong. A way to show she believed in him.

In a final light of blinding realization, Logan decided he didn't want Alexander Santell's company. He wanted Chandler. Her heart and her soul. He wanted her to know he would choose her every time, no matter how many millions were at stake.

Logan made the decision, then turned to the next problem at hand. He hit the intercom buzzer and barked a few words to Connie. Minutes later, Richard Thorne walked in.

His attorney looked at ease as he strolled into the office. Logan felt a brief flash of regret before it quickly flickered out. He'd used Chandler, lied to her, and would have happily trapped her into a loveless marriage.

So Richard Thorne would have to pay.

The two men nodded at each other. "You wanted to see me," Richard said.

"Yes."

"What's up?"

"You're fired."

Richard blinked, then smiled. "Hmmm. Sure about that, boss? I thought you liked keeping your enemies close."

"Only when they have use. You've now outlived yours."

The smile turned to ice. "We both lost, Grant. Probably overplayed our hands. There's no use messing up a good partnership over a woman. Let's just move on."

Logan shook his head. His lip lifted upward.

"Game's over. I just got off the phone with Santell. He's signing his company over to me with no provisions. You see, Thorne, it was a test, and you failed. Her father was looking for the man to pick her over the money. You played into his hands, therefore, you lost." He chuckled. "And you sure as hell won't be invited to our wedding."

The attorney looked somewhat desperate. "I'll convince her you're both lying."

Logan's eyes narrowed. "You will never see her again. If you do, I can promise you won't ever find work in Manhattan. There's a small computer firm I contacted, who I think you'll be perfect for. Cause any trouble, and I'll call in my favors." He paused. "You're finished, Thorne."

"You son of a—"

Logan buzzed the intercom. "Connie, get security to escort Mr. Thorne back to his office. This is his last day."

"Yes, sir."

Logan switched off. "Get your belongings. Then get out."

He turned back around in his chair as he heard a snarl of rage. The attorney was personally escorted out of the office by two burly guards. As the door slammed, Logan allowed himself to feel relief.

Game over.

It was time to claim his woman.

● ● ●

She was dreaming.

A part of her knew the scene unveiling before her was just a misty image of her sub consciousness, but the rush of pleasure and happiness that surged in her blood made her go along with the fantasy.

She watched Logan undress beside the bed, quickly shedding his clothes as he revealed the hard muscled length of his body. With a murmur of pleasure, she reveled in his masculine power, greedy to absorb his image as she knew once she awoke her lover would be gone. Naked, he slipped under the sheets and pulled her into his arms, taking her mouth in a hungry kiss.

She responded heatedly to the embrace. Her heartbeat thundered as his hands drifted down her body and pulled off her nightgown. He caressed the ripe flesh of her breasts, lowering his mouth to take the hard crests between his lips, sucking with slow, teasing motions that urged her hips to press into his, her thighs opening to welcome him.

In her dream, he made love to her with all the passionate intensity she remembered, exploring every inch of her skin with his hands and lips and tongue, driving her into a wild frenzy of need, until she begged him to take her.

Then with a single, powerful thrust he drove deep inside of her. The pounding rhythm escalated so rapidly she dug her nails into his shoulders as the tension grew, her head arching backward into the pillow as the tempo increased faster and faster, making the blood pound through her veins. Then the climax came, hard, pushing her over the edge until a scream broke from her lips, and she heard her name being whispered in her ear as she floated through the air.

Knowing once she opened her eyes the image would be a distant memory, she breathed in the scent of male sweat and musk, reveling in the feel of his sleek muscled length pressing against her, his weight covering her.

Then she realized she wasn't dreaming.

Chandler's eyes flew open in disbelief as she took in the sprawling male figure on top of her. His lips curved in a satisfied smile. "Logan!"

His hand stroked her breast with lazy motions. "It better be me, lady. If you had screamed the wrong name, I would have had something to worry about." She blushed at the wild, open response she had given him. "What are you doing here? It's the middle of the night. Have you gone crazy?"

"I was crazy to let three weeks drag on in the first place." He moved upward and pressed her deep into the pillows, moving her wrists above her head so she was trapped beneath him. Smoky gray eyes burned in the darkness. "I was crazy to let my pride and your stubbornness come between us. I spoke with your father today."

Chandler kept her voice neutral. "What did he say?"

"He offered me his company. No strings attached. He gave me a tidy little speech about trusting me to make him a profit."

"What did you say?"

His lips traveled down her neck. "I told him to go to hell."

"What?"

A laugh rumbled his chest. "I told him I never wanted the contract in the first place. That's when I realized you were behind the whole thing. You convinced your father to give me what you thought I wanted." He trailed kisses along the side of her jaw, then moved over her lips, his tongue slipping inside her mouth to kiss her hungrily. She clung to his shoulders and met each thrust of his tongue with one of her own.

When he broke away Logan spoke in a fierce tone. "You little fool, don't you know the only thing I ever wanted was you? Not your father's company or his money."

Chandler smiled radiantly as the realization finally dawned on her. Even after he was offered a contract by her father that did not include marrying her, he declined. Logan Grant had given up the opportunity to rule a financial empire because he wanted her more.

"What about Richard?" she asked.

"Thorne will never bother us again. Now he's going to be looking for a new job."

She winced. "You fired him?"

"Yes. He's a good worker, sweetheart, but I can never trust him again. And I want him far away from you."

She nodded, knowing it was the only logical action Logan could take. "I love you," she whispered. She ran her hands over his hard features. "I was afraid I'd lost you, that I had pushed you too far when I said I would never believe you again."

"You could never lose me, Chandler. The moment I realized you had set up the offer I knew I had to come to you."

"So you decided to sneak into my bedroom in the middle of the night?" she asked teasingly. The crisp hairs on his thigh tickled her as he entangled his legs with hers.

"Of course. What else do rational, logical business-men do when they are crazy in love, and want to make love to their women?" His palm settled over the curve of her hip. "I'll never give you a reason not to believe in me. I love you too much." He paused. "You've changed me, Chandler. You looked past all the barri-ers, found my soul, and loved me anyway. I like the man I am with you." He smiled.

His lips rubbed over hers, sweetly, lovingly, as all the emotions suddenly burst from between them, shedding all the doubts and fears for the very last time. What remained was a pure, lighthearted joy and a rag-ing passion that sent Chandler's soul soaring high above the heavens.

"I think we still have something important to dis-cuss, Mr. Grant." Her eyes sparkled with happiness.

His palm coasted from the curve of her buttocks to dip to her inner thigh. She moaned. "Yes, Ms. Santell?"

"The contract."

His finger lightly tested the liquid heat as he found her core. Her breath came in short pants. "Ah, yes, the contract. I'm sure we'll be able to work up something beneficial to us both. Of course, this time there will be no escape clause. The arrangement will be on a more permanent basis."

"No trial period?"

A wicked grin transformed his features. With one quick movement, he moved inside of her and joined his body with hers. Slowly, he started a teasing rhythm that coaxed throaty moans from her lips.

"Logan!"

"This trial period ends on our wedding day," he growled, raining tiny kisses over her cheek.

"Where do I sign?"

Logan gave a husky laugh and interlaced his fingers with hers, starting a sensual journey of love as old as time.

THE END

Jennifer Probst

I've always wanted to be a writer. At twelve, I took a pen in hand and wrote my first love story. I haven't stopped since. Those heroines taught me valuable lessons that served me well. I learned to keep my head up high and surge forward when I was afraid; I learned to demand respect in a relationship; I learned about compromise and dreams and independence. Those are the stories I want to write, and I can only hope I give back some of the joy I received over the years.

I live in the beautiful Hudson Valley in upstate New York. I've traveled to many places but always seem to be drawn back to the mountains. I graduated with a proper business degree and a master's in my passion, English Literature. I've pursued many career paths such as travel agent, yoga teacher and insurance salesperson. I've wanted to be an airline pilot, a cat burglar, a dancer, an archaeologist, and a vineyard owner. I have been all of the above through romance novels, and intend to explore many more.

I met the love of my life when I had finally given up on my own romantic journey. The first time he asked me out he promised to buy my book if he could buy me dinner. We had dinner and fell in love over sushi and haven't been apart since. I learned it wasn't about happy endings. It was about happy beginnings.

I welcome any response to the following email address romancewriter121@yahoo.com. Please visit me on the web at www.jenniferprobst.com.

"Delightful opposites attract. Complex, interesting characters with a refreshing bonus of a hero. Logan Grant tugged at my heart. A high-stakes gamble worth every reader's time. Highly recommended."

— Eileen Charbonneau, Author

"A compelling read, highly sensual and very enjoyable. The romance between Chandler and Logan held me captive."

— Janet Lane Walters, Author
Mysteries and Romances

Logan Grant knew he was in trouble the moment Chandler Santell walked into his office. He agrees to her crazy deal only when she risks all and guarantees him a profit. Behind the scenes a dangerous game of love, power and greed begin to play out—a game Chandler knows nothing about. The payoff is worth millions to the man who can win Chandler's heart.

Chandler Santell avoids men—especially the rich and powerful ones who believe more in money than people. Desperate to save her struggling Yoga & Arts Center, her last hope is the most powerful man in the finance industry, a man reputed to have a "heart of steel."

"Heart of Steel" is a wow! You will love the sexual tension and conflict…wonderful characters…well-crafted twists. Jennifer Probst is one talented writer."

— Nan Doporto, *Romance at Its Best*